THE OMICRON KILL

AN OMEGA THRILLER

BLAKE BANNER

RIGHTHOUSE

ISBN-13: 978-1-63696-343-3

ISBN-10: 1-63696-343-9

Cover design by: Damonza

Printed in the United States of America

www.righthouse.com

www.instagram.com/righthousebooks

www.facebook.com/righthousebooks

twitter.com/righthousebooks

THE OMEGA SERIES

ONE

Lambda, Mu, Nu, Xi...Omicron.

I wrote the names down on a paper napkin, and then the symbols: λ, M, N, Ξ...O. O-mega and O-micron. Big O and small o. Did it mean anything?

Outside, the desert was an endless, shapeless glare of heat, sand and scorching sun. Inside, the bar was still, cool, dark and quiet. My beer glass, standing on the dark, high-polished wood, was empty, the inside stained with dry froth. Further down the bar, the bartender was leaning by the pumps, staring at his phone, occasionally poking the screen.

"Get me another beer, will you?"

He lifted one elbow, sniggered at his cell, read a little more, then sighed. He set down his phone and shuffled over to the pumps. As he set down the beer beside me, he glanced at the napkin. "What's that y'writin' there? Remind me of the symbols..." He paused, waiting for his brain to catch up with his mouth. "What was that place? ...Roswell, just a little ways from here, where they found the UFO. I juss read a book 'bout it. Had symbols juss like that."

I studied him a moment. His beard reached his paunch in the two prongs of a long fork. He was bald on top but had a long, scraggly ponytail down his back. I shook my head. "Letters from the Greek alphabet. Lambda, Mu, Nu, Xi and Omicron," I said.

"Huh... This book..." He leaned his elbows on the bar and stared across the empty saloon at the desert outside. "Says all the most powerful politicians and royal families and all that shit, they's all smart dinosaurs that learned to shape shift and look like humans. And that's who rules this world. That's why they's so cruel. Reptiles is all cold-blooded."

I gave a small laugh. "It's a nice theory, but in my experience the most depraved, predatory, cruel and cold-blooded species on this planet is us. Look around you. You're not seeing lizards living in their millions in the cities, it's all humans."

He gave me a curious look and nodded. The door opened onto the blistering afternoon and four men walked in making noises about beer and heat. They were big, hard guys, used to working cattle in an unforgiving desert for a living, who rode longhorns and broncos for sport. They were men I had a basic respect for, but not a lot in common with. I didn't pay much attention to them. Three went over to a booth and the fourth slapped his hand on the bar and said, "Gimme four of your coldest beers there, Gastank!"

As he moved away, I said, "And give me a whiskey chaser when you get a chance, will you?" and turned my attention back to the paper napkin.

I could feel the newcomer staring at me. I ignored him,

but after a moment he spoke. "You mind waitin' till he's finished serving me before you give him your order, pal?"

I turned to look at him a little more closely. I figured six one in his boots. His T-shirt revealed a strong torso and powerful arms. His neck was thick and his freckled face had two pale blue eyes, though there didn't seem to be an awful lot going on behind them. I guessed he just wanted to be respected. I nodded. "Sure."

I turned back to my Greek letters, in particular Omega and Omicron, but his voice broke in on my thoughts.

"See, I think it's disrespectful."

I turned to look at him again.

"If I'm talkin' to Gastank here, makin' my order, and you butt in makin' an order of your own. See? That is a lack of respect toward me."

Gastank sighed. "Let it go, Jesse. Man didn't mean nothin' by it. We was just talkin', he didn't butt in."

"You should shut your mouth there, Gastank. Man can talk for hisself. You can talk for yourself, can't you, mister?"

I calibrated him a little more carefully. He'd be slow and telegraphic. He'd waste a lot of energy. I was pretty sure he'd charge like a bull and go for a take down. There was a warmth in my belly I recognized as adrenaline, and I was surprised to realize I was hoping he'd attack me.

I gave my head a small, sideways twitch and spoke quietly. "This isn't a problem for me either way. I meant no disrespect by ordering a whiskey chaser. But if you want to take it that way, that's your problem, not mine."

He looked over his shoulder at his buddies, who were watching him and looking bored. "Does that sound respectful to you? That don't sound like a sincere apology to me."

I sighed and turned back to my napkin.

His petulant voice broke in again. "Don't you look away from me when I'm talking to you, you goddamn pussy."

I knew then there was no way out. I was going to have to neutralize him. I felt a stab of excitement in my gut that I didn't like, but accepted anyway. I climbed off the stool and turned to face him. "Why don't you put your estrogen back in your ovaries, Jesse, pick up your beer and go and sit quietly with your pals."

He obviously knew what estrogen and ovaries were, and wasn't down with gender fluidity, because his freckled cheeks flushed and he reached for the scruff of my neck with his left hand, while he drew his right back for a massive cross. If it had connected, it would have taken my head off. But for that I'd have had to wait around while he put the punch together and delivered it.

Instead, I snatched hold of the baby finger of his left hand and bent it back against the joint. He could feel it was about to snap and went up on his toes. His eyes and mouth opened wide and he went, "Ah... ah... ah..." a lot.

I took hold of his wrist in my left and bent the finger harder, pressing gently down. He started to bend at the knees. I looked over at the booth, where his pals were standing up. I shook my head and they paused. Jesse was kneeling now, staring at his finger, still saying, "Ah... ah..."

I said, "Right now, from here, there are eight simple ways I could kill you with a single move. There are three simple ways I could dislocate your arm and too many ways to break it for me to go through them all. The number of ways I could put you in hospital with broken bones and fractures runs into hundreds. And you know what's worrying me, Jesse? I actually want to do it. Now, you came looking for trouble with me, and you found it, and it was more trouble than you reckoned on. There is no shame in that. So, why don't you go on over to your friends and drink your beer, and leave me in peace to enjoy mine? You've had your warning, Jesse. Next time I'll break your shoulder."

I let him go and he staggered to his feet. His face was flushed red and for a moment I thought he was going to come at me, but his friends surrounded him and led him back to the booth, taking their beers with them. I returned to my stool, looked at Gastank and said, "How about that whiskey chaser, Gastank?"

As he poured it, he was watching me from under his eyebrows. "That was a pretty neat move. What was that? Kung Fu or somethin'?"

I shook my head, still trying to focus on the napkin. "Path of least resistance."

He nodded and corked the bottle, with his mouth slightly open. "Like Zen..."

I smiled. "Something like that, yeah."

He nodded a lot, like he understood, said, "Neat," and walked back to his cell phone. But what he'd said had started me thinking.

Zen: jhana in the original Pali language. It was a state. It was a state which you achieved through meditation, in which you experienced a kind of timeless, shapeless sense of simply being; being now. And this state was expressed in ancient Greece with the sound 'Ou', meaning entity, being, existence. O-micron, meant small being, contraction, or small existence. Whereas O-mega, meant big being, expansion, or major existence.

I sipped my whiskey, felt it burn and realized I hadn't eaten since five that morning. I made a mental note to eat something, and wondered why it mattered that Omega and Omicron were like opposites of each other. Either way, Omega, the organization, was broken, crippled, all but finished.[1]

All but.

I had spent the last six months drifting across the southern States, with no fixed purpose, not ready to go back to Weston, not ready to go home, and somehow not ready to accept that Omega was finished. Though for over six months they had give no signs of life.

Omicron. They had contracted in on themselves.

If Omega was big and expansive like the sun, then what was Omicron? A seed? More to the point, I told myself, who? Who was Omicron? In the Omega cabal of men and women with too much money and too much power, who liked to form secret societies, manipulate world power, and give themselves quasi-mystical names drawn from the ancient Greek alphabet, who was Omicron?

Whoever he or she was, they were based in South America. Assuming, I told myself, as I sipped my whiskey again, and this time enjoyed the burn, assuming that Omega III, which controlled Latin America, had not collapsed along with Omegas I and II.

I knew I had his name somewhere. I had a full list of the names of the members of Omega. I had one copy at my

---

1. See *Kill: One* and *Kill: Two*

house in Weston, and I had given another copy to Jim Redbeard in Los Angeles, less than six hundred miles to the west. I drained my glass of whiskey and waved it at Gastank to refill it.

Jim Redbeard, the philosopher-cum-Viking master of chaos who had helped me bring down Omega II in Europe. He would know whether Omicron was significant. He would probably also advise me to let it go, go home and take up fishing.

Gastank shuffled up and refilled my glass. I said, "You can leave the bottle."

He hesitated a moment. "I don't want no trouble in my bar, mister."

I eyed him a moment, feeling unreasonably irritable. "You won't get any, if you leave the bottle. You got any food here?"

"In about an hour," he said with a twist of resentment in his voice. "Carmen comes in 'round six. She'll cook you whatever you want."

"I'll have a beef burger and fries when she gets in."

He went away and I sat staring at the glare outside the window. I had the idea of cycles nagging at my mind, cycles of time. But I couldn't pin down why. I had picked up somewhere that 'O' or zero somehow symbolized eternity, infinity or great cycles of time. But I had never had time for philosophy, much less mystical BS. I could just about stomach the Zen I had learned while studying martial arts, and that was mainly because they advised you, "Don't think, do." That was my kind of philosophy.

But you need to know your enemy and understand how he thinks, and there was no doubt in my mind that Omega, whatever was left of it, was founded on mystical principles; mystical principles that were rooted in ancient Greek philosophy. Somebody, somebody connected with Omega, had spouted something at me about cycles of time being associated with the letters of the Greek alphabet. Was it Ben? Ben had had a taste for that kind of thing—they all had—but it had not been him. It had been after I'd killed Ben[2]. So it must have been Timmerman.

Then it came to me. We'd been on the train, traveling from Paris to Madrid, and he had told us, me and Njal, that Omega was not an organization. He'd said it was a protocol. Each protocol, he'd said, covered a period of social and technological development, and we were at the end of protocol twenty-three, Psi.

I pulled a pack of Camels from my pocket, shook one free and poked it in my mouth. Gastank looked at me and shook his head. "Hey, man, I can't let you do that..."

I gave him the dead eye. He sighed and walked away. I didn't light up.

Njal had asked him what protocol Psi was. What had he answered? I turned my ancient, battered brass Zippo around in my fingers, reaching back with my mind. He'd said it was the time when the technology for mass production and mass distribution expand and stabilized free markets. I had no damn idea what the hell that meant. I poured myself another shot and sipped it, allowing my mind to go back to the train again. Njal had asked him what came after Psi. Timmerman had told him that after Psi came Omega. Omega was the end. When technology surpassed human understanding.

---

2. See *Kill: One*

The end. So if Omega was the end, what the hell was Omicron?

Jim Redbeard would know. If he didn't know, he could work it out.

It was nearly six, the light was fading outside the window and I was surprised to see the level of whiskey in the bottle had dropped. I could hear noises coming from the kitchen and realized I felt sick with hunger, I had drunk too much and my head was not clear. Worse than that, I had a pellet of hot anger building in my belly, and I didn't know why.

A loud hiss from the kitchen, followed by the smell of singed meat and onions, told me Carmen was cooking my burger. Gastank was further down the bar serving drinks. The place was filling up. Jesse and his pals were still in the booth.

I said: "Hey, Gastank, get me another beer, will you?"

He pulled it and put it in front of me. "This one's on the house. Now, don't you think you've had enough? How 'bout you eat your burger, drink your beer and go home to sleep it off for a bit? I'll look after your whiskey for you."

I frowned at him. "What's your problem? I'm not disturbing anyone, I'm not causing a ruckus, I'm just sitting here having a drink."

He sighed. "You ain't causin' a problem, but Jesse's pals are comin' in soon, and you really riled Jesse, the way you humiliated him in front of his friends. You'd be smart to leave sooner than later."

"I'll have my burger, and my beer, in peace. Then I'll pay you what I owe you and go on my way."

He sighed again, a little more deeply.

I smiled a smile that couldn't have been nice to look at. "Don't worry, I'll pay for any damage, too."

He went away. The door opened behind me and people came in. Gastank came back after a while with my burger. He gave me a pleading look which I ignored and he left. The first bite of the burger made me feel better. But as I took a pull of the cold beer and a second bite, I was suddenly aware, through some sixth sense, of Jesse getting to his feet and crossing the room toward me. A couple of seconds passed and the room started to go quiet. I glanced at Gastank and smiled at the expression on his face. I stuffed the last piece of burger in my mouth, took my time chewing it and then drained my beer.

After that, I turned on my stool to see Jesse standing, staring at me.

"You and me got unsettled business," he said. "We gonna settle it right now."

All my training and all my instincts told me to walk away, but right then that pellet of anger and frustration in my gut was stronger than my instinct and my training; and it told me that people like Jesse get away with being assholes too often.

I shook my head. "I have no business with you, Jesse. If I bruised your..." I smiled and labored the words, "...little finger, like I told you before, that is your problem, not mine."

His cheeks colored. "You better get off that stool, mister, an' face me like a man, or I'm gonna haul your ass off it and bullwhip you till you weep like a girl."

"You and your friends?"

"I figure I got this."

I looked over and saw that his pals had all stood up. There were six of them and they were all grinning. I nodded. "OK," I said. "Come and haul my ass off my stool and bullwhip me. I think your friends would be amused by that."

His frown said he didn't understand what was happening, but he was going to pile right in and whoop my ass anyway. He came at me as I knew he would, with both hands reaching for my collar. I let him do that and when he had a firm grip, I slammed my left forearm down hard on his elbows, forcing him forward, and smashed the heel of my open hand into his jaw. He let go of my collar and staggered back a couple of steps. He was strong and he could take it. That was fine by me. I was in no hurry. I had some anger and frustration to work off. I climbed off the stool and walked to the center of the floor. Somebody locked the door. Everybody else gathered around. It didn't feel like a lynch mob. It felt like sport.

Jesse shook his head to clear it, then snarled. He rushed at me, swinging his right fist in a big arc. I could have written *War and Peace* in the time it took to reach where my head should have been. I weaved back and let it pass, then laughed.

"Man, you are not telegraphing, you are sending me a letter. C'mon! You can do better than that."

He charged again.

It takes a fist the same time to travel a full yard, as it does for your core and your shoulder to travel an inch. I planted my feet, flicked my hips and my shoulder and smashed my fist into his nose with the combined force of my two hundred and twenty pounds and his mammoth charge.

He went up on his toes and his knees did a little in and

out dance as he staggered back with blood streaming down over his mouth. I could see his pupils were dilated and he had a dull, stupid look on his face. I didn't waste time. I took two steps toward him and drove my fist straight into his solar plexus. He went down vomiting.

I looked at his six friends. They weren't sure what to do. The three who'd come in with him looked like they just wanted to get back to drinking beer. But there was one guy, bigger than the rest, whose face said he had a mean disposition and he'd decided he didn't like me. Jesse was getting to his feet, holding his belly, and he didn't look to me like he was out either. I guess men in New Mexico are made of hard stuff. I pointed at the big guy. I was grinning.

"What's your name, son?"

He didn't like me calling him son. He said, "My name's Billy, and I'm gonna whip your ass till you bleed."

I shook my finger in the negative. "I'll tell you what we're going to do. I'll take you both, and a third if anybody wants to join the party. And whoever goes down buys a round of drinks for the bar. You too chicken for that, Billy?"

There was a cheer. One of Billy's friends, a Mexican in a blue shirt and a cowboy hat, decided he felt like buying a round that night. He pulled off his hat and rolled up his sleeves. I was wondering what the hell I was doing, but I told myself this was living Zen. Don't think. Just do.

Jesse looked very pale, but he wiped his mouth on his sleeve and moved toward me. Billy and the Mexican started to circle, Billy on my left and the Mexican on my right. They were going to grab me and let Jesse have his revenge. That was their plan.

I laughed again and said to Jesse, "Third time lucky, huh,

Jesse?" It wasn't subtle. An experienced fighter would have seen it coming. But these guys were used to wrestling bulls, not professional killers. I'd spoken to Jesse, so their attention was on him. They didn't expect the charging side kick at the Mexican. It caught him in the floating ribs, lifted him off his feet and sent him crashing through the ring of watchers and into a table, sending the four chairs flying. He didn't get up.

But by the time he'd hit the floor, I was already closing on Billy. I knew Jesse was basically the walking dead, and the crowd was looking forward to their beers. The only man I had to worry about now was Billy.

I figured a bit of boxing would be fun. I run at least five miles every morning at about five AM and I have near zero body fat. I've also learned to develop a kind of trance-state, where I can just keep going for hours without getting tired.

Billy must have weighed in at two hundred and seventy pounds. He was muscle strong and I was pretty sure if he landed a punch it would be lights out for anyone. But I didn't think he had staying power, and every punch he threw was using up precious energy. I leered at him and got in close.

"C'mon, Billy. What's troubling you? You afraid of spoiling your looks for your boyfriend?"

That did it. He powered in, swinging right and left with massive crosses and hooks. I ducked and weaved and stayed a few inches out of range while Jesse followed along, trying to get his wind back. Billy's breathing was getting heavy and his face was flushed. He threw another right hook and as it went past, I leaned forward and flicked a nasty left jab at his right eye. He backed up a step and winked a few times. I stepped forward and as he threw his right again, I crouched and drove both fists into his floating ribs, one after another. He doubled up.

As I came upright, Jesse was charging me. I snatched Billy's right wrist, pulled and twisted savagely and palmed his elbow, so he stumbled and collided with Jesse. Jesse staggered back. Billy was still doubled over and I had a firm grip on his wrist. It was time to buy a round. I drove my right boot into his belly and he went down.

Jesse was gaping at me. I stepped forward and jabbed the tip of his chin. He went straight over backward.

I was surrounded by a ring of very silent men. I knew some of them were thinking about it. I gave them a couple of seconds. Nobody moved. I said, "Looks like these boys owe you gentlemen a drink."

There was a moment's silence. Then somebody laughed. Then they were all laughing and Gastank was pulling beers and looking relieved. Several guys went to drag the fallen to their feet. Gastank called over to me, "What about Billy and Jesse, and Nestor?"

"They look to me like they could use a drink. Give me one too, will you?"

And that was when the door opened and the sheriff walked in.

"What the hell is goin' on in here?" He looked around, saw me and said, "Oh, I might have guessed. You again!"

TWO

"WHAT IS WRONG WITH YOU, WALKER?"

The sheriff was sitting on the edge of his desk beside his hat, looking down at me where I was sitting in a bentwood chair. He was big, his eyes were narrowed and his arms were crossed. He looked more like an angry barn than a man. He was wearing a gray uniform shirt with a star, but he had on blue jeans and boots. He was everything you wanted your sheriff to be. I decided I liked him.

"I'm not sure what you mean, Sheriff."

"You've been in my county for almost a month. I don't know what the hell you think you're doing here, but you've busted up three bars in as many weeks."

"I didn't start any of those fights, Sheriff. And I paid for all the damage that was caused, even though I didn't start the trouble."

"Which is the only reason you're still in my county. You say you don't start these things, but look how you always find your way to the roughest joint in whatever town you're in! Can't you spend your leisure time at Ma Bennett's coffee shop, or the Blueberry Family Restaurant, instead of Gastank's Hog Bar?"

"Mrs. Bennett makes damn fine pie, Sheriff, and the steak at the Blueberry is second to none I've ever eaten, but they don't sell whiskey, and they don't sell beer. So if a man wants to sit and have a quiet drink in your county, there are not many places he can choose from."

He sighed. "Well, no offense, Mr. Walker—and I do take your point—but perhaps you'd be more comfortable in another county where the local population take a more relaxed view of alcohol." He stood, walked around behind his desk and dropped into his chair. "What *are* you doin' here, anyhow? I know you ain't short of money, and I know for a fact you ain't lookin' for work!"

"I don't know, Sheriff. Maybe I'm looking for the answer to that very question."

He stared at me for a moment like he didn't know whether to backhand me or buy me a drink.

"I don't know what personal baggage you're carrying, Walker. I do know that it's my responsibility to keep the peace in my county. Twice I've cautioned you because it genuinely did seem you hadn't started things, and you made handsome reparation without being asked. But this is the third time you've managed to find yourself in a fight. You may not look for trouble, Walker, but you sure as hell find it."

I nodded. "I can't deny that, Sheriff."

He frowned. "You got a home somewhere?"

"Yeah, yes I have."

"Go there. Sort out whatever it is that's causing all..." He gestured at me. "*This!*" Then for good measure he wagged a finger in my direction. "If a man goes through life getting into fights that he ain't lookin' for, that means he's sendin' out some kind of bad message. You go home, Walker, and sort yourself out. I don't want to see you in my county tomorrow. You understand me?"

"I understand you, Sheriff. Is there a fine I need to pay...?"

"You just pay Gastank for the damage to his bar. Then get out of Cottontown."

I stepped out into the cold night and the door banged closed behind me. The sheriff's office was on the edge of town, set in a large lot that had been fenced off but not asphalted, so you had the feeling you were out in the desert. Up above, there was an astonishing number of stars, the moon was rising fat and orange in the east, and you could hear the coyotes howling at it, away in the distance.

I stopped outside the perimeter fence, by the municipal museum building, and paused to pull a Camel from my pack and light up. The sheriff had advised me to go home and sort out my problems. He had probably assumed my problems were wife-related. But all my wife-related problems had solved themselves, when my wife and my potential wife had walked away. My problem was a deeper one than that. My problem was that Omega lived on, either out there in the world, or inside me, in my mind, and I had to find the way to kill it, for once and for all.

I started walking the mile or so to the Hampton Motel, where I had a room and where I had left my car. As I walked, I called Jim. He sounded pleased to hear from me.

"Lacklan. I am just enjoying a glass of Bushmills on the

terrace. I was wondering how long it would be before you called. Where are you?"

"Cottontown, New Mexico. I just got thrown out of the only bar in town, and the sheriff told me he wanted me out of his county by sunrise."

I heard the weathered rasp he used for a laugh. "Nice to know there are still places like that left. What's on your mind?"

"Omicron."

He grunted. "General Francisco Ochoa, supreme commander of the *Brigada de Operaciones Especiales*, second only to the *Secretario de Defensa Nacional*. Or at least, that's what the Secretary of National Defense thinks."

I turned into 2nd Street and started walking south. The road was long and straight, and there was no lighting except from the stars, the moon that was creeping over the horizon, and what little light filtered out through the closed drapes of the sparse, one story houses that flanked the road. The silence was heavy, like a palpable thing that made the echo of my footsteps loud, almost startling in the stillness.

"You been doing your homework?" I asked.

"I had a feeling you'd be calling soon to discuss the Greek alphabet."

"You going to tell me what the Sheriff of Hidalgo County told me, to go home and sort out my problems?"

"That's good advice."

"Yeah, only my problems aren't at home."

"How far are you? Six, seven hundred miles?"

"About that."

"In that electric monster of yours, you could be here in five or six hours. Spend a few days here, swim in the ocean, enjoy some time with Mioko. We'll eat and drink and talk about Omicron."

On an impulse, I turned and looked behind me. There was nobody there, just the long, lonely road I had already walked, and beyond it the desert. Ahead of me the same long, dark road with no end in sight, flanked by the silent, dark houses.

"Sounds like a plan, Jim. Will Njal be there?"

"He's away on business at the moment. But we can call him back if we decide it's necessary."

"Yeah, good."

"I'll expect you for an early breakfast then."

"See you, Jim."

I arrived at the motel parking lot shortly before ten. The monster Jim had referred to was a matte black 1968 Mustang Fastback. Only, under the hood it had something different. This was a modified Zombie 222, from Bloodshed Motors in Texas. There was no roar when you fired her up, no thunder, no sound at all. But its twin engines delivered eight hundred bhp and one thousand eight-hundred foot-pounds of torque, instantly, directly to the back wheels. The acceleration was insane: from 0-60 in one and a half seconds, with a top speed of 200 MPH. And she was totally silent.

I opened the trunk and checked my kit bag. I hadn't replenished it since the affair in Freeport. I had my two Sig Sauer p226s, the Smith & Wesson 500, my Fairbairn & Sykes fighting knife, the suppressed Maxim 9 and my take down bow, but there was little else. If I decided to go after Omicron I'd need to replenish my arsenal.

I closed the trunk and went to pack my bag and check

out. For the first time in six months, I felt suddenly cheerful again.

———

I TOOK the I-10 via Tucson and Phoenix and drove through the night. It was just over six hundred miles and though there were places where I had to go slow, from Phoenix to Riverside, the road was straight and mostly desert, and I was able to hit speeds of 120 MPH, and peaked outside Blythe at 150. I guess it averaged out at around a hundred and ten, because I left the motel at midnight and pulled up outside Jim Redbeard's house on Paseo de la Playa, in Malaga Cove, at fifteen minutes before six. The sun was rising over the San Gabriel mountains in the east, turning the pale blue sky slightly pink and washing the ochre walls of his house with bronze light. I grabbed my bag from the trunk and made my way to the door. It was already open and he was waiting for me on the step.

He embraced me, took my bag and asked, "How long can you stay?"

The smell of coffee and freshly baked bread was strong on the air. Through the large, open space that was his living room, I could see the glass doors open onto his terrace. Before I could answer, he leaned into the kitchen, gave some instructions and led me out to the terrace with his hand on my shoulder. Out there, he had a huge, old wooden table set in the shade of some palms above a garden that sloped down, threaded by a winding path, toward the edge of the cliff over-looking the cove. The ocean was vast and dark, reflecting the early sun in a winking sheen of broken light. He sat at the head of the table and I sat facing the ocean.

"I don't know," I said in answer to his earlier question. "That's kind of why I am here."

"You are feeling lost. You brought down Omega, and now you don't know what to do with yourself. All you know is warfare, and fighting."

Two young girls who might have been Filipino came out with two pots of coffee and several baskets of hot bread and croissants, creamery butter and cold pressed honey. They deposited them on the table and left. I helped myself to a hot roll and broke it open while he poured the strong, pungent black brew.

"That's just it, Jim. I am not sure that I have brought down Omega."

He grunted. I spread butter on the roll and watched it melt, spooned on thick, waxy, aromatic honey and bit into it. While I chewed, he gazed out at the ocean.

"Do you know," he asked without looking at me, "how William the Conqueror defeated the Saxons at the battle of Hastings?"

I wiped my mouth and sipped coffee. "The legend is that a Norman archer shot King Harold in the eye with an arrow."

He shrugged and turned his attention to a hot roll. "That may or may not have happened. Harold had formed an impenetrable wall of shields and spears, a common tactic of the time. The Normans, who were, as I am sure you know, Danes and Norwegians, not Frenchmen, charged again and again, with infantry and cavalry, but they were unable to break the Saxons' wall."

He bit into the soft, crusty bread and chewed thoughtfully for a while. Eventually he drained his cup and refilled it, and I began to wonder if he was going to finish his story. But he started speaking again.

"Harold's men were exhausted. They had just, only recently, defeated Harald Hardrada at the battle of Stamford Bridge, less than three weeks earlier, and had had to march almost three hundred miles to confront William's forces, where they had formed a beachhead at Hastings, on the south coast of England. Harold had about seven thousand men, many of whom he had recruited during the march. They were practically all infantry, with very few archers.

"William, a true Danish tactician, like his great grandfather, Ganger Rolf, had a well balanced army. He had about ten thousand men, barely half were infantry, and the rest were divided between cavalry and archers.

"Battle was joined on October 14th, some miles from Hastings, near the village of Battle. It lasted all day, from nine in the morning until dusk with, as I say, wave after wave of Norman attacks being repulsed by this impenetrable wall of exhausted, but determined Saxons.

"Finally, after what seemed to be one final, desperate attack, as dusk was falling, the Normans turned in disarray, and fled. Fresh from defeating Hardrada, exhausted from the march and the day-long battle, the Saxons were exultant, and they made a mistake which was to shape the history of the entire planet for the next thousand years."

Now he turned to look at me and said: "They broke ranks and they charged, pursuing their enemy. But it had been a ruse. The fleeing cavalry promptly turned and charged. The impenetrable wall had been broken, not by

Norman attack, but by the Saxon decision to pursue their enemy. The Saxons were decimated, Harold was killed, William marched on London and, despite pockets of resistance, he soon subjected the country and sowed the first seeds for what would become the British Empire."

I sat in silence, staring at the gleaming ocean, chewing hot bread and sipping strong black coffee. Eventually, I said, "I am not sure what you're trying to tell me, Jim."

"It would be presumptuous of me to tell you anything, Lacklan. You have proved yourself to be a supremely capable warrior. What I am doing is illustrating a fact which you already know: that sometimes it is advantageous for your enemy to think you are stronger than you are, sometimes it is an advantage for your enemy to think you are weaker than you are. What you never want is for your enemy to know your actual strength.

"Harold lost the battle of Hastings because he went after William, having underestimated his strength. Are you sure you are not at risk of making that same mistake?"

I shook my head. "No, I am not sure." I thought a moment longer and added, "I'm not sure of anything, Jim. I left the SAS because I was tired of killing, and all I've done since I set up in my house and my workshop in Wyoming is get rich and kill people. Is this all I am capable of? Do I feel lost because there is nobody left for me to kill?"

He leaned back in his big, wooden armchair and regarded me from under hooded eyes.

"In the first place, that is not all you have done. You inherited your money, legitimately, from your father, and you have used your energy and your resources to help bring down one of the most dangerous political organizations since the Third Reich. But..." He stroked his long beard. "It is interesting that in your eyes, that is all you've done."

"What's that supposed to mean?"

He shrugged. "Was bringing down Omega just incidental? Was the real thing for you the fight? Perhaps it didn't really matter to you, deep inside, who you were fighting, just as long as you were fighting. It can become like that for some men."

I peeled a pack of Camels and extracted a cigarette. I offered him one and he shook his head, waiting for me to answer. I flipped my Zippo and leaned into the flame. Then as I let out the smoke, I said, "I've been thrown out of almost a dozen bars in the last six months. I've been arrested six times and thrown out of three counties. All for brawling. I should have gone home to Kenny and Rosalia at Christmas, instead I've been drifting across the southern states, drinking and getting into fights. I'm worried, Jim. How long will it be before I kill an innocent man? Why can't I accept that the job is done, and it's time to enjoy the peace?"

He was laughing, but it wasn't a happy laugh. "That's a lot of different questions, Lacklan. For a start, there is no such thing as an innocent man. How long before you kill a man you did not intend to kill? That has been a question hanging over you since you were eighteen. You are just more aware of it now, because you have no defined enemy. You are a gun looking for a target, and that makes you dangerous."

He looked up at the sky, as though he were seeking guidance from the gods. "Why can't you accept that the job is done? I have no doubt, Lacklan, that if you asked a psychoanalyst that same question, he would point to your unresolved Oedipal complex and your need to kill your father and possess your mother. And no doubt there would be some truth in that. But for me, the explanation is simpler."

"I'm not crazy about the psychoanalytical explanation."

"Few people are. Personally I think Freud had it about right. But my own view, Freud aside, is that you are a warrior. Warriors are a thing the modern world has little use for. That is true of men in general, in fact. This is now a woman's world, where the great virtues are empathy, compassion, dialogue.." He made a vague gesture with his hand. "Good men are men who are caring and sensitive, who know how to listen, who emulate women. Men like you and me are largely obsolete, we are anachronisms, viewed with disfavor. The world has little use for us, and let's face it, we have little use for the world." He sighed. "As long as you were fighting Omega, you could ignore this fact. But with no enemy to fight, you look around you and wonder where the hell you are supposed to fit in. Especially..." He paused, nodding slowly at the table. "Especially since you lost your wife and Marni." He turned his eyes on me. "They, either one of them, might have given you a sense of purpose. Serving women is about the only purpose men seem to have left these days. We are born, we go to university, we get a job. Somewhere along the line we find a woman to adore and serve, and she and her children become the focal point of our lives. The highest a man can aspire to in modern society is being a good husband. That is the modern way."

I burst out laughing. "That's a pretty unorthodox view, Jim."

"That's the word, unorthodox. Does it help at all?"

I took a drag on my cigarette and thought about it. "You're right, I do feel that I have no place and no purpose.

With Omega gone, Marni and Abi, I feel like I don't know what my purpose is. Yeah, that's all true." I smiled and shook my head. "But I'm not so sure the solution for me is finding a woman and devoting my life to her."

"I wasn't proposing that, Lacklan. Omega are hurt, but they are not finished. There is a chance they are pulling a 'Battle of Hastings' ruse. I just want you to be sure, if you decide to go after them, that you know why you are doing it. If Harold's men had known why they were chasing the Normans, they might have timed it better and won the day. Don't go after Omicron because your head is full of murderous passion, go after him because you have decided to destroy him. Be systematic."

I eyed him a moment. "They are not finished?"

"You know they're not. They still have their Asian branch, their African branch and, above all, their South American branch. They may be down, I have no doubt you damaged them badly when you took out the computer system in Brussels[1], but they are far from out. In fact, I would say that right now they are possibly at their most dangerous."

My coffee had gone cold, but I drained my cup anyway. I studied the black dregs a moment, frowning, and finally said, "So you think I ought to go after them, and finish them?"

"Oh yes," he said. "I think you should study your attack carefully, then you should go in and kill Omicron, and all the rest of them; but especially Omicron."

---

1. See *Kill: Two*

THREE

WE STEPPED OUT AFTER BREAKFAST, CROSSED THE parking lot at the end of the road and found a trail leading down the cliff to the beach below. It wound, with no real sense of purpose, through a scrubland of small bushes that looked like thyme, rosemary and lavender, rocks and small boulders. And, further down the cliff, closer to the sand and the sea, it wound among bigger bushes and small trees that I could not identify. Above, seagulls wheeled and cried out to the wind. Below, large breakers were rolling in off the Pacific and, though they were a good hundred and fifty or two hundred yards away, the roar and the spray were carried on the brisk morning breeze, and both reached us.

Halfway down, Jim stopped to sit on the steps that had been hewn out of the living rock and gazed out at the immensity of the ocean beneath us. I sat on a boulder nearby and listened for a while to the huge, heavy sigh of the waves thundering onto the shore, and then retracting back into the deep.

"If I understand the way they think," Jim said suddenly, "Omega is not the organization. Omega is the state the organization is in at the present time." He raised a hand. "Was in, until you came along."

"Timmerman said words to that effect," I said. "Each letter of the Greek alphabet represented a period of development in human society. Omega was the last stage, the stage we were at."

He nodded. "Right, so Omega, or, in English, Mega O, the big O, is the end. It's the final stage of expansion or dilation before everything collapses in on itself."

"That sounds about right. That's what they were about, wasn't it? Preparing for the big collapse."

"Yup..." He squinted at the horizon, like he was having some internal dialogue. The wind whipped his hair across his face and his beard crawled over his shoulder. "Then, you showed up..." He turned to look at me. "You didn't actually show up, did you?"

"No, my father sent Ben to get me."

"But we now know that your father was Gamma in the organization, and Ben was Alpha. And even though Ben was acting as your father's secretary, that was just a front. Ben was in fact your father's superior."

I frowned. "I guess he was."

"So it doesn't make much sense that your father would send Ben to get you..."

I stared at him. A sudden gust battered my face, carrying with it the smell of the sea. My mind reached and strained, but couldn't grasp it.

"My father..." I said, and faltered. "Marni had disappeared. She'd taken her father's research into..."

"Into what?"

"Into climate change, into the activities of Omega... Nobody is really sure."

"Except Marni."

"Yes..."

"And she had gone missing."

"She'd disappeared, left me a coded message that she was in Colorado..."

"And your father told you that he had sent Ben to get you, to go and look for her.[1]"

"Yes, but obviously, if Ben was Alpha, it must have been his decision, not my father's..." I frowned at him where he sat, turned slightly back toward me, with his hair and his beard flapping erratically across his face in the wind. "Why? Why would he do that?"

He grunted and stood. "If you'll forgive me saying so, that's a question you should have asked yourself when you first realized he was Alpha. It's an important question."

I watched him descend the steps for a while, toward the beach two hundred feet below, then I rose and followed him.

I caught up with him when we had reached the bottom of the long flight of steps, and he was standing on the sweep of white sand with his arms crossed, looking out at the towering waves, rolling, foaming and crashing in onto the shore. He glanced at me as I drew level and we started to walk, pushing through the sand. He said:

"So Omega is the end of a process, the final dilation, expansion, exhaustion of a process. Omicron—micro O, is

---

1. See *Dawn of the Hunter*

exactly the opposite. It is the contracted, initial stage of a process."

"Like a seed."

"Exactly like a seed. A seed is an omicron."

"So the implication is obvious. The new process—the new Omega, for want of a better name—will be born from Omicron."

"That's what I think."

"But why not Alpha? Omicron is the fifteenth letter of the alphabet. It is well over halfway through. Why is that the beginning?"

He smiled at me and placed a huge hand on my shoulder. "Will you, do you think, when you are finally too old to go around beating people up, will you become a philosopher?"

I shook my head. "I have no time for navel-gazing, Jim. No offense intended, but to be eternally asking questions you know you can never answer..." I shook my head again.

He rumbled a laugh. "That is mainly the European rationalists," he said. "The English empiricists were a whole different kettle of fish. And Newton was an alchemist, you know? But to answer your question, does a child begin in his mother's womb? Does it begin in the egg? Both of those are omicron. But the child, the process of the child, begins before that. It begins with alpha, the blade, penetration, insemination. But in reality, Lacklan, there is no beginning and no end. The whole thing is a cycle, and it perpetuates itself to infinity, like Jörmungandr, the Midgard Serpent, that eats its own tail."

I raised a hand. "OK, let me get my feet back on the ground. What we are saying is that, according to the doctrine of Omega, their South American arm, and in particular Omicron, is charged with putting them back on the map if somebody like me comes along, takes out the leaders and destroys their computer network."

"Yes, you could put it like that."

"Then I have to agree with you. It is essential that we take out Omicron."

"Mh-hm." He nodded a few times, watching his feet as he walked. "But it is not enough to take out Omicron. You have to take them all down, Lambda, Mu, Nu, Xi *and* Omicron. The whole South American operation will have to come down. Then, *then*, we can say that Omega is finished. It won't be easy. You'll need Njal."

We had come to a large, yellow canoe that was lying on the sand. Here Jim stopped, turned and walked a few paces toward the sea, and there sat on the sand. I sat beside him. He picked up a strand of seaweed and started turning it around in his fingers, frowning slightly.

"General Francisco Ochoa, supreme commander of all Mexican special forces. You may sneer, but they train with the Seals. They are combat hardened and very tough. He has them all at his command. And as of right now, he is the supreme commander of Omega, as well." He wagged the piece of seaweed a few times. "And you should also bear in mind that South America is not Europe or the United States. Different rules apply, and far fewer of them. It is a very thin veneer of civilization overlaid on absolute anarchy."

"I have worked there."

"Of course you have."

"Do you know who the others are?"

"Raul Rocha, Minister for Mines and Energy in Brazil." He smiled at me with hooded eyes. "They have one of those over there, a minister for mines and energy. That's Lambda, obviously he works and lives in Brasilia. Mu, Narciso Terry, Minister for Scientific Development in Argentina, based obviously in Buenos Aires. The other three are in Mexico. Nu is Felipe Gonzalez, the governor of the free and sovereign state of Sinaloa, Xi is Samuel Zapata, nicknamed '*El Vampiro*' because he is said to drink human blood. He is the current head of the Sinaloa cartel."

We were silent for a while, listening to the waves crash and thud, and feeling the spray on the wind. After a bit, I said, "It's a major operation. It will take a lot of planning, and support."

"Yes, and we have to be very careful that word does not reach them. This plan has to be hermetic. As far as the world is concerned, you are satisfied that Omega is finished, and now you're letting your hair down, having some fun, learning to be a playboy. The plan has to be developed in absolute secrecy."

"What about Njal?"

He thought for a while and answered obliquely. "Take a few days to familiarize yourself with their bios, their photographs..." He glanced at me. "I have them back at the house. You know the routine: get to know them, who they are, who their families are, what they do each day, how they spend their weekends..." He twisted up the piece of seaweed in his hands, tied it into a knot and dropped it in the sand. "Meantime, be seen around town, take some girls to dinner, go dancing, try to get noticed by the society pages. You're a rich playboy, behave like one. While you're doing that, I'll contact Njal. I'll arrange a get together somewhere discreet in a few days' time, and we'll discuss the plan." He paused, then added heavily, "Put some flesh on the bones."

———

BEING a playboy isn't something that comes naturally to me. Instead, I developed a routine of rising at five AM, running down the steps to the beach, training for an hour in the surf and then running back up the steps for breakfast at seven. After breakfast, I would take the photographs and bios of one of the heads of Omega III and digest them. I also tried to familiarize myself as much as I could with their homes, towns and workplaces via Google Earth and Google Maps. It wasn't much but it was something.

On the morning of the third day, Jim joined me for breakfast on the terrace. He asked me how I was getting on. I told him I had a pretty good basic knowledge of Raul Rocha and Narciso Terry and was working on the others. He squinted out at the sea for a while and then grinned.

"If I were Omicron—General Ochoa—I would have men watching you. I don't know if he has. I haven't seen anyone. Maybe he doesn't know where you are. But considering the damage you have caused so far, I would definitely have somebody looking for you, and ideally watching you." He turned his long, pale, blue eyes from the sea to look at me. "If he has, what is he going to see? He's going to see Bruce Lee. Up at five to run up and down cliffs and fight with the Pacific surf, then locked in Professor Redbeard's house all day. And who is this Professor Redbeard we have never heard of till now? Perhaps we should look into him..."

I sighed. "Playboy... How do you do that? It's not something that comes easily to me."

"Even if I had a damn, Lacklan, I wouldn't give one. Take Mioko out tonight. I'm pulling strings and booking you a table for two at Mélisse, in Santa Monica. It's one of the most expensive restaurants in town. After that, go to a club. Dance. And tomorrow I want you going to a show or a play or a concert. I don't give an amoeba's fart where you go, but you better be seen in town or I'm pulling the plug." He pointed at me. "Omega is dead and you are celebrating. Get over it."

He stood, slapped me on the shoulder and returned to his study.

So for the next three nights, I went out on the town with Mioko. She didn't talk a lot, but agreed with everything I said and did. At first I found that annoying and even tried to get her to complain about how Jim treated her and used her and the other girls, but she seemed to find that amusing and in the end I gave up and started to relax. We had fun, and every night, when we went home, she would come to my bed with me. She seemed to take it for granted.

On the morning of the fourth day, when I got back from training on the beach, Jim joined me for breakfast again on the terrace. We were served bacon, fried bananas and pancakes with cold pressed honey by the two Filipino girls. Jim poured himself coffee, drank and asked:

"How are you coping with the stress of having fun?"

"I'm coping. Mioko is a nice girl."

He chuckled and his long eyes swiveled to look at me as he cut into his bacon. There was something that bordered on leering malevolence in them. "I wouldn't advise you to fall in love with her."

"I don't plan to."

"You think they are my slaves?"

I shrugged. "It's none of my business. They seem to be happy."

"Mioko tells me you tried to incite her to rebel against me."

"Maybe I did. She seemed to find the idea as amusing as you do."

He chuckled again as he finished his bacon, then leaned back in his chair holding his coffee cup. "We'll go this afternoon and meet with Njal. He has a house in Arizona which we bought recently. It is secluded and off the grid, so we'll have privacy there. I've booked you on a private jet to D.C. for the sake of appearances. Somebody who looks like you will take your place, and Mioko will accompany him."

"Does this somebody know why..."

"They don't even know they are setting a false scent. They think they are going to D.C. for a perfectly legitimate purpose, to handle some business for me."

I nodded. "You're subtle, Jim. I only hope you're on the side of the angels."

He shook his head. "I'm not. I'm on the side of the valkyries." He laughed, like he'd told a joke, but his long, pale eyes were watching me. He stood and patted my shoulder. "Pack a bag and make whatever preparations you need to make. We'll leave as soon as you're ready."

An hour later, he rolled out a gray Wrangler Moab and we put the Zombie away in his garage. I threw my bag in the back, climbed in and slammed the door, and we set off through town. He didn't talk much until we'd joined the I-15 at Etiwanda and we were headed north out of town toward Victorville. Then he said, "Are we being followed?"

"No."

"Njal is at a place called Cadiz. It's about ninety miles east of Barstow, in the Mojave desert. We should be OK there. The few people he comes across, he tells them his name is Pierre and he's from Paris, the French one. That explains his accent."

"He has a Norwegian accent."

"You think they can tell in Cadiz?" He grinned at me.

"I guess maybe not."

"I want to put some flesh on the bones of our plan there. I think we might need to strike sooner rather than later."

"Why?"

"Why do I think that, or why do we need to strike?"

"Both."

"Njal has some intelligence that suggest Omicron may be active. And if he is, we may have a problem."

"Active how?"

"I'll let Njal explain that."

FOUR

SHORTLY AFTER ELEVEN THAT MORNING, WE turned east at Barstow, onto the I-40. The road was long and straight, flanked on both sides by scorched desert and gnarled shrubs as far as the eye could see, with only distant ridges of purple-tinted mountains to break the endless prospect. The air was dry and, in the growing midday heat, it shimmered and warped above the ochre dust.

"You might want to close the windows and turn on the AC," Jim had said at one point, "but personally I prefer to sweat and let the desert air cool me as we drive."

We drove on for almost an hour, until we came to Ludlow and there turned south and east along the National Trails Highway, going ever deeper into the desert. An hour after that I spotted an hacienda, surrounded by tall palms and eucalyptus trees, enclosed within yellow adobe walls, about a half mile from the road, on the left. Jim slowed shortly after and turned off the road onto a pitted, dirt track which we followed, trailing a great plume of red dust, on a winding course to the hacienda gates. Those gates were steel and electronically controlled, set in walls that were some ten feet high. Jim smiled. "It might look like a quaint adobe hacienda, but this place is a high-tech fortress. Make no mistake."

Tall palm trees towered over the walls and as the gates rolled back I could see sprawling gardens with yucca plants, aloe, Saguaro cacti and tall eucalyptus groves. Set among the palms and the eucalyptus, at the end of a dusty driveway, some eighty or ninety feet from the gate, was a white, two story house with a veranda completely shrouded in vines hung with huge clusters of purple flowers, and to the left, also in the shade of the trees, a vast terrace with a gleaming, turquoise swimming pool.

Three steps rose from the drive to a covered arbor outside the front door, where Njal sat on a step, smoking and watching us.

We pulled up in the shade of a palm, Jim killed the engine and we climbed out. Njal approached on his long, thin legs, smiling, with his cigarette hanging from the corner of his mouth. He embraced me and then Jim, and we made our way up the steps to the house.

"We are alone, my friends. We have much to talk. I have couple of chickens in the oven, beer in the fridge, we eat by the pool in half an hour. Lacklan, I show you your room."

We were in a large hall with deep terracotta floors and white walls. A dark wooden staircase rose to a galleried landing on the upper floor. Jim said he was going to get a drink and Njal led me upstairs to a heavy oak door. There he slapped me on the shoulder.

"Have a shower, change your clothes. I see you downstairs in twenty minutes." He said that but he didn't walk away. He stared at the door, sucking his teeth, then added, with a nod, "Maybe this is the big one, you know? Maybe we die this time." Then he gave his head a small twitch. "But it's a good way to die."

I didn't know what to answer, so I watched him make his long, lanky way to the stairs and descend them two at a time at a slow run.

The room was large and bright, with a large window overlooking the desert, heavy beams on the ceiling and a large, comfortable bed. I took a fifteen minute cold shower, dressed and went down to join Njal and Jim by the pool. Jim had stripped down to some tropical Bermudas and was in the turquoise water. Njal was by a brick barbeque with a tray of roasted, quartered chickens which he was dousing with herbs and olive oil from a stone jug.

In the dappled shade of some trees there was a table set up, and beside it a large metal bucket full of ice, encrusted with bottles of beer.

"Take a brew, Lacklan. Bring me one, too, yuh?"

He said that and dropped a chicken leg on the iron grill. It hissed and flames leapt and soared, licking at the flesh and singeing it. Seven more pieces followed as I pulled two bottles from the ice, opened them and set one down on his work table as he poured more of the sauce over the dismembered fowls. More flames leapt and seared their flesh. I heard the slosh and slap of water behind me and Jim pulled himself out of the pool. For a moment, I had a strange sensation that I had stepped into an especially weird chapter of Alice in Wonderland. As Jim toweled himself dry, I said to Njal, "What's the intelligence you've got?"

He pointed at the table where I'd put his beer. There was a terracotta dish with an aluminum lid. "There you got potatoes fried in olive oil, with cayenne pepper too. Take that to the table. I bring the chicken. Then I tell you about these guys."

I sighed, picked up the fries and carried them to the table. He followed with the quartered chickens. Jim had finished toweling himself and was pulling the cork on a bottle of wine. As Njal set down the chicken and sat, he said, "We godda kill these guys." He looked up at me. "And we godda kill them soon, man. Siddown."

I sat. He reached into the dish and pulled out a chicken breast and a wing. I helped myself to a leg while Jim spilled fried potatoes onto his plate and passed the dish to Njal. He helped himself and passed it to me as Jim filled our glasses with rich red wine. Njal drained his glass of beer, sat back and belched, then tore into the meat with his hands and teeth. As he chewed, he spoke.

"I'm gonna take these guys one at a time and tell you what I have found out. Some of this shit you know already, some of it will be new, but what I tell you about Felipe Gonzalez, Samuel Zapata and General Francisco Ochoa, this is all gonna be new to you. That's Nu, Xi and Omicron. This is bad shit, man."

Jim said, "Tell us."

"OK, first, Lambda: Raul Rocha, Minister for Mines and Energy in Brazil, lives in Brasilia, Shis QI 12, Conjunto 15, that's how they are making addresses in Brasilia. Crazy shit. It's on Lago Paranoa. He works at the Ministry of Mines and Energy, Esplanada dos Ministérios. He gets driven every day to work in his Bentley by his chauffeur, who is also his personal body guard. The car is bullet-proof and bombproof, but latest intelligence suggests he is not on red alert. Security at his house is high, security at the ministry is moderate to high. My source tells me that morale is complacent. Every Wednesday evening he goes to see his mistress at her house on Shis Qi Conjunto 6."

Jim raised an eyebrow at him. "Complacent? That is surprising given the fact that Omega I and II have recently been put out of action. We must be sure not to be the same."

I nodded. Njal grunted. "We can view footage later in the house. Initial analysis suggest the ideal spot for a hit is at the gate, as he exits in the morning, or in his office. But we need to do some brainstorm for this."

He picked up his chicken and bit into it.

I asked, "How secure is your source?"

He looked at me with no expression for a moment, then said through a mouth full of food, "Dead, so pretty secure." He shrugged and swallowed. "He was drunk, driving his car. You shouldn't drink and drive."

I sipped my wine. "OK, what about Mu?"

"Narciso Terry, Minister for Scientific Development in Argentina, works at the Ministry of Scientific Innovation, Avenida Cordoba, Buenos Aires. Lives at 42 Calle Parera, penthouse apartment, five minutes from the ministry on the other side of the Avenue 9 de Julio. Status of morale, again, complacent. Level of security moderate both at the ministry and at home. Wife, fifteen-year-old daughter, seventeen-year-old son, both at boarding school."

I narrowed my eyes. There were alarm bells going in my head. "Why are they complacent?"

He shrugged and shook his head.

I said, "Mistress?"

He stuffed fries into his mouth and shook his head again. "No. More like random, occasional trips to clubs and whorehouses."

"Recommended hit?"

He thought about it while he chewed, then picked his teeth with his tongue. "My personal opinion, at home. Kill the wife too."

Jim stopped chewing, with the chicken breast in his hands, and watched Njal. "Why?"

"Because she will probably be a witness, and also it is probable she is involved with the organization."

I said, "I don't like it. We'll discuss it. What else?"

"We look at the details later, in the house. Now, Nu, Xi and Omicron: Felipe Gonzalez, Samuel Zapata, *el Vampiro*, and General Francisco Ochoa. They all in Mexico, all in the Free and Sovereign State of Sinaloa."

Jim grunted. "Sounds like the HQ is in Sinaloa."

"You ain't kidding. Gonzalez is based in Culiacán, the capital city of Sinaloa State, in a walled, gated fortress on the Avenida Alvaro Obregon. Zapata and Ochoa are living in Mazatlán, a luxury beach town, hundred and twenty miles south of Culiacán , at the mouth of the Gulf of California. They are like an hour away from each other and they are always in touch, by telephone, using telegram, or visiting each other in person. And once a month they get together. And more or less once a month, they go to Zapata's country villa. It's like a palace, yuh? In the mountains near the border with Durango, near a small village called Cosalá, where the Sinaloa have a big fuck off airfield in the middle of the goddamn village."

I said, "Let me get this clear in my mind: we have Lambda and Mu, respectively, in Brazil and Argentina, working in the government and living in the capital cities. Meanwhile , Nu, Xi and Omicron live in Mexico, not in the capital, but in the region of Sinaloa; Nu, the governor of the state, lives in the capital, Culiacán, while Xi and Omicron live an hour's drive away in the coast town of Mazatlán. They stay in touch with each other and once a month they all get together at Zapata's—that's Xi—country villa in the mountains near a large landing strip in the village of Cosalá."

Njal nodded. "You got it."

"What about security?"

"Kind of lax..."

"Them too, huh?"

"Yuh, they have bodyguards and basic security at home and at work, but it is not great high tech stuff, you know? Basically electronic alarm systems and guys with guns. It's like they feel, so long as they are in Sinaloa, nobody is gonna touch them."

We all ate and drank in silence for a few minutes while Jim and I assimilated the information. Finally, I said, "OK, so why the urgency?"

He reached for another leg and broke it in half. "Because the word I get from my contact is that there is a lab at the house in Cosalá, in the mountains. They bringin' equipment in, regular, you know? To the airstrip, takin' it up to the house in boxes, doin' some kind of work up there. They don't let nobody into the lab, but they got some scientists workin' and livin' there."

"Developing drugs?"

"That's what I said. But my source says they don't think so. Is something different. Something more than that."

"Something more, like what?"

"The equipment is all electronic."

Jim said, "We can only speculate. You need to go and get eyes on it."

Njal shrugged. "I agree. My contacts don't know what it's about, but just that fact, that they don't know? That means it is something out of the ordinary. Something that they are spending big money on. We need to see it, and we need to destroy it."

I sighed. "OK. So we start with Mu, Narciso Terry in Argentina. We make it convincing as an accident, or natural causes. We arrive in Argentina separately, we meet up for the kill, we leave separately. Same thing in Brazil, one of us goes to a five star hotel, the other to a hostel, backpacking, whatever. But it's not enough to make Rocha's death look natural. Nobody in Omega is going to buy two deaths by accident or natural causes so close together. So we have to keep it quiet for at least a week."

Njal nodded. "We can do that."

"Then we travel to Mexico. That's going to be more complicated. Sinaloa is not a place you go to as a tourist or on business, unless you're buying drugs."

Jim was stroking his beard. "So you have to make your approach as somebody interested in buying large quantities of heroin and cocaine, with something very valuable to sell in return. We'll have to arrange fake IDs, too."

I said, "Yeah, fake IDs are essential. Buying drugs may attract too much attention. We could be naïve journalists for Rough Guide, something like that. Whatever we decide, we'll have to strike fast, because news of Terry and Rocha's deaths are going to come in pretty quick. We'll have just a few days to make the three hits and get out."

Njal said: "So we time it for when they are all at the villa, and at the same time as we take them out we check out the lab, see what the hell is going on there, maybe destroy it, yuh?"

"Yeah, that's good. We are going to need a lot of firepower and explosives. Getting that into Sinaloa is not going to be easy."

Jim said: "We'll have to bring it down from Arizona by plane or by boat from California. Leave it to me. I'll sort it out. We'll need a drop and collection point, and a place where you can store the stuff till the hit. Maybe..."

He looked at Njal. Njal nodded with his mouth full. "Sole. We fly the material down by sea plane. She can meet the plane in a boat and bring it ashore."

Jim looked at me. "Make a shopping list." Then to Njal, "You too. Let me have it by tomorrow morning." He wiped his mouth. "OK, that's good, we have the makings of a plan. I'm going to make some calls and have a sleep. I'll see you gentlemen this evening."

He stood and we watched him walk back across the terrace, through the glaring sun, toward the shade of the house. Njal refilled our glasses with wine.

"Now he's gonna..." He paused, gave his head a shake. "I don't know, maybe he's gonna sleep or maybe he's gonna meditate, but he's gonna process the whole thing in his mind. It's like his mind is a computer, you know? He inputs the information, leaves it while he sleeps or while he meditates or some shit, and then it comes out couple of hours later: 'OK, you got this problem, that problem, the way we do this is like this and that...' He's an amazing guy."

"How long have you known him?"

He shook his head. "Need to know, man. I like you, I trust you, but information is the weak links in security, right?"

I nodded. "Before we go, I need to talk to Senator McFarlane."

His face went hard. "You need to clear that with Jim."

I spoke calmly, but there was an irrational pellet of anger in my belly. "I don't need to clear shit with anybody, Njal. There are no ranks here and no bosses. This is not the army."

"You talk to the wrong person you put all our lives at risk."

"I'm aware of that. McFarlane is not the wrong person."

He spoke to his glass, and there was something dangerous in his face. "Do me a favor. Lacklan. Talk to Jim before you talk to anybody else, yuh?"

FIVE

NJAL WENT TO HAVE AN AFTERNOON SLEEP. I SWAM in the pool for an hour, then had a cold shower and went for a run in the desert. After that I spent a couple of hours training in the shade of the palms by the pool.

When the white walls of the house were turning copper and pink, and the shadows of the eucalyptus were lying long across the terrace and the turquoise pool, Jim emerged from the house again.

"Let's talk." He said it and his voice seemed to echo slightly in the evening. I didn't answer. I dived in the pool, touched the bottom and erupted at the far end. There I pulled myself out, showered in cold water and toweled myself off while he stood waiting. I walked past him toward the house.

"I need to get dressed. Give me ten minutes."

"Lacklan."

I stopped and turned to face him. "Yeah."

"No rebellion is required here. What's eating you?"

"Nothing."

"You've got people's lives in your hands. I need you stable."

"I need me stable."

"Of course you do. But so do I and so does Njal. You fuck up on your own, that's your fucking problem. You fuck up while we depend on you, that's our problem. If something's eating you, I need to know about it."

"Nothing's eating me."

"Ten minutes, in the study."

Fifteen minutes later, I came down the stairs, crossed the terracotta hall, through the large, modern drawing room and found the study through a solid, dark wood door. There was a heavy Castilian desk, the walls were white lime wash, there was a six foot fireplace and several free standing, low bookcases. There was also a nest of gray, thick linen armchairs and a sofa set around a coffee table. Jim and Njal were sitting there looking at me as I came in. I joined them and sat.

Jim spoke first.

"What I'd like to get resolved this evening is a concrete plan detailing how you intend to make each hit, and how you intend to transition from one hit to the next without alerting the remaining members of the cabal. Of course we might alter and amend the plan as we get closer to execution, but I want the basic structure down this evening, with the essential details."

I didn't wait for Njal to answer. "I approach the ministry of scientific development with a proposal that will appeal to Omega. It might be the development of some form of green energy, cyborg technology, something of that sort. We let it be known that it is highly confidential and that Argentina is especially well placed to help us develop it in Latin America. We also let it be known that it has the private support of Senator McFarlane, who is known for her green credentials. Her sanction—and ideally an introduction—will also ensure we get an audience. We request a private, non-official meeting outside Buenos Aires, intimating that this way it will be financially more beneficial for Narciso Terry himself. We book him into a luxury hotel. On the way to the meeting he has a car crash. Meanwhile we have also booked a high-class hooker into his room so it looks as though he crashed on his way to a rendezvous with a woman."

Njal nodded. "Sounds good. We need to make sure the card used to book the room is untraceable, and that the initial communications regarding the meeting are also strictly confidential and untraceable. We approach him initially by confidential telephone call, via McFarlane, so there is no record of what the contact is about."

"Agreed."

Jim said: "What about the accident itself?"

I said: "We'll have to select a stretch of road, look at the features—ditches, undergrowth, woodland, distance from town, all that stuff—and decide the best way to set it up. We don't want to tamper with his car, the risk is too high, and with forensic techniques they can detect it. What we need is to interrupt his journey, either with an obstacle on the road, or with another vehicle. Maybe a rendezvous."

"OK. What about Rocha in Brazil?"

I thought for a moment and Njal said, "Similar sort of thing. We make an appointment with him in the same way, using Senator McFarlane. Like Narciso Terry in Argentina, we inform him it is confidential and we suggest that if he keeps it quiet there can be benefits for him financially, a bribe. We arrange a meeting with him somewhere quiet and private, maybe at an hotel, like Terry. Maybe use a woman's name, yuh?"

I nodded. "That's possible. Makes him feel safer and provides a red herring for anyone investigating his disappearance."

"When he shows up, you approach him and tell him you gonna take him to meet with whatever her name is—Dr. Elizabeth Strada..."

I shook my head. "Let's not get bogged down in details at this stage."

"OK, whatever, you take him to the kill site. We get whatever information we can from him about Omega 3, kill him and hide the body."

I glanced at Jim. He was nodding slowly. I said, "We need to get access to his personal computer and his phone, send messages to his wife and kids that he's been called away on business."

Jim said: "Buy some postcards, get him to write them out. You provide the text. Send them from Mexico."

"Again, too soon for details. On the ground it doesn't always play out the way you plan it. Let's keep it simple and use the same basic plan for both."

Njal sighed. "OK, so we approach them both in the same way, lure them to a quiet spot and kill them. We godda choose the kill sites for both, and a way to dispose of Rocha's body."

Jim watched him write some notes and asked, "How do you want to tackle Gonzalez, Zapata and the General?"

I spoke before Njal had finished writing. "We time it for

one of their visits to the ranch, where they have the lab. We execute it like a military assault. We insert undetected, recon and then take the place by surprise. We kill everyone except Omicron, we photograph and film the lab, then we destroy the whole place and we bring Omicron here. We interrogate him and then eliminate him."

Njal narrowed his eyes at me. "You want to kill a prisoner?"

"Yeah, Njal, but I don't want to kill his wife."

They both raised their eyebrows at me.

I sighed. "He's not a normal prisoner. Right now he is the most dangerous human being on the planet."

Jim spoke the thoughts I knew were in Njal's mind. "Right now, Lacklan, I'm thinking that person might be you."

My belly was hot but I kept my voice level. "He has to die, Jim, and we also need the information he has."

"Do we?" He gave me a moment, then went on: "Once Omicron is dead and that lab is destroyed, Omega will wither and die too."

I shook my head. "No. Omega III must be using some kind of back up computer network that was not linked to the primary one. That's how they survived. All the data from this lab, whatever it is, must be on that network. They must also have bank accounts, money laundering networks, distribution networks—all connected to that back up computer system. All of that needs to be accessed and destroyed."

Jim shrugged. "Or simply destroyed."

I flared, "We can't destroy it without accessing it, Jim! We need to interrogate him and get access to their computers, the same way we did with Timmerman."

Njal shook his head. "I don't agree to another neutron bomb. The risk with the last one was huge. As it was, it caused massive damage to the European stock market. A lot of innocent people lost their business and their livelihood because of that. Also, Lacklan, I godda tell you man, I am not cool with torturing people. OK, with Timmerman it was necessary, but with Ochoa..."

"Do you know what the Sinaloa cartel do to their enemies? Not just their enemies, anyone who gets in their way..."

"Yeah, I know. That's why I don't wanna become like them."

The burning in my belly turned to cold. "What the hell is wrong with you, Njal? You are going to jeopardize the success of this mission because you're feeling *squeamish?*"

Jim came out and said it. "I'm worried about you, Lacklan."

"Why?"

"Because murdering the members of Omega seems to be becoming more important to you than eliminating what they stand for."

"That's bullshit and you know it!"

"I don't know it, Lacklan, and I think you need to examine your behavior over the last six months."

There was a pressure in my head and my breath was coming short. My voice came out too loud. "What is this, a damned intervention?" I stood. "You invited me on this jaunt, remember? If you think I'm not suited to the job, what the hell am I doing here?"

He raised an eyebrow at me. "Getting mad, by the looks of it, and losing perspective."

I hesitated. "What's that supposed to mean?"

"It means that for the last six months you've been on a short fuse. How many bars did you say you were kicked out of? How many times arrested? This is the most important hit you have ever made in your life, or are ever likely to make again. You need to be clear and you need to be sharp. I don't believe you are either right now. And more serious than that, Lacklan, your motivations are not clear. I am not sure why you are doing this job, and neither are you. How much of this is about anger and revenge and how much of it is about putting an effective end to Omega? You don't want that kind of uncertainty going into this operation."

He waited, watching me. I didn't say anything. I knew he was right and I had nothing to say.

After a moment he sighed. "Njal said you wanted to talk to Cyndi McFarlane. I think that's a good idea. Go to D.C., discuss the operation with her, get her support for the introductions. Make her understand it goes no further than her. Like you, I know Cyndi and I trust her." He spread his hands. "Meantime, Njal and I will be gathering more intel, preparing the groundwork, doing some initial recon of the areas. I'll get your documents ready, tickets, the rest of it."

I nodded. "OK."

"But do me a favor, Lacklan, give this some thought: what's motivating you? We don't need to torture anybody, and we sure as hell don't need a loose cannon."

I nodded again, and said again, "OK. Agreed."

I left the study and climbed the stairs to my room. There I started putting things in my bag. There was still a hot rage in my belly, and I wasn't sure who that rage was against, or what. I was vaguely aware that I had gone there in Jim's truck and that my own car was back in L.A. That made me dependent on Jim, put Jim in control, which somehow made the anger worse. I was struggling to remember that Jim and Njal were not the enemy.

I was zipping up my bag and I heard a footfall behind me, then Njal's voice.

"What are you doing?"

"What does it look like, Njal? I'm packing. I don't see any point in hanging around."

"You're mad."

"You better stop telling me that. You made your point, I got it."

"We still got a lot of details to discuss. You can go tomorrow. Nobody is asking you to leave, Lacklan."

"Don't patronize me, Njal."

"Is what you're doing right now."

I squinted at him, like I couldn't see him clearly. "*What?*"

He jerked his head at me, but spoke slowly and calmly. "You think I need to walk on fuckin' eggshells with you? You think I'm scared of you? If I thought you was no fuckin' good you wouldn't be in this fuckin' house, and sure as hell I would not be talking to you. In my opinion you are the best damn warrior I ever met, and coming from me that means something. I don't want nobody else on this job with me. I want you to get your fuckin' shit straight and do the job. But I don't need to fuckin' patronize you or walk on fuckin' eggshells. I ain't scared of you."

I sighed. I had my bag in my hand and dumped it back on the bed. "What do you want to talk about?"

He crossed his arms and leaned on the doorjamb. "How about women?"

I gave him a look that said if he wasn't scared of me, he should be, and walked to the window. The desert evening was closing in fast and stars were starting to wink over the horizon. I pulled a cigarette from the pack and lit it, then turned and sat against the windowsill. "We going to play psychotherapy now? You going to be my counselor?"

He almost smiled. "Believe me, I don't want to look inside that shit hole you call a head. But you and me, we both know Marni fucked you up on the Timmerman job. That is still burning in you, man. That's not psychotherapy, that's common fuckin' sense."

I threw him the cigarettes and the Zippo. He caught them left handed and lit up. I didn't say anything. He inhaled and as he blew out the smoke, he said, "But that ain't everything, Lacklan. Marni is just the surface."

"What do you mean?"

He tossed the cigarettes and the lighter on the bed. "I'm talking about your father and your mother. Your dad *was* Omega! That's a lot of betrayal, man, going back a long way. You don't need to be Freud to see what's goin' on there. And Marni wasn't just the straw that broke the camel's back. She was more than that." He pointed at me with the smoldering cigarette stuck between his fingers. "You got some dark shit going on, and you need to understand that and get a grip on it in the next couple of days."

I watched the red tip of my cigarette burn for a moment, then I said, "How do I get from here to D.C.?"

"Take one of my cars to Barstow airport. Is an hour west from here. There you get an air taxi to D.C. We can book it online." He paused. "Call Cyndi. Go in the morning. Then come down. We'll have a drink before dinner."

He left and I heard his feet on the stairs. After a moment, I pulled my phone from my pocket and called Cyndi.

"Lacklan, this is a nice surprise. I suppose it's not a social call."

"I'm afraid it's not. I need to see you tomorrow. Can you squeeze me in? It's important."

"You have such a sweet way with words. How long do you need? Will ten minutes do?"

"Let's make it dinner. Are you free in the evening?"

"I am dining with Judge Henshaw and his wife. They have set me up with an oil billionaire from Texas because they think it's time I should start dating again."

"Cancel. This is more important."

"You know, masterful behavior in men is frowned upon by right-thinking people these days, Lacklan."

"I'm serious."

"You are, and no fun. Fine. I'll cancel."

"I'll pick you up at eight thirty. I'm sorry to have spoiled your evening."

"You haven't spoiled it yet, Lacklan. You can still make it right. Remember Route 66? That was fun, right?"

"The Carolyn Inn, in Bristow. You took us to that cute Mexican restaurant. You wore a black leather jacket and no makeup."

"My goodness! You remember!"

"How could I forget?"

"You see? You *can* be romantic."

"It was a careless oversight. Don't get used to it."

"You were nice that night. You didn't kill anybody, at least not in the restaurant."

"Noted. I'll see you tomorrow."

"I look forward to it, I think. Black tie."

"You're on."

I hung up and stood looking at the darkness outside the window for a while. Then I crushed out the cigarette in the ashtray on my bedside table and made my way downstairs, feeling like a child returning from the naughty mat.

SIX

THE FLIGHT TOOK FIVE HOURS AND WE TOUCHED down at Ronald Reagan National Airport in D.C. at four PM. From there I took a cab and crawled through the late afternoon rush hour to the Willard, on Pennsylvania. On the way, I passed by Gieves & Hawkes on Rhode Island Avenue and picked up an off the peg evening suit, while the cab waited. At the hotel I showered and dressed, had a martini in the bar and took another cab to Cyndi's apartment on New York Avenue.

Dusk was turning to evening as we turned into the street. Street lamps and headlamps cast a diffuse, amber glow over the city. I pulled out my cell and called her. She was waiting in the lobby of her apartment block, stepped out onto the sidewalk and waved. We pulled in and I got out into the evening air to open the door for her. She kissed me on the cheek and climbed in the back of the cab. I got in the other side while she was telling the driver, "The Kinship, 7th Street, it's half a mile up the road..."

"I know it, lady."

I closed the door and we took off. I smiled at her. "Either you were really keen to see me or you don't want me in your apartment."

Her smile was slow. "Both."

"Then that's half nice to hear."

"You going to start flirting with me again, Lacklan? I know your heart belongs to another."

I raised an eyebrow and grunted. "You haven't heard the gossip?"

"I heard something. I wasn't sure how true it was."

I didn't answer for a moment. Outside, there was a feeling of evening gearing up for the night, with bright lights and thoughts of exotic booze. When I spoke, I didn't meet her eye.

"I planted information with Marni. I told her we were going after Emanuel Van Zuydam."

"The President?"

"Yeah. It was a deliberate lie. I was going after Timmerman, the Commissioner." I turned to check her expression. She was just staring at me. When she didn't say anything, I went on. "I wanted to see if the information got back to Van Zuydam. It did."

"How? And why on Earth did you suspect her?"

"She told Gibbons, Gibbons told Van Zuydam." I shrugged. "I always thought she was too close to Gibbons. I never trusted him."

"I'm sorry."

"She believed in Gibbons, idolized him. I think she cast him in the role of her father..."

"And you in the role of yours?"

It was my turn to stare. "I'd never thought of that." Then, "Yeah, maybe. Either way, I told her not to pass the information on to him, and she did. So that was kind of the end of it."

She was quiet for a moment. "You're not big on forgiveness, are you, Lacklan?"

I shifted in my seat so I could look at her. "It depends on what I'm forgiving. Betrayal is a hard thing to forgive."

"Are you sure she saw it as betrayal?"

"Does it matter? Not realizing that what you're doing is contemptible doesn't make it less contemptible."

"That's pretty harsh. Are you still in love with her?"

"I'm not sure I ever was."

"Liar." She smiled and her smile said she hoped I was telling the truth. "Is this what you wanted to talk to me about?"

I shook my head, but we were pulling up in front of the restaurant. I paid the driver and we climbed out. The doorman knew her, as did the *maître*, who asked if she wanted her usual table. She said she did and he led us across hardwood floors to a booth with a table and two upholstered couches. Cyndi sat and I told him we'd have two martinis dry and he went away with a happy, busy face.

As I took my seat, she said, "So what *did* you want to talk to me about?"

I studied her face, wishing for a moment that I had come to talk to her about something else—anything else: her, us, my divorce from Abi, my empty house that I couldn't bring myself to return to. I smiled. "You mean apart from wanting to catch up and see how you are?"

She raised an eyebrow.

I sighed. "OK, I know." I hesitated. "I'm going to South America."

She sat back and frowned. "Oh..."

"Brazil and Argentina, then Mexico. I need an introduction to Narciso Terry and Raul Rocha."

Her face went hard. "That's a big ask, Lacklan. I know them both. And Narciso, though he's not a close friend, he's more than just an acquaintance."

I nodded. "He was a friend of your husband's, right? They both were."

She seemed to sag and looked away. "Yes."

"He is Mu, Rocha is Lambda."

She closed her eyes. "Jesus..." She stared at the wall for a moment. The lights, the diners, the waiters and the soft background music all suddenly seemed surreal. She asked, "What are you going to do?" I didn't answer and she turned to meet my eye. I remained expressionless and after a moment she said again, "Jesus, Lacklan. When does this ever end?"

"The other three are in Sinaloa. They have a lab in the jungle, but we don't know what they're using it for or what kind of experiments they are conducting out there. I just figure whatever it is, if the John Richard Erickson Institute was anything to go by, it's not aimed at ending world hunger[1]." I gave my head a small, sideways twitch. "Not by providing food, anyhow."

She narrowed her eyes and seemed to scrutinize me. "You're a son of a bitch, aren't you, Lacklan?"

"My father would probably have agreed with you. He

---

1. See *To Rule in Hell*

wasn't really fond of my mother. He wasn't really fond of me, either."

"These are people you're talking about, Narciso, Rocha, these others..."

"Don't lecture me, Cyndi. If you don't want to be a part of this, I respect that. But don't lecture me about these bastards being human beings. First of all, in my experience, human beings tend to be somewhere below paramecia on the evolutionary scale; second, these particular human beings are murdering sadists who are happy to destroy women and children to make themselves richer and more powerful, third—I've been there, seen it and done it. As far as I am aware, the closest you have got is reading the reports on your desk."

She went rigid. The waiter arrived and placed our glasses in front of us. He smiled. "Are we ready to order?"

Cyndi's face said she was ready to stand up and go home. She took a deep breath and said, "Give us another ten minutes, will you, Paul?"

He left and I said, "I apologize. That was uncalled for."

She was quiet for a long moment. Then sighed. "Yes, it was, but I should not have lectured you. You're right. Apart from our jaunt down to Texas, I have never experienced violence first hand. But I *have* read the reports and I *do* know what Omega are capable of."

"This is a particularly brutal branch of Omega, Cyndi. General Francisco Ochoa, head of the special forces division of the Mexican Army, Felipe Gonzalez, governor of the Free State of Sinaloa, and Samuel Zapata, known as '*El Vampiro*'. These are the senior members of this cell. Samuel Zapata is the godfather of the Sinaloa cartel, and he didn't get his nickname because of his excellent teeth, believe me. The heroin and cocaine trade are at the heart of their operation and they are making hundreds of billions of dollars from it every year, which by the looks of it is being plowed into the resurgence of a new Omega, pared down, revitalized, stronger..." I shrugged again. "They have to be stopped."

"But, like that? Is there no other way?"

I raised an eyebrow at her. "Yeah, we could enter into a meaningful dialogue with them. They're probably not bad people at heart. They probably just feel disenfranchised, that they haven't got a voice in this world. They're merely victims of Western exploitation."

"Remind me why I like you. I keep forgetting."

I smiled. "Don't ask me, I never could work it out."

I pushed the menu across the table to her. She gave me a baleful look and after a moment, she picked it up and started leafing through it and sighing like she couldn't make up her mind. Eventually I called Paul over and I told him, "The lady will have the caviar followed by the Maine lobster. I will also have the caviar, but followed by the pan seared venison. We'll have a Dom Perignon with the caviar, the lady will have an Alain Chavy white Burgundy with the lobster and I'll have a bottle of Savigny-Les-Beaune Burgundy."

Paul gave Cyndi a look you could only describe as fearful. She narrowed her eyes at the menu, then handed it to him and smiled the way only politicians know how. He gave a small bow and hurried away. To me, she said, "Are you trying to provoke a fight with me for some reason, Mr. Walker?"

I turned my glass around a few times, watching the olive

bob. I spoke without humor. "I don't honestly know." Then I raised my eyes to meet hers. "Maybe."

"Why?"

"I don't know that either. I almost had a fight with Jim and Njal just before I came here. I've been thrown in the cooler five times in the last six months, for brawling."

She smiled, then started to laugh.

I went on. "Three times I was actually arrested, and I've been thrown out of six bars from Texas to Arizona. I keep getting into fights. I don't think it's intentional, I'm not aware of provoking it..."

Her laughter subsided, but not the smile. "Well, you were definitely provoking *me*. The last time a man ordered my meal for me was..."

I watched her, waiting. I was smiling too now, because I knew what she was going to say.

"Oh, yes, it was you."

"In Corpus Christi. Then I was definitely trying to annoy you."

She spread her hands and shook her head, wide-eyed. "Why, for heaven's sake?"

I sat looking at her, smiling, thinking that she was actually very attractive and I had never allowed myself to notice before. "Maybe I feel there is unresolved sexual tension between us and this is my way of expressing it."

Her face flushed. Her eyes were bright but her expression was scandalized. I found myself enjoying that and wondering why. She was shaking her head. "Lacklan! That is so... That is *awful!* It's *primitive!* That is *not* the way to seduce a woman!"

"I don't like being told how to do things. Maybe I am

primitive and awful." I leaned forward with my elbows on the table. "You're so good, so moral, so upright. But you are also very attractive. I want to rough you up a bit, make your cheeks burn."

Her face lit up like a Christmas tree and her cheeks burned red, but she was laughing. "Lacklan! Stop that *immediately!* My *God!* What has got into you?"

I shook my head. "I told you, I don't know. Maybe I am just learning to speak my mind. Maybe I've realized life is too short for anything else."

She wagged a finger at me. "You, mister, are on the rebound, and a very dangerous man. You are *still* in love with Marni."

"Is that what you believe or what you hope?"

"I don't know, to be honest. But don't you come marking my territory until you know for sure what you feel."

I knew she was right and let my face say so. "Deal."

She sighed. "Now, you had better tell me about your plan."

I gave her the outline we had worked out at Njal's place, then said, "So I need an introduction to Rocha in Brazil and Narciso Terry in Argentina. Obviously the introduction has to be convincing enough for them to bite, but deniable enough so that if it comes to light, you can distance yourself from it."

She stared down into her drink. After a moment, she said, "Yes, I can do that." She raised her eyes to hold mine. "There are unacknowledged channels for this kind of thing. We all know about them, we all know how to use them. It's how business gets done in certain countries. I'll get you your introductions. Are you going to kill them?"

"Yes. You know I am. All five of them. They are too dangerous to leave them alive." I hesitated a moment. "Besides, Cyndi, somebody has to speak for all the victims: all the kids, all young girls forced into prostitution, the murdered men and boys, the bereaved mothers, all the grief, all the people whose lives have been destroyed because of those men. There has to be some comeback, some retribution."

A small frown creased her brow above her nose. "I agree, but what makes you the judge, jury and executioner?" The question wasn't hostile. It wasn't a challenge. It was a genuine question. She added, "Aren't you playing God?"

I gave my head a small twitch. "If God ever starts doing his job, maybe I can give up mine." She didn't like that and her face showed it. A couple of waiters arrived, one with our caviar and the other with a bottle of champagne in an ice bucket. He popped the cork and poured, then went away.

I sighed. "I'm not a philosopher, Cyndi. I've been to some dark places and I have seen men, women and children in extreme situations most people wouldn't believe. I have seen cruelty and savagery most people couldn't begin to imagine, and I have seen honor, courage and compassion that beggar belief. I have seen human beings digging deep and finding that cruelty and that compassion and courage inside themselves. But I'll tell you what I have never seen. I have never seen a devil rise out of a fiery pit and force anybody to be cruel, and I have never seen an angel or a god come down from the sky and rescue a baby from the hands of a killer." We were quiet for a moment, staring at each other. After a moment, I picked up a piece of toast and stared at it. "And I never saw an animal that understood morals. The whole damn show is something we invented, so that people would abdicate responsibility."

She frowned. "What do you mean?"

I spooned caviar onto the toast and put it in my mouth. I spoke around it as I chewed. "Morality is something we invented so that people would hand responsibility for their actions over to the kings and the priests, appointed by God to judge mankind. But it's a fiction. Morality does not occur in nature. Balance, pain, pleasure—all of those do; but morality does not. These five men have crossed my path, what they do offends me and causes pain to incalculable numbers of people. So I will eliminate them. Nobody else is responsible, Cyndi. Nobody gets to judge me or send me to hell or heaven. I do that, and go there, travel the path, all on my own."

I drained my glass, refilled it and spooned more caviar into my mouth. She watched me do it and, with an odd expression on her face, said: "You are a very frightening man, Lacklan."

I smiled.

After a moment, she shook her head. "If what you say is true, how do you decide what is right and wrong? How do you decide who is good or who is bad? If there is no morality, what makes *El Vampiro* a bad person, or General Ochoa?"

"Nothing. They are not bad people. They are just people. They are people who murder and torture, and destroy lives. They are people who cause suffering on a massive scale. As long as you're using ideas like good and bad, moral and immoral, you are in the land of smoke and mirrors and you will never see anything clearly. These men are not bad, they are cruel. They make people suffer and they enjoy it. End of story. I don't want these people in my world, so I take them out."

She narrowed her eyes. "Are you telling me you have no moral code *at all?*"

I shrugged. "Be kind."

"That's it?"

"That's it."

"Are you going to be kind to these five men?"

"I am going to be kind to the world they have raped and pillaged." Then I hesitated, thinking of Jim and Njal, and added, "Yeah, I'll be kind to them. I won't torture them," and added in my mind, 'unnecessarily.'

After a moment, she turned her attention to her own caviar and said in a small voice, "I'm glad you're on my side."

I sat back and sipped my champagne, watching her eat. "Yeah," I said, "I'm glad you're on mine."

SEVEN

IT WAS MIDNIGHT AND THE AIR WAS COOL WHEN we climbed out of the cab and stood at the door of her apartment block. The city was quiet but for the desultory hiss of tires on blacktop on the avenue behind me. Behind her were the plate glass doors of her block, with the amber reflection of the streetlamps in them, and our own dark shapes, standing close, looking at each other.

She placed her hand on my chest and said, "You know I want to ask you up."

"Are you going to?"

"No."

"That's a shame."

"You're all kinds of trouble, Lacklan. I can't do that." She smiled. "I'm not a one night stand kind of girl, and you are a lifetime of trouble kind of guy. Can we be friends?"

I bent and gave her a kiss on the cheek. "Always."

I watched her step inside and disappear toward the elevators, then I started down New York Avenue. My hotel was a fifteen minute walk down 14th Street and I needed to think. The last four hours of conversation with Cyndi had been all kinds of interesting, but they had done nothing to clear my mind or resolve the issues that were troubling Jim and Njal.

I took it easy, with my hands in my pockets, watching the sporadic traffic hiss past, listening to the occasional noises of the closing night: car doors, a rattling roller-blind coming down, shouts of laughter across the dark city. My mind wandered back, trying to recall something Njal had said. He had thrown my Camels and the Zippo on the bed and pointed at me with a smoldering cigarette between his fingers:

I'm talking about your father and your mother. Your dad was Omega! That's a lot of betrayal, man, going back a long way. You don't need to be Freud to see what's goin' on there. And Marni wasn't just the straw that broke the camel's back. She was more than that... You got some dark shit going on, and you need to understand that and get a grip on it in the next couple of days.

My father's betrayal was clear enough to see. He just hadn't liked me and I hadn't liked him. Our life together had been a constant battle which he had resolved by sending me to boarding school. It was something I had grown accustomed to many, many years ago. So why should it start troubling me now?

I turned into 14th Street and started south. A red and white taxi sighed past. Its brake lights glowed, it slowed and turned right. A hundred yards ahead, a car was parked with its hazards on. There was a man standing by the open door talking to a woman. She was gesticulating at him. He was gesticulating back.

I logged it as a failed date, a lovers' tiff, and thought about my mother breaking up with my father. It was a thing that had happened by degrees, while I was boarding at school. She was always there when I came home for holidays, but they were always a little more distant, a little less involved with each other. I never questioned that she spent so much time at the apartment in New York, or that she started traveling back so much to visit her family in England. All the while she had been leaving, without telling me. Was that betrayal?

The car was a BMW. It was fifty paces away now and I could see the couple and hear them clearly. She was leaning forward slightly, talking loudly, staring into his face. She was mad. He was leaning back, but the expression in his eyes said he was reaching his limit. She told him he was a loser and followed up by telling him he had a small dick and was shit in the sack.

His voice came out through his teeth: "*You fucking bitch!*"

He stepped forward and shoved her. She staggered back a couple of steps and screamed louder than was justified. He shouted, "*Shut up!*" and took another step.

I was closing on them and said, "Hey, pal, take it easy."

He turned to look at me and his face was ugly. I saw he was in a suit. It looked expensive. "Take a hike. This doesn't concern you."

I was drawing level. I smiled. "If I see you push a lady, that concerns me. Get in your car and go home."

The girl was scowling at me and scowling at him. He stepped toward me. "I'm telling you to mind your own goddamn business, *pal!*"

Now the girl was stepping up. The smell of alcohol was strong from both of them. She was shouting, "Did you see? He hit me! Did you see him put his hands on me?" To him she said, "You're going *down*, you motherfucker!"

I fixed him with my eye. "Go home. Now."

"Mind your own fucking business!"

He thrust his face at me and the blow came out of nowhere, of its own volition. I slammed the heel of my hand into the tip of his chin. His eyes rolled back in his head, his legs folded and he sank to the sidewalk. I frowned down at him, wondering why I'd hit him. I looked up the road to see if there was a cab. There wasn't. I looked back at the woman and saw that she was gaping at the guy on the ground. She kneeled and took hold of his head.

"Jerry? Jerry, sweetheart? Are you OK?"

I said, "He's fine. He'll have a headache in the morning, but he'll be fine."

She stared up at me and her eyes were wild. *"You fucking maniac! You fucking animal! What have you done to him?"* Next thing, she was on her feet screaming, *"Help! Help! Somebody help me! Police! Somebody get an ambulance!"*

I sighed. This was life. This was love. This was loyalty and betrayal. I asked myself, who needs it, crossed the road and continued on my way back to the hotel, hearing her cries and shouts behind me. We imbue our memories with drama, but when they happened, most of them were tawdry and banal.

I reached the hotel ten minutes later and pushed through the doors into the plush, almost archaic lobby. I was about to head for the elevator and go up to my room, but went to the concierge instead. "What time does the bar close here?"

"Not till two AM, Mr. Walker. Not for another hour and three quarters." He leaned across the counter in a way that was conspiratorial. "And to be honest, as long as there are customers in the bar, we keep it open."

"My kind of bar."

I crossed among the pile carpets and the palms to the sober green and dark wood of the bar. There was still a quiet hum of conversation. Half a dozen tables were occupied, so I climbed on a stool and the barman approached.

"Give me a vodka martini, extra dry."

He went away to put it together and I sat looking at my thumbs. Suddenly I was sick of soul searching, sick of asking irrelevant questions about my emotions and my parents and Marni, Abi and Cyndi. I had a damned job to do—a difficult damned job—and I couldn't afford to be contemplating my navel and questioning my motivation. And as far as Omicron was concerned, if he had information I needed and he wasn't prepared to talk, I was going to make him talk, whether Jim and Njal liked it or not. That wasn't morality, it was reality.

The barman came and placed my drink in front of me with a bowl of peanuts. I sipped and considered the possibility of doing the operation on my own. If they were going to get squeamish, Njal could become more of a hindrance than a help. With Cyndi's introductions I could get close enough to Rocha in Brazil and Narciso Terry in Argentina. Setting up a couple of accidental deaths was certainly not beyond my skills. Maybe I should tell Njal and Jim the op was off and I would do it myself.

I felt the presence move and sit next to me on the next stool along from mine. Instinctively I glanced at the other stools around the bar. Most of them were empty. Then I looked at the woman who had sat next to me. She was dressed in Levis, a University of Oxford sweatshirt and a denim jacket. Her hair was in a ponytail and she was watching me. The barman approached her and she said, "Vodka martini, very dry." Then she turned to me. "Do you mind if I join you?"

"Marni." I frowned. "How did you know I was here?"

She picked up a pinch of peanuts and put them in her mouth. "What makes you think I knew?"

"I don't believe in coincidences."

"You've got a big ego, Lacklan. I come to D.C. regularly, remember?"

"And you happened to be staying at the same hotel as me?"

She shook her head. "No, but I happened to be in D.C."

"So you were in D.C. to meet with Cyndi and she told you I was here."

"Or maybe I just happened to walk into the Round Robin, saw you and decided to join you."

I watched her face a moment while she popped peanuts in her mouth and watched the barman. I said, "Is that what happened?"

"No."

"So...?"

"I was here in D.C. for a meeting with Cyndi. She phoned me after you called her and told me you were coming. She called me again half an hour ago and told me I should come and talk to you."

"What about?"

"I don't know." She turned her head to face me. "You tell me."

The barman brought over her drink and set it in front of her. When he'd gone, she picked out the olive and put it in her mouth. I thought how pretty she looked and immediately felt a twist of bitterness and anger. "I can't imagine what you would have to talk to me about, Marni."

"Really?" She didn't look at me. "What about Gibbons? You think maybe I might have something to say about Gibbons?" Now she turned on her stool to face me. "What about the fact that I told Gibbons you were going after Van Zuydam when you had asked me not to, and he passed that information on to Omega? You think maybe I have something to say about that?"[1]

"I don't know. What could you say? You have a greater loyalty to Gibbons than you have to me? I know that already. That you and Gibbons are prepared to negotiate with Omega? I found that out too. That those six months we spent together in Wyoming, when you shared my bed and my home, and we were..." I shook my head and looked down at the ice in my glass. "Whatever. You could tell me that none of that means anything to you anymore, but I already know that too. So, I don't know what Cyndi thinks you need to talk to me about, but I am pretty sure I know everything you have to say. So I am sorry you wasted your time."

She sighed and gave her head a small shake. "You are one hell of a piece of work, Lacklan. Forgiveness doesn't come easy to you, does it?"

---

1. See *Kill: Two*

"I can forgive most things, Marni, but not betrayal. I find it hard to forgive betrayal."

She was quiet for a long time. Eventually she said, "I didn't betray you. I am no longer involved with Gibbons. I am working on my own now. When I realized what he had done, what he was doing, I broke off all contact with him. I had no idea..."

I turned to face her. "Marni, I gave you the name of my target and asked you not to tell Gibbons. I specifically told you not to tell Gibbons. And you immediately went and told him. Omega were alerted so fast you must have picked up the phone as I left your apartment. Don't tell me you didn't betray me."

"You have to understand, Lacklan..."

"Understand what, exactly?"

"I had no idea he was in contact with Omega! I thought we were all on the same side!"

"Why did you tell him after I had asked you not to?"

"Because I was worried about you!"

I narrowed my eyes at her. "*You* were worried about *me?* Well, that's what I call ironic. Because it turns out all along it should have been me worried about you."

"That's harsh."

"So was sitting in that bar in Brussels watching the news about how the cops had received a tip off that Van Zuydam was the target of a hit."

She went quiet again. "I can imagine."

"Can you?"

"Yes, I can." She looked at me and held my eye. "You forget that you were not the only one betrayed, Lacklan. I was also betrayed. I had grown to love Gibbons as a surrogate father. I trusted him implicitly. He was a hero, a mentor, a guide and a friend. You don't get this because you are so wrapped up in your own pain, but when he betrayed you, he betrayed me too." I didn't say anything and after a moment she went on. "You're not an easy man, Lacklan. You are so sure that you are right all the time. You are so sure that your way is the only way. But your way is so *extreme* sometimes... You walk in and tell me—like you're telling me it's going to rain tomorrow, or you just bought take out—'I'm going to assassinate President Van Zuydam!' And you expect me just to take that and say, 'Oh, yeah, OK, Lacklan, what time do you think you'll be through? Maybe after, we can go grab a meal!'"

"It wasn't like that."

"To *you* it wasn't like that. You did all the preparation and all the planning. *You* were ten years in an elite black ops unit. I didn't do any preparation and I am just an academic. I solve problems by analysis, discussion and swaying public opinion through debate. Oxford professors don't shoot their enemies, they *talk* to them!"

I couldn't bring myself to look at her because I knew what she was saying was true. I stared into my glass instead and said, lamely, "You can't talk to men like Timmerman. You can't talk to Omega..."

"I know that, Lacklan. I get that. But it still scared the bejaysus out of me when you stepped into my apartment and announced that you were going to assassinate a European president. I couldn't turn to *you* because you weren't *there*. I had *nobody* to turn to. I was terrified of what you were doing. The only person I had was the man I trusted implicitly. So I made the mistake, the *serious* mistake, of confiding in him. And he betrayed me and he betrayed you. But in my heart and soul, Lacklan, I didn't betray you."

I drained my glass and thought about going up to my room. Instead I signaled the barman for another drink. I still couldn't look at her, but I looked at her hands, where she was clasping her drink.

"There has to be trust, Marni. Maybe betrayal is the wrong word. Maybe Gibbons betrayed us both, like you say. Maybe you didn't betray me." Now I looked up into her face. "But what happened to the trust we had?"

"I don't know."

"We loved and trusted each other, since we were kids. What happened?"

She shrugged and looked away. "You went to England with your mother. You joined the SAS. I felt I had lost you. I didn't know how to reach you. You remember I went after you? I went to London and I offered you my heart and my home..." She smiled at the melodramatic turn of phrase. "But you said no. You sent me back to Boston. You closed the door and I have never been able to reach you since. You have no room for me in your world, Lacklan. I don't know who you are anymore."

"I didn't close the door." But I didn't say it with much conviction.

"Yes, Lacklan, you did."

"I didn't mean to..."

"Yeah, like I didn't mean to betray you. And let me ask you this. Where was the trust? When I came to see you in London, and asked you to come home, and you said no, because, in your words, you didn't want to subject me to what you had become, where was the trust?"

My voice was barely a whisper: "I wanted to protect you..."

"It's still the same question, Lacklan. Where was the trust?"

After a long while, I said, "I'm sorry."

"Me too, buddy." She reached over and took my hand. "I'm working on my own now. Cyndi and I hook up regularly. Gibbons is not on the scene anymore. I am learning who to trust. How about you do the same?"

I squeezed her hand and looked into her eyes. My mind was on fire and I could feel my heart pounding in my chest. I gave my head a small shake. "I don't know, Marni," I said. "I don't know."

EIGHT

The sky was blue-white. The desert was ochre and gray, with small bushes like gnarled hands reaching out of the parched dust in search of water they were never going to find. A billowing red cloud twenty feet high trailed me down the road toward Njal's house. As I approached the gate, it rolled back. I slipped through and it slid closed behind me as the tires crunched to a halt outside the double garage.

Njal was on the porch, squinting at me through the glare when I climbed out. "How'd it go?"

"Good. No problem." I slammed the door. "I need to let her know the names I'm using. She'll make the introductions and get back to me."

He didn't say anything, but turned and went inside the shaded house. I followed him to the study, where he opened the door and I went in. Jim was sitting by the cold fireplace with a half empty pint glass of beer, and his reading glasses perched on the end of his nose. He looked up and smiled as I came in.

"How was Cyndi?"

"Cooperative. She needs the names you're putting on my ID papers so she can make the introduction."

"Naturally." He rose and went to the desk, where he rummaged in a drawer.

Behind me, Njal said, "You wanna drink?"

"Yeah, whiskey."

Jim came back to the table with three manila envelopes. He pointed at a chair. "Sit down." We sat. Njal joined us. He had two glasses of whiskey, one of which he handed to me. As I sipped, Jim pulled out the contents of one of the envelopes.

"In Argentina you are Nicholas Eddington, you are a British national and you are an IT engineer. Build yourself a back-story that makes sense to you and that you will remember if you need to. Your address is at 286 Ladbroke Grove, London W11. Everything else you provide yourself. I am sure you know the drill."

I nodded, sipped and took the papers from him. There was a passport, a driving license and a credit card. I inspected them closely. They were good.

Next he took out a number of photographs and a slip of paper. He handed me the paper first.

"That's a PIN for the credit card. Reasonable expenses only, please. It is not unlimited."

"I'll reimburse any expenses I have."

He glanced at me and went on. "These are photographs of your house, you better familiarize yourself with them. That's your girlfriend, put that in your wallet, dream up a name and a back-story for her. Destroy everything when you move on to Brazil."

I reached over, took the envelope and put the stuff back inside it, then scrawled on the outside, 'Argentina'. Jim opened the second one.

"In Brazil you will be Jason Devries, a U.S. mining engineer from Nevada. You live in Vegas. This is your passport, ID card, credit card, PIN and driving license." He handed me the documents, along with a handful of photographs. "As with Nicholas Eddington, you have photographs of places, things and people that should be familiar to you, build your back-story around them."

I studied the Brazilian documents, put them in the envelope and scrawled 'Brazil' on it. Jim said, "And finally, for your entry into Mexico, you are Bill Rogers, an insurance salesman from New Jersey, address, passport, et cetera all there." He handed me the third envelope. "This back story doesn't need to be so complete because as soon as you get there you'll be going to ground."

I took the envelope and studied the documents, then leaned back in my chair. "Have we got a date for the Mexican trio's next gathering at the house in Cosalá?"

Njal nodded. "Yuh, Thursday, July 4th. They will typically stay there till Monday, making a party."

"So that gives us three weeks and three days to finalize our plans, make the Argentine hit and the Brazil hit, and then get ourselves to Sinaloa."

Jim pulled a cigarette from a pack and lit it. "Can you do it?"

I nodded. "I've been doing some homework." I stared up at

the ceiling, speaking my thoughts aloud: "We arrive in Argentina separately. Njal goes ahead, economy class, puts up at a hostel, writing an article for a travel blog, or Lonely Planet, something like that. I stay at the Hilton on Macacha Güemes, an expensive room, a suite, but not too expensive. I'll arrive from London Heathrow..." I paused a minute to think. "27th June." I looked at him. "Njal, you arrive 25th. Don't tell me where you're flying from or what your ID says. We don't know each other and I don't want to know anything about you. We each carry a burner. If we need to communicate, we use the burner."

"Cool."

"I'll make contact with Terry according to Cyndi's instructions. I'll call her this afternoon. After the initial contact, I'll invite him to the Hotel Las Garzas. It's just outside the town of Navarro, about forty miles west of Buenos Aires. We'll have booked a room in his name and arranged for a couple of expensive escort girls to meet him there. When we make the reservation, we'll alert the management that this is a government minister who expects discretion, and for the girls to receive him in his room with a bottle of champagne.

"I'll arrange for him to arrive alone and at night. The hotel is remote, in the countryside, seven miles north of Navarro itself. To get there he'll have to take the RP47. On that road there is an intersection which is signposted to Las Garzas. A mile from the intersection there is a bridge over a tributary to the River Plata. You and I meet on that road before nine PM. I stop him, we pour half a bottle of whisky down his throat, break his neck, put him behind the wheel of his car and push him over the bridge. Then we each make our separate ways to Brazil. That's the rough outline of the plan."

Njal thrust out his bottom lip. "I have two questions: one, why should he meet you in such a remote place? He could find that suspicious. Second, what about his wife?"

Jim nodded. "My questions too."

"OK, first of all, you said his state of morale was complacent, plus I come recommended by a U.S. Senator. Also, you said he likes to visit whorehouses. So as well as the promise of a large bribe, I'll tell him I've arranged for some high class hookers to spend a couple of days with us while we arrange the details of the deal."

Jim asked, "What's the deal?"

"My IT company wants a contract with the Argentine government for the supply of security software. We are damned good but we also like to sugar the pill. He will get a very substantial commission, plus a lot of other inducements along the way. His greed will overcome whatever misgivings he might have. We also make the deal attractive to Omega, by giving the software an edge. What we, as a company, are seeking to do is to integrate biological components into computer security systems in order to achieve authentic artificial intelligence, so that cyber attacks like the one that brought down the stock exchanges in Wall Street and Brussels, can never happen again."

Jim pursed his lips and nodded. "Good, that's good."

"As to his wife, she is not on my hit list, Njal. I don't care if she is corrupt. She is not one of Omega. I don't want to kill her if I don't have to."

He shrugged. "OK. We kill him away from his house, it's not a problem. What about Brazil?"

I took a pull on my whiskey and peeled a pack of Camels. I spoke as I pulled off the wrapper.

"We have no choice but to arrive on the same day, but we'll fly in with different airlines. Again, you go to a hostel, I'll book in at the Windsor Plaza. It's close to the ministry and to Rocha's house, and it's where he would expect me to stay. Again, I'll contact him according to Cyndi's instructions. Meantime, you set up a watch on his mistress."

"Joelma Santos."

"1st July, when you are satisfied she's alone, you break in to her apartment and you take her hostage. You'll need a gun."

"We have a contact in Brazil. I can arrange it."

"Good. I'll arrange to meet Rocha, probably for lunch, and on the pretext of introducing him to my partner so we can discuss the details of his bribe. Once there, I'll get a message saying that my partner wants to meet us for cocktails or whatever. We go in my car and I take him to Joelma's apartment. There we kill him and frame her. Then give her a substantial sum of money and fly her to Los Angeles. She'll need a fake ID and a ticket. I see Joelma off at the airport, and Njal and I make our separate ways to Mexico, arriving late on the night of the 1st July, or early in the morning of the second. That gives us two days to get to Sinaloa."

Jim was shaking his head. "Your plans for Joelma are very high risk. That can go wrong in so many ways."

"I know. The alternatives are to kill her, which I won't do, or take him out of the city, which is going to be very difficult to persuade him to do. And we haven't got the time to build up a relationship of trust. If she is faced with the threat of going to a Brazilian jail for killing a Brazilian minister, she'll take the option of moving to L.A., believe me."

"It seems extravagant."

"All other options just take too long, Jim. We could rent a safe house, but that leaves a trail and again, takes time we haven't got."

Njal had been nodding slowly. Now he said, "OK, I agree, if we kill the woman it causes more problems. If we frame her and she disappears, it is better."

Jim said, "All right, if you're both on board with it, I'll trust your judgment. What about Mexico?"

"We haven't got the time to pose as dealers looking to buy, and in any case that would draw too much attention. All we can do is make our way to Cosalá, set up camp in the forest, collect the weapons from your contact and develop a plan of attack once we are on the ground. We will need a lot of fire power."

Njal puffed his cheeks and blew. "If we are camping in the forest, collecting weapons and explosives from the Gulf of California is not going to be easy."

"You said you could arrange for somebody to collect them and bring them ashore."

"Yuh, we can." He glanced at Jim, who ignored him. "But then we gotta go with a pick up truck and collect the guns and explosives and take them into the forest without being seen and without arousing suspicion. Getting them from the plane to the shore is the easy bit. Getting them to our camp ain't so easy."

I thought for a moment, then shrugged. "You get your contact to collect the weapons and deposit them wherever he figures is safe. We rent a truck in Mexico City. We pick up the weapons in Sinaloa. We drop the truck in the woods near Cosalá and carry the weapons the last few miles. We're talking about two kit bags. It's down to us not to arouse suspicion or get caught. If we do, we shoot our way out or we bribe our way out. That's the best we can do."

Njal shrugged his agreement. "Jim, you talk to Sole this afternoon."

"Sure, Njal."

"Good. As to the hit on the *Vampiro's* place and the lab, we can rough out a general idea for a plan using satellite images, but any kind of detailed plan of action will have to wait till we're there."

Jim sighed heavily. "Good, now, what will you need?"

I sipped my whiskey and thought for a moment. "Two Heckler & Koch 416 assault rifles fitted with the AG-HK416 grenade launchers and infrared telescopic sights. And we'll need plenty of ammunition with that." I looked at Njal. "You happy with the choice or you have some other preference?"

He shook his head. "It's fine."

I went on, "Obviously we won't be able to take our handguns on the plane, so you better add a couple of Sig Sauer p226 for me and whatever Njal uses."

"Glock 17."

"With the extended magazines, two per gun, same for the Glock. Also, two Fairbairn & Sykes fighting knives, one for me and one for Njal. I want a take down bow, hickory or orange osage, sixty-five pound draw weight and a dozen aluminum arrows, broadheads. You want a bow?"

Njal shook his head again. "But you better get us a

couple of Maxim 9s. If I have to be silent, I prefer to be silent with a gun."

"Yeah, good. I'd like to take a heavy machine gun, but it's going to slow us down too much, so we make do with the 416s and the grenades. But we are going to need explosives, so you better add in eight cakes of C4 each."

Jim laughed. "That's twenty pounds of C4! You planning to level the place?"

I smiled. "Yes. I've had prior experience of Omega labs, Jim, and if past experience is anything to go by, I plan to level the place to the ground."

"OK, no argument from me. Anything else?"

"Detonators, remote and mechanical. Night-vision goggles for both of us, binoculars. I think that's it. The plan is simple, go in, kill everybody, destroy everything and leave. The strategy is to use surprise, attack from a distance with extreme violence and move in gradually, so they never know who or what they are up against, until we have them boxed in. Then we unleash unholy hell on them. The precise details will have to wait till we are on the ground." I looked at Njal. "You have anything to add?"

He shook his head. "Not yet." Then as an afterthought, he asked, "You planning to torture anybody for information?"

I shook my head. "No."

Jim pursed his lips at his glass of whiskey. "You had concerns about their computer network and their bank accounts..."

"I still have, but I need your support for this operation and you won't give it if I torture Omicron, Xi or Nu. That's a decision you will eventually regret, but as it stands, what choice have I got?"

He sighed. "If you turn rogue on us once you're in the field, Lacklan, the consequences could be catastrophic, you understand that?"

I studied his face a moment without expression. "Is that a threat?"

"No, it's not a threat. For God's sake, man! We are not your enemies, we are your friends. All I am saying to you is that we need to work together."

I shrugged. "OK, so work with me to get the passwords to access whatever computer networks Omega has left, and the passwords to their bank accounts. As long as they have those resources intact, Omega will not die. You know that as well as I do."

"We plan to, Lacklan. We just plan not to use torture."

I nodded. "Sure. So I have no choice but to toe the line. We'll do it your way."

He raised an eyebrow at me. "Just talk to me or Njal before you do anything that might jeopardize the operation, Lacklan. I'm trusting your professionalism here."

"You can trust my professionalism. Relax."

"OK, so I am going to arrange the delivery and collection of your shopping list. Then I'm going to head back to L.A. and leave you to work on the fine details of the plans. Meantime, anything you need, let me know."

He rose and went up to his room. Fifteen minutes later, he came back down again and told us it was sorted. We walked him out to the porch, watched him climb into his Moab and drive out of the gate and away, across the desert, trailing a lazy plume of dust behind him. Njal stared up at the near white sky as the gate rolled closed. "I'm gonna talk to Sole about collecting the weapons."

I nodded. "Good. I'll call Cyndi."

He slapped me on the shoulder. "Catch you later by the pool, we can start putting details on the plan. You cool?"

"Yeah, Njal, I'm cool. Stop worrying."

He nodded. "Good. Catch you later."

He went upstairs, but I stayed a while, staring out at the scorched desolation of the desert, thinking. It was time to start planning in earnest.

NINE

I TOUCHED DOWN AT THE MINISTRO PISTARINI International Airport in Buenos Aires at just after nine o'clock on the morning of the 27th of June. I picked up a nondescript Toyota Corolla from the Hertz office and headed out on the General Pablo Ricchieri Highway under a mild blue sky, across pleasant green fields, toward the city. The road changed its name a couple of times, but it was pretty much one long, gently curving arc over the rooftops of Buenos Aires, with a brief descent through Chacabuco Park, until it came, as the 25 Mayo, to the river. There it frayed like an old paintbrush, sending twisted tendrils in all directions. I took the one that led to Ing Huergo Avenue, turned right over the bridge and followed the canal for five hundred yards till I came to the Hilton.

There I let a kid with spots and big, brown eyes park my rental car while another with red hair and freckles carried my bags into reception. I checked in at the bank of brown and beige desks, where pretty receptionists with standardized smiles welcomed me to the mass-produced luxury that only the Hilton knows how to provide. Everything was shiny and nothing was too much trouble. My personal receptionist handed me the key to my executive suite with a tilt of her blonde head and a big, happy smile.

I rode the elevator to the tenth floor with Red Freckles. After he had opened the curtains and shown me where everything was, I gave him ten bucks and closed the door on his retreating, grinning form. Then I pulled my cell from my pocket. Cyndi had contacted Narciso Terry and told him I was interested in meeting him. She must have made it convincing because it seemed he was keen to meet me too. He'd asked her to give me his private cell number and call him as soon as I arrived. That was what I did. I checked my watch as the phone rang. It was ten thirty, local time.

A voice that was surprisingly agreeable answered. There was an accent, but not much. "Hello, Mr. Eddington?"

I took a second to think of my mother, her friends, and my commanding officers at the SAS, then spoke in perfect, cut glass English from England. "Good morning, Minister."

There was a small, indulgent laugh. "There is no need for formalities. Please call me Narciso, and if you will allow me, I will call you Nicholas. I hope you had a comfortable flight."

"Perfect. I slept all the way."

"You are comfortable in your hotel? Is there anything you need?"

"A shower and a large whiskey, but it's a little early for that." I laughed. "But I was hoping you would allow me to invite you to lunch, Narciso."

"Absolutely not. I insist you are my guest. You are at the Hilton?"

"Indeed."

"I will have a car collect you at twelve o'clock and lunch will be my treat."

"That is extremely kind of you. I look forward to it very much."

"It is my pleasure. Any friend of Cyndi's is a friend of mine, and she speaks very highly of you. Until lunch, then."

I told him again I was looking forward to it, hung up and switched on the burner I had brought with me to receive messages from Njal, if an emergency cropped up. We had arranged to switch them on three times a day for not more than five minutes. The precaution was probably excessive, but excessive caution can save lives.

Either way, there were no messages, so I switched it off, stripped, had a long shower and changed my traveling clothes for a business suit and tie. By that time it was eleven o'clock, so I went downstairs for an early cocktail of black coffee laced generously with Jameson's.

At twelve on the button, a man in a black suit with black knee-boots and a black cap came into the bar and approached me.

"You are Mr. Eddington?"

I told him I was and he said he had the car waiting out front. I followed him out into the gentle sunshine. It was a pleasant sixty degrees, more like seventy in the sun. The car he had waiting turned out to be a dark blue Bentley Mulsanne, with the extended wheelbase. That was three hundred and fifty thousand bucks right there, without any extras. He opened the door and, as I went to climb in, I saw there was a man already in there. He was what you would call groomed. Even his pencil moustache was groomed. He spread his groomed hands and smiled, so I could see his teeth were groomed too.

"Nicholas, forgive me for not getting out," he said. "One has to be discreet in Argentina. Please, come in, make yourself comfortable." I did, wondering how showing up in a Bentley Mulsanne qualified as discreet, and the door closed behind me with an expensive clunk. "A drink? It is not far to the restaurant, but you certainly have time for a drink."

I smiled. "Thank you. Scotch, on the rocks."

"Macallan?"

"Who could say no to the Macallan?"

The glasses were leaded crystal and the Macallan eighteen years old. He handed me a glass, we toasted and he sat back and sighed with pleasure. I looked around the car and raised an eyebrow. "What does the president drive?"

He snorted in a way you could describe as derisive. "A Mercedes." He gave a small, self-deprecating shrug. "Money and office, Nicholas, they are the trappings of power. They are not power itself. The president is a good man, we are good friends, but his preeminence will wane and a new president will come along. Why? Because his power is not his, it comes from the people. They give it and they take it away; and with it the trappings and much of the money."

I sipped and studied his face, wondering absently how well he had known Ben and my father. "You say that as though it didn't apply to you. You are also an elected member of Congress."

He glanced out the window as we turned onto Tucumán. The street was narrow and the buildings modern, with brick and marble facades. It could have been Paris or Madrid, or any of a dozen Mediterranean cities.

"When Caesar made his comment about bread and circus, the circus he was referring to was the one where the lions ate the Christians." He turned his gaze back to me and smiled. "Currently we are not allowed to do that kind of thing, so instead we use the television and the democratic process." He gave a laugh, like he was sharing a private joke with himself. "Neither one is enough on its own, but used together, they are a very powerful intellectual anesthetic. The people are lulled into a dream where they believe they are somehow involved in the process of government."

I offered him my best debonair, English smile. "That is pretty ambiguous, but I don't want to pry. As far as I am concerned, the function of government should be to facilitate business and trade. So according to that criterion, you are doing a first class job."

He raised his glass. "Here's to that."

We crossed the massive central esplanade, crisscrossed by the Avenida 9 de Julio, Cerrito and Carlos Pellegrini running north to south, and just about every other avenue in Buenos Aires running east to west, forming a grid pattern of small parks stretching north and south from the Plaza de la Republica. At the opera house we turned right down Libertad, and I was struck again by the feeling that this was a European city somehow transposed to another continent.

Narciso had been quiet for a while, watching the crowds on the narrow sidewalks as we cruised past. "It is not ambiguous, Nicholas. I have perhaps been vague, but not ambiguous." He turned to face me and smiled. "Most architects have only the most rudimentary understanding of physics, most physicists have only the most rudimentary understanding of relativity and quantum mechanics..." He shook his head and shrugged. "Most doctors have only the most basic understanding of what is health. It is the same with politicians. Most politicians do not understand the fundamentals of power. Do you know what power is, Nicholas?"

I frowned at the ice in my glass. "A wise man once told me that the source of all temporal power was the ability to deploy violence."

He gave a small laugh that sounded indulgent. "He was right, of course. But power and the *source* of power are two different things. True power is the ability to achieve pleasure and avoid pain. Temporal power is the ability to make people do what we want them to do—usually to provide us with pleasure and avoid pain!—and of course, as your wise friend pointed out, the way to motivate people is to deploy violence, or the threat of violence." We had been traveling up Avenida Santa Fe, and now turned in to Pueyredon. He gestured with his hand and said, "We are here. I hope you like Spanish food. As an Argentinian, I sometimes grow tired of steak! We did have a superb French restaurant here for a long time. Sadly, it closed. But the Oviedo is very good too."

Another turn into Antonio Beruti and we came to a halt outside a restaurant with a long, blue awning and big, broad windows. The chauffeur opened the door and let us out, and as he climbed back into the Bentley and drove away, the head waiter of the Oviedo opened the door to the restaurant to let us in. I began to wonder if, after all, the nature of power wasn't having people everywhere opening doors for you.

The place was quiet and elegant, with a lot of dark wood

and very white linen, and waiters in white jackets with bowties. The head waiter led us, in a walk that was half-bow, to 'el Señor Ministro's usual table in a quiet corner where we were given a couple of leather bound menus the size of small encyclopedias, and Narciso ordered two more single malts on the rocks. Then he gripped the waiter's arm and said to me, "Will you allow me, Nicholas? I can recommend for you the king prawns in garlic, and for the main plate, Patagonian lamb with Sardinian gnocchi, it is superb here."

He didn't wait for me to answer, he spoke to the waiter in Spanish and I heard him say the words 'Vega Sicilia noventa y nueve', a wine from the Ribera del Duero region of Spain that was going to set him back over four hundred U.S. dollars.

The head waiter went away with his instructions, delegating to his subordinates as he went, and Narciso smiled at me. "I am fortunate," he said, "to have the power to achieve pleasure and avoid pain."

I raised an eyebrow at him. "I am fortunate that I like prawns in garlic and lamb."

"Even if you didn't, you would like this. It is food fit for gods." The waiter brought our drinks. Narciso sipped and seemed to study my face a moment. "So, how can I help a friend of Cyndi's?"

"It's more a case of how I can help you."

"Indeed?"

I nodded and sipped my own drink. "You recall the recent crash of the stock markets in Europe and the U.S.A."

"Naturally. The repercussions were felt worldwide."

"It was caused by the collapse of a series of linked computer networks that spread across government and administrative bodies, through a series of banks and billion dollar corporations."

I paused and watched him. He had gone very still. I waited for him to say something. He didn't. He just waited, so I went on.

"It was a miracle the collapse wasn't more widespread. It had the potential to bring down world banking and international trade. The consequences could have been truly catastrophic, on a global level. Fortunately, our company was able to establish that the networks that did go down were..." I hesitated, searching for the word, "*Hermetically* sealed, isolated from other networks."

His voice was wooden: "What else did your company discover?"

"That the crash was triggered by a virus. We suspect it was Islamic cyber terrorism." I delivered the statements with a show of perfect innocence, holding his eye throughout. Before he could answer, I went on, "We think that, because the point of introduction seems to have been within the government computer systems of the European Union. It was a very rare virus that had been considered almost mythical up to that point. It is known as the neutron bomb, a wildfire virus that spreads from computer to computer, from network to network, but is virtually undetectable until it stops spreading. Once it stops spreading, then it self-activates and within minutes, takes down every computer in the networks it has infected."

He kept his eyes on his glass, turning it slowly around on the table cloth, and for a moment I wondered if I had been too smart and overplayed my hand. After a moment, he said,

"That is very interesting, but how does it affect Argentina? Islamic terrorists have little interest in us."

I sipped, nodded vigorously and set down my glass, smacking my lips. "Oh, sure, that is true—for now at least—and in a sense, that is why our proposal could be of mutual benefit."

He frowned, then laughed. "Which of these statements do we pursue first? For now? You think we will soon become of interest to Islamic terrorists? Why? And what is this proposal of yours?"

I held up a hand. "Let me answer the first point first, because it is, for now, of least interest. Our analysts tell us that though the Trump administration is coming down hard on Mexico, this is just the Trump style of negotiation. The end game is to build much stronger ties with Latin America with a view to commercial and political integration in the long term. That could, conceivably, lead to Mexico and Argentina eventually becoming targets for enemies of the U.S.A. But that is very much long term. In the shorter term, Argentina being off the radar and a little isolated from the major Western economies affords us, my company, opportunities for research and development that we cannot pursue in Europe or the States."

His eyes were narrowed and sharp. He was thinking, as I had intended him to, that enemies of the U.S.A. equated to enemies of Omega, and whoever had taken down Omega 1 and 2 might now come after them, however low their profile was. So our supposed research was now of major interest to him. Having us develop that research in Argentina, where he could keep tabs on it, was suddenly very attractive to him indeed.

The prawns in garlic arrived and the wine waiter brought us a glass of chilled dry sherry to accompany it. He sniffed the sherry, twitched an eyebrow and sipped it.

"What exactly is this research you want to conduct, Nicholas? You understand that we cannot contemplate anything unethical or immoral."

I smiled blandly. "Naturally. Ours is a very ethical company, Narciso. Our only objective is to make the world a better, safer place. Of course..." I broke a hot roll and soaked up some of the hot, spicy sauce, then stuffed it in my mouth and chewed. "Of course," I repeated with my mouth full, "the problem is that too often politicians and legislators lag behind scientists when it comes to adapting to new, socio-economic developments. What we are seeking to do is to integrate biological components into computer systems to achieve authentic artificial intelligence, so that cyber attacks like the one that brought down the stock exchanges in Wall Street and Brussels can never happen again."

He went very still. I smiled. He said, "You are talking about cyborgs..."

I winced. "That has dramatic connotations, but in a very limited sense you are right. However, think of it this way, a bloodhound's brain which interprets data from viruses, even dormant wildfire viruses like the neutron bomb, as smell."

"Wow..."

"Exactly. Smell, taste, touch, images and sounds are simply the brain interpreting data from subatomic particles, right? So you program the brain to respond to certain data, and you can have a pack of bloodhounds surfing the net hunting for hostile viruses. This is a proposition which is undoubtedly of benefit to humanity as a whole, but the bleeding heart brigade in the West will simply not allow that kind of research."

He was quiet for a long time, eating methodically and sipping his sherry. After a time he glanced at me sidelong and said, "This could be of interest to Argentina."

I smiled like I was relieved and spoke a little too quickly: "We would naturally be very keen to meet any fees and expenses that might arise in presenting the proposal to ministers..."

He looked me in the eye and said flatly, "We do not need to be coy, Nicholas. I require a bribe of one million pounds sterling. I will provide you with the details of my offshore account."

I sighed again and smiled. "It is so good to do business with somebody who does not beat about the bush, Narciso."

He laughed. "Of course. You know the definition of an honest businessman?"

"Tell me."

"One who does not lie about being bribed. So where do we take it from here? I would like to meet your principal."

I didn't answer straight away. I mopped up the last of the sauce from my prawns and stuffed the bread in my mouth. "And he would like to meet you. But we need to be discreet. MI6 and the CIA are both interested in his research, and we have competitors in the field, especially in Japan, who are also watching him with interest."

"What do you suggest?"

The waiter came and took our plates away. The wine waiter approached with the bottle of Vega Sicilia and there was a small ritual while Narciso smelled the cork, then the splash in his glass, and then he tasted it. After that, he nodded and grunted.

"Superb." He said it shrugging and shaking his head, like he didn't know why it was superb, but it was. "Superb," he said again.

The waiter filled our huge glasses with a couple of inches and went away. Then the lamb arrived. We didn't talk again until we had tried the lamb and savored the wine. I made suitable noises, which were heartfelt, and after an appropriate period of reverence, I dabbed my mouth with my napkin and said, "He has chosen a place for a meeting. Only he knows where it is. Not even I know. When I tell him you are interested, he will tell me where and when, and I will tell you. I have to ask you not to tell anybody else either, so that only we three know the time and place of the meeting. There he will fill you in as to the full range of benefits to you personally." I smiled. "The million is just the tip of the iceberg—and what he is looking for from the Argentinean government in terms of freedom to conduct research and development."

He nodded, gazing down at his plate as he ate. After a while he looked up and raised his glass. "I think we can do business, Nicholas."

I raised my own glass and they rang out as we knocked them together. "Here's to a successful conclusion to the enterprise," I said.

"Here's to that!" he replied, not knowing that he was drinking to his own death.

TEN

We talked about everything from the scourge of socialism and the benefits of free market anarchy, to the death penalty and the virtues of the British monarchy. Then, at four PM, he dropped me off at the hotel and I made my way up to my suite. There I ordered a pot of black coffee and sent Njal a message saying simply, '*Call me*'.

Then I had a cold shower, changed into jeans and a sweatshirt, drank the pot of coffee and went for a walk around the Plaza de Mayo and the Plaza Colon, taking the burner with me. Njal called at just after six. He said:

"What?"

"It was quicker than expected. He's enthusiastic, waiting to hear from my principal."

"You want to bring it forward?"

"I think we should. I'll call him tomorrow morning, set it up for Saturday, 29th. You good with that?"

He was quiet for a count of three. Then said, "Yuh. I call you Saturday morning, eight, to confirm."

He hung up.

I spent the rest of the day visiting museums and reading English language newspapers on pavement cafes, giving Narciso's men time to bug my room and my phone. I made no effort to keep a low profile. I was an English businessman doing business in Buenos Aires with a government minister. I had nothing to hide and no reason to feel nervous, or to suspect I was being spied on. That was my front, and that was my persona. When I had left the hotel I'd spotted my tail, but it was low key and low tech. I didn't figure Narciso was suspicious, I figured he simply wanted to make sure I was who I said I was.

At six that evening I made my way back to the hotel and called a London number Jim had given me. A pretty voice answered after the third ring and said, "Soft Solutions, how may I direct your call?"

I said, "Hi, Pam, it's Nicholas, put me through to Jerry, will you?"

"Hello, Mr. Eddington, just putting you through. How's Buenos Aires?"

"Great. Loving it. Thanks, Pam."

There was a click when the call was put through to L.A., and Jim's voice came on the line. "Hey, Nick, how's it going?"

"Good. Mr. Terry seems to be very interested in our proposition. He wants to meet Phil. How soon can he be here?"

Jim laughed. "He's already there. I swear that guy is paranoid. How soon do you want to meet up?"

"I'd like to strike while the iron's hot. You think tomorrow is too soon?"

"I don't see why. I'll call Phil and get back to you. Listen, how much is he looking for to grease the wheels?"

Now was the time to bait the hook and make it irresistible.

"He asked for a million."

"Cool, less than we expected."

"Yeah, I told him there would be other benefits, but I didn't specify what."

"Good. If there's anything left in the kitty, that's for you and me, pal."

I laughed, said I'd be waiting for his call and hung up. I had absolutely no doubt in my mind that the conversation had been recorded and listened to. It would all go toward reassuring Narciso and whetting his appetite.

Jim called back ten minutes later.

"Nick, I spoke to Phil. He's ready to go ahead as soon as you are. He said he'd call you on your cell to give you the details."

"Cool, thanks, Jerry. I think we have a deal here."

"Glad to hear it. Take it easy."

I hung up again and settled down to an evening of watching TV. At eight I ordered a steak and fries in my room and by ten I was in bed reading about how the ancient city of Troy had not been in Turkey at all, but in Cambridge. Who knew?

———

I was up at six and went for a run. At eight I had coffee and croissants sent up to my suite and called Narciso on his private line.

"Good morning, Nicholas. I see you don't hang around. That is good. What news have you for me?"

"Good morning! Now, Phil, that's my principal, is very keen to meet you. He has asked me to apologize to you if his methods seem a little cloak and dagger, but the industry we are in is cut throat, and a product like the one we are working on..."

I hesitated a moment and he cut in. "I know, Nicholas, it could be worth billions. I am aware of that."

He labored the words, implying that he was going to be expecting a much bigger reward than the million I had promised him. I smiled to myself, but my voice was hesitant and a little nervous.

"Well, yes, if it takes off."

"So where and when would Phil like to meet?"

"Is tomorrow evening too soon? I know you must have a busy schedule."

"Tomorrow evening will be fine. Where?"

"OK, there is a small hotel called Las Garzas. It's a few miles west of the city, near the town of Navarro."

"I know the town, but not the hotel."

"That's OK. What Phil would like you to do is to drive, in a nondescript family saloon, not a Bentley!" We both laughed and I continued, "Drive up to Lujan, and from there take the RP47 south and west toward Navarro for about twenty-eight miles. There you'll come to a junction where I will be waiting for you and I'll lead you the rest of the way to the hotel. As I say, it's a bit cloak and dagger, but that's Phil, you know? And I guess he has a point, there is a lot at stake. He asks that you come alone. He will be alone too. I'll leave the both of you to it, and he will have a private discussion with you."

He was quiet for a while, like he was thinking, and I wondered for a moment if he was going to back out, but finally he said, "Yes, that sounds fine. I will be in a white Focus."

"Can you be there for nine thirty?"

"I will be there." Now he hesitated a moment. "Nicholas."

"Yes, Narciso?"

"If this is a trick, a trap, a kidnapping... You understand the consequences will be catastrophic for you."

I managed to sound genuinely astonished. "Good heavens, Narciso! We might be a little secretive about our product, but we don't go around *kidnapping* people! Least of all government ministers!" I burst out laughing. "We wouldn't get very far in business if we behaved like that, would we!"

He chuckled comfortably. "Forgive me, Nicholas. We learn to be very careful. Argentina is not England."

"Yes, well, rest assured, the only place we want you to be is in your office, facilitating our research!"

"Very well, very well. I shall see you tomorrow evening, then."

"See you then. Should you need me for anything, I'll be at Las Garzas, but you can always get me on my mobile."

He hung up and I sat for a while with my feet up, smoking and drinking coffee—and thinking. So far everything was going according to plan, easier than I had expected, and that worried me. But however much I turned it over I couldn't see a flaw in it. I'd been introduced to him by a U.S. senator, he'd bugged my phone and I'd said all the right things while he listened, and from the way he was speaking, he was buying into the story he'd heard, and wanted a piece of the action.

So everything was going according to plan.

I called down to reception and had them bring my car around to the front. Then I grabbed the book I'd been reading and went down.

I left Buenos Aires headed south, through Lanús and Lomas de Zamora. From there I took a roundabout route along the RP10 and then the RP6 to a small town called Cañuelas. It was a modern grid pattern town that could have been any small town in the U.S.A. I drove around the streets for a while, enjoying the sunshine and noting that the VW Gol that had been on my tail since I left the hotel was still with me.

Eventually I stopped on Rivadavia and waited for him to pull in a few cars behind me. Then I got out and walked up San Martin to the Scachi Bar, where I sat outside, ordered a coffee and settled down to read my book. A minute later I glanced up and saw my shadow arrive and sit at the Bar Rocklets across the road. He was short and overweight. He looked like an ex-cop. I gave him a couple of minutes to order his coffee and settle in, and then I called the waitress. I explained to her in elaborate, bad Spanish that I wanted a beer, I would pay now but I needed to run across the road to the supermarket, could I leave my book and my beer there? Would she keep an eye on them? She smiled and said she would. In my peripheral vision I could see my shadow watching, alert.

I got up, leaving my book on the table, and sprinted across the Avenida Libertad and up the stairs into the big supermarket. I bought a pack of three bars of soap, paid for them at the check out and left via the parking lot at the side. Then I ran fast along Libertad and down Del Carmen back onto Rivadavia, where I had parked. I approached the back of his VW, peeled the wrappers off the three bars of soap and stuffed them up his exhaust. After that, I sprinted back the way I had come and sauntered back to my table, which now held a beer as well as my book. My shadow across the road was looking worried, but relaxed when he saw me return.

I spent another ten minutes drinking and reading, then made my way back to the car. While he was trying to start his, I drove past him, like I was going back toward Buenos Aires, but instead I looped around the town at the Cañuelas Roundabout and took the 205 south. There I floored the gas all the way to the town of Lobos, and put twenty-five miles between me and Narciso's watchman.

For the rest of the drive I kept my eyes glued on the mirror, but there was nobody following me. I figured my ex-tail still had his head stuck in his engine trying to find out why it wasn't starting, and he was too scared to tell his boss.

A mile and a half after Laguna Navarro I turned right onto the RP47, a narrow road with acres of empty fields on either side. I followed that for three miles and finally came to the turn off for the Hotel Las Garzas. It was a broad, dirt track, and after seven hundred yards there was a turn off to the left and a large copse of tall trees. I pulled in and found Njal sitting, smoking, in a Ford pickup with the window open. I climbed out and walked over to him. We shook and he grinned at me. "You're late."

I pulled out my phone and called Narciso Terry.

"Nicholas, I did not expect to hear from you until tonight. Is everything in order?"

"Almost. But I think there has been some misunderstanding, Narciso. I had asked you yesterday for discretion, and I stressed that Phil was quite strict on that point. Yet today I went for a bit of sightseeing and the sight I saw was a rather clumsy ex-cop tailing me in full sight. That makes me uncomfortable, and worst of all, it makes Phil very uncomfortable. There has to be trust between us, Narciso, or this is not going to work."

"I understand. It was an oversight. The Secret Service, you know, they try to keep an eye on anyone who meets with a minister. I will take care of it."

"For crying out loud, Narciso! Are you telling me the Secret Service know about this?"

"No, no! Please, listen to me. They have orders to watch me. They see me go out and have lunch, so they watch the person I have lunch with for a few days, to see if they are an enemy of the state. That is their only interest. But I will call them off."

"You'd better. That is *not* the kind of attention we want. I have to say I am surprised, Narciso. I thought we had an understanding."

"We have. Please rest assured that the problem is solved."

"Good. And tell your guy that the reason his car won't start is because he has three cakes of soap rammed up his exhaust."

There was a long silence, then, unamused, "Yes, I see. I understand."

I laughed. "Everybody in this game is smart, Narciso.

Let's play nice, OK? Are we still on for tonight or should I call it off?"

"No, no! We are still on. As I said, it was an oversight, but I will deal with it right away."

I hung up. Njal was still grinning. "You put soap in his exhaust?"

"Potatoes just get blown out. Soap starts to melt with the hot moisture and forms a kind of mush that yields just enough not to get blown out, but blocks enough of the gases to choke the engine. You need three cakes for it to be really effective. Don't say I never taught you anything. Now, what have you got?"

He opened the door of the cab and swung down. He had a flask of coffee and offered me some. I shook my head.

"I booked a room at the hotel for tomorrow night. The most expensive suite they have. I told them it is for the minister, Narciso Terry, but it's very confidential. We want the best service, but absolute confidentiality. If they are good, we come back. If they are not, there will be consequences. My Spanish is not so good, but his English was great."

"Good. Were they cooperative?"

"Very. So then I found a high class escort agency and I booked two girls. I told them it was for the minister." He laughed. "The madam who took the booking asks me why Pedro is not making the booking like usual. I said this was a private company providing entertainment for the minister. We need absolute discretion and we pay a big bonus if everything is good. She was very happy, so we have Carmen Zeta and Rosa Mari coming tonight. I call the hotel again and tell them that the minister has two companions tonight and I want them booked into his room. He says no problem."

"What time are they arriving?"

"Eight PM."

"Good, that gives us time to set up. He'll arrive at nine thirty. I'll meet him at the intersection and we'll drive down to the bridge. Let's go and have a look."

We climbed into his truck and pulled onto the dirt track again. The bridge was another six hundred yards down the road. When we got there, I was surprised at how big it was. It was a good sixty feet across over a deep canal, but it was not a bridge in any conventional sense of the word. There were no barriers at the side, and there were no sidewalks. It was just a concrete arch with dirt on top. It was a gift.

I peered down at the dark, green water. "Have you checked the depth?"

"Yuh, ten feet."

"Couldn't be better. The gods are smiling on us. Let's hope it lasts."

I scanned the fields all around us. We were still almost four miles from the hotel, and there was just empty fields and occasional copses as far as the eye could see. I looked back the way we'd come. "I'll meet him at the intersection in my car. I'll tell him to follow me. I'll drive slowly. When we pass the copse where you are parked now, you pull out behind him, across the road, so he can't reverse. Get out and start waving your arms like you need help. I'll stop in the middle of the road so he can't get past. I'll walk back toward you, asking you what the hell is going on. I'll make like I don't understand you and ask him to translate. He gets out, we do the job."

"OK in theory, but what if he will sense a trap? What if he will panic, lock the doors, try to escape?"

I nodded. "Be prepared. Do what I did to his man. Have a plug ready for his exhaust, and a hammer for the window. But let's try to avoid that."

He echoed my nod. "OK. What car is he using, do you know?"

"Ford Focus, why?"

"I make a good plug, that fits good with duct tape. But be careful, Lacklan, you have to assume he will be armed."

"Yeah, I know. I'll be ready. OK, let's get out of here. I'll see you tomorrow night at seven."

We drove back to the copse. I got in my car and headed back toward Buenos Aires via a long, circuitous route to the south.

ELEVEN

That night I dined in the hotel dining room. When I had finished, at about nine thirty, I went to reception and asked one of the male receptionists where there was a nice club where I could have some fun. He recommended the Jet Lounge, which was a short taxi ride from the hotel. The place was noisy and expensive. I found a table and made an effort to enjoy myself with a couple of girls, and even danced a bit, mainly for the benefit of my new shadow. He was more discreet than his predecessor, but still not what you'd call a real pro. He sat most of the evening over a beer and looked unhappy, while I had all kinds of fun he couldn't afford.

At one AM I had them call me a cab and left with a girl on each arm. I let him and the receptionist see me go up to my room with them, and then I ordered a bottle of Dom Perignon, a bottle of vodka and a bottle of single malt from room service. It wasn't really my scene, but sometimes you have to make sacrifices in order to convince your enemy you are for real.

At nine the next morning, we had Eggs Benedict for three and at ten I sent them home, a few hundred bucks richer than they had been the day before.

At midday I called Narciso.

"Nicholas, I am not sure you should call me so often."

"Keep on the way you're going, Narciso, and this will be the last time I call you. I thought we had an understanding, but your lack of trust is very disturbing. I am on the level here. I want to do business and have a little fun, as your man last night must have seen. But I am getting the feeling this is a one-sided relationship."

"Please, Nicholas, let's not be hasty. You don't understand, a man in my position..."

"You said you had real power, Narciso. Let me see that. The meeting tonight was due to be a cordial, relaxed affair. Now you are making me take precautions."

He was quiet for a moment. "What kind of precautions?"

"If we see anybody with you, anybody at all, the deal is off and we go to Brazil. Period."

"That is not necessary. We simply had a man on you. It is standard proced..."

I cut him short. "Be at the junction at the agreed time. I'll meet you there and lead you to the hotel. If I see anybody else with you, the deal is off. Irrevocably. I need you to understand that, Narciso. You said it yourself, there are billions of dollars riding on this deal. Play smart and you can be a part of that. Play too smart, and we are out of here. Do we have an understanding this time?"

"We have an understanding, Nicholas."

"I'll see you this evening."

I hung up and stood for a while looking out at the view of the vast mouth of the River Plata, thinking. Narciso's biggest worry now, after the call, was that he might lose out on the deal that was going down. We were talking now in billions, not millions, and he would be desperate to get cut in on a share of that deal. Any residual doubts he might have, he would keep going back to the fact that this introduction had been made by a U.S. senator—a senator whom he knew personally. References don't come much better than that.

The attempts he'd made to tail me had been half-hearted at best, and had shown him exactly what he must have expected to see, that I was a successful businessman having fun in Buenos Aires. And the tap on my phone showed him the same thing.

He would be there that night. And I would kill him.

That afternoon I booked a three AM flight to Brasilia in the name of Jason Devries, using Jason Devries' credit card. Then I went through the suite, wiping my prints off everything I had touched, and making sure there was none of my hair left in the shower, the sink or the bed. I packed my bag, went without lunch, because hunger will give you an edge of aggression on a hit, and at twenty to six, I was downstairs with my bag, settling the bill. Twenty minutes after that, as the sun was setting, I headed off in my car, taking a winding route through the evening city, as the lights came on and the sky grew dark, watching my mirror to see if I was tailed. I didn't expect to be, and I wasn't.

I wound up eventually on the RP200, leading through

Marcos Paz and General Las Heras to Navarro. By the time I got there it was seven thirty, and dark. I crossed through the town and covered the last seven miles in a leisurely ten minutes. There I parked on a piece of wasteland beside the road in the cover of some trees. It was seven forty. I sent Njal a text: *OK?*

The reply came almost instantly: *10/4*

I settled down to wait. At eight o'clock, a limousine approached from the direction of Buenos Aires. It turned onto the dirt track and I watched its red taillights disappear toward the hotel. I waited another twenty minutes and the limo returned and took off again back toward the city.

When it was gone from view, I got out and jogged the seven hundred yards to the copse. There was no moon, and the Ford was hidden from view in the darkness. I stepped close to a tree, so I made no silhouette, and whispered, "*Njal?*"

His voice came out of the shadows. "OK, I am here."

I heard a footfall and a deeper patch of blackness moved. Next thing, he was standing in front of me.

"We have an hour, but there is not much to prepare. I have a plug for the exhaust if it is necessary, and I have the hammer. Better if you take it."

He gave it to me and I slipped it in my waistband, behind my back. Then we walked the short distance to the road and picked out markers so I would know exactly where to stop and Njal could cut Narciso off, leaving a minimum amount of room for maneuver. After that, we spent half an hour discussing possible things that could go wrong, the worst, and most likely, of which was that he might turn up with a couple of wagons of soldiers. If he did that, we decided, we'd kill them all and head for Uruguay, just across the river.

With half an hour to go, I jogged the short distance back to my car at the intersection and waited.

He was punctual. At nine twenty-five, I saw a bright light approaching from the north. At first I thought it was a bike, but then the single light split like a glowing amoeba and resolved itself into two lamps. I climbed out of the car and leaned on the roof, watching. If there was any trouble, the car would give me some cover, and I could make for the ditch and the trees behind me.

The lamps drew closer and soon I could make out that it was a white Focus. It slowed and soon turned in to the dirt track and stopped. The windshield was black. I waited. After a moment, the door opened and Narciso leaned out.

"Nicholas?"

I raised my hand. "Good evening. Do me a favor, Narciso. Just switch on the light inside your car, would you?"

He put on the light and I could see the seats were empty. I smiled at him and walked over. As I shook his hand, I looked in the back. There was nobody there, either. I grinned. "I guess we're all getting a bit jumpy, huh? A lot riding on this deal. C'mon, follow me. Phil's at the hotel. I think you're going to have a nice evening. I wish I could be a part of it."

There was no mistaking the complacency in his face. "Maybe next time, Nicholas."

"Yeah, maybe next time."

I walked back to my car, climbed in and fired her up. Then I pulled slowly onto the track, doing maybe fifteen miles an hour, with Narciso close behind me. After a minute or so, my headlamps picked out the turn off with the copse beside it. I rolled past and dropped to second gear, keeping my eyes on the mirror. I saw him pull level with the copse and then move past. I slowed to a crawl, like there were bumps ahead in the road. Narciso came right up a couple of feet behind me, and then I saw the lane flooded with light and Njal's truck roared and plunged across the road, came to a dead halt short of the ditch, and he clambered out the door, shouting and waving his arms.

I stopped and climbed out, shouting at him angrily, "*Que pasa? Que pasa?*" Through his windshield, I could see Narciso frowning. His hood was three feet from my trunk, and his trunk was six feet from Njal's door. I gestured to Narciso to stay put and walked toward Njal, still shouting at him, "*Que pasa?*"

Njal was coming toward me, burbling loudly in something that might have been Spanish. We made noises and gestures at each other for a moment longer and finally I went over to Narciso's car, knocked on the glass and made a motion to wind down his window, saying loudly, "I think the damned idiot is drunk! Can you translate for me?"

He opened the door to get out. "Nicholas, this is not England! You have to be careful!" And that was when I saw he had a 9 mm Glock in his hand and was pointing it at Njal. He snapped, "*Quien eres? Que haces aqui? Que buscas? Habla!*"

I had seconds. As soon as Njal opened his mouth, Narciso would know he wasn't Latin American. Half a second after that, he'd know he'd been stung. My instinct was to snatch the gun, but it was pointing straight at Njal's chest. If it went off, it would kill him outright. Instead I shouted at Narciso, "What the hell are you doing? You want this man to go to the cops? You know what low profile means, right?"

He glanced at me. It was all Njal needed. He wailed, "*No! Por favor, no me mate!*" and dropped on his belly. As Narciso turned to look at him, I grabbed the barrel in my right hand and his wrist in my left, and wrenched hard down. He cried out in pain as his index finger snapped. The weapon came free and I smashed it into his face. He staggered back and I tossed the Glock over to Njal. Narciso was looking at me in horror. For a second, pity twisted my gut. I ignored it and took two large steps toward him as he backed against the hood of his car.

He was stammering, "What are you doing? What is this?"

I jabbed him in the chin with my right. His eyes rolled and his legs went wobbly. Then I grabbed him by his shirt collar and dragged him toward me. He made no effort to fight back. He just whimpered, "Please, Nicholas... why?"

I stepped behind him and slipped my right arm around his neck, wedging my elbow under his chin, and grabbed my own wrist with my left hand. As I squeezed I spoke into his ear. "You want compassion, Mu? Go ask for it from all the people Omega has destroyed, and all those it was planning to destroy. I'll see you in hell, Mu."

I squeezed hard, lifted and twisted savagely. I heard his neck snap and dragged him to the Focus. There, we bundled him in the back. Njal reversed his truck into the cover of the trees and then ran over and got behind the wheel of the Focus. I saw he was wearing gloves. I got into my rental car and we drove the eight hundred yards to the bridge. When we got there, Njal climbed out and we put Narciso behind the wheel. Njal said, "I brought a bottle of whiskey for him. That was the plan."

I shook my head. "If we could have forced him to drink it, that would have been good. But if there's an autopsy and they find it's all in his mouth and on his clothes, but none in his belly or his blood... That's a bad look."

He shrugged. "OK, it's a dark night, there is no moon and no barrier on the bridge. It's good enough."

We rolled the car to the edge of the canal. Njal had longer arms, so while I held the door open, he got down on his knees, depressed the clutch with his left hand and the gas with his right, getting the revs up high. I leaned in, across Narciso's limp, staring body, and moved the gear shift into third. Then Njal released the clutch and the gas pedal, and the car lurched violently forward, tipped over the side and toppled, upside down, into the water, with a huge splash. We watched it a moment as it sank among a rush of froth and bubbles.

When it had settled, we got in my car and sped back along the dark track to the copse where Njal had left the pickup. As we drove, with the headlamps picking out the rushing ribbon of road, but throwing everything around it into blackness, I spoke fast.

"OK, we are a day ahead of schedule. So change of plan. We don't want to hang around Buenos Aires while his body is found and they start investigating. Here's what we do. You drive now to Uruguay. If you cross at Fray Bentos, it shouldn't take you more than four hours to get there. From there you get the first flight to Brasilia. Have you got another car? That pickup is going to look conspicuous."

"Yeah. I got a normal car prepared with luggage. I had thought this already. What are you gonna do?"

"Nobody is going to miss the minister till tomorrow morning. There won't be an alert out for him till midday at the soonest. I'm going straight from here to the airport. I'll see you in Brazil. Wash your truck. Message me as soon as you're in Brasilia."

"You are teaching your grandmother to suck eggs. I have done this before."

"Yeah? You'll have to tell me about that one day."

I pulled up at the copse. He climbed out, slammed the door and ran in among the trees where his vehicle was waiting, invisible. I didn't wait. I took off back toward Lobos via Laguna Navarro, where I dumped Nicholas Eddington's passport, credit card and driving license. From now on I was Jason Devries. At Lobos I would pick up the 205, which would carry me all the way to the airport.

I felt sick. I told myself it was because I hadn't eaten, but all I could think about was Narciso staring at me, frightened and confused, not even trying to fight back. He had trusted me. More fool him. He'd been complacent and stupid. And all I wanted was to get out of the goddamn city, out of the goddamn country, and finish the job. So I could go home.

Wherever the hell that was.

TWELVE

AT SEVEN O'CLOCK THE FOLLOWING MORNING I disembarked at Brasilia's international airport, in need of a few hours sleep, a shave and a shower. The rental company had given me a choice between an Audi sedan and a Jeep Renegade. It was no contest. Audis are German and designed for middle managers who play golf. Jeeps are cool.

I picked up the Renegade at the hire office and, after I had persuaded the SatNav to stop talking to me in Portuguese, I headed into town. I had never been to Brasilia before, and my first impression was that Lúcio Costa and Oscar Niemeyerit, the guys who'd designed it, had done too much ayahuasca while watching H. G. Wells' Things to Come, before designing it. The whole city is in the shape of an airplane, its fuselage is the Monumental Axis: two wide avenues flanking a massive park five miles long, while the cockpit is the *Praça dos Três Poderes*—the Plaza of the Three Powers—which holds Congress, the Supreme Court and most of the ministries. The wings are two vast, parabolic sectors with broad avenues and boulevards, and towers of steel and glass rising among wide gardens and parks. The whole thing was planned and developed between 1956 and 1960, when it was inaugurated as the capital city of Brazil. It should have been beautiful, and I guess to an ant or an android it might be.

At half past eight I pulled onto the ERL Sul, one of the three avenues that form the starboard wing of the plane, and headed for the commercial sector of the city, where my hotel, the Windsor Plaza Brasilia, was located. The skies were very blue and already, at that time of the morning, we were in the low seventies.

As I drove, I ran over in my mind where we stood and what we had to do. Though we were ahead of schedule, it was now only by a few hours—I had arrived in Brasilia early Sunday morning, instead of late Sunday afternoon—which meant we had four days before the next meeting between Nu, Xi and Omicron in Casalá, and three days before Raul Rocha, Lambda, next visited his mistress, Joelma, at her place on Conjunto 6.

We were always going to have to act fast, but since the night before, I had felt an urgency to get the job done, go back to my house in Boston and put Omega, and my father's whole sad, twisted legacy behind me. But before we could put our plan into action, I needed to hear from Njal. I had departed from the plan by sending him via Uruguay. I don't like to vary from my plan; more often than not it can start a disastrous chain reaction of events. But on this occasion it seemed an unnecessary risk to me to stay in Argentina after the job was done. Now I had to wait for him.

I pulled up outside the hotel on Via S2 and walked into the gleaming white and blond reception. I had phoned the night before to say I would arrive early, and my executive suite was ready for me. I handed over the keys to have my car parked, and my bag brought up, and was taken to my room by a kid in a uniform. When he'd left, ten bucks richer, I ordered eggs and bacon and a pot of black coffee, stripped and stood under the shower for ten minutes.

I toweled myself dry, and as I was dressing the burner rang and there was a knock on the door. I shouted, "It's open!" and answered the phone. Njal's blunt voice said, "You there yet?"

A guy in a white jacket and bowtie wheeled in my eggs and bacon. I pointed out to my balcony and he wheeled the trolley out there and started to set my table for breakfast. To Njal I said, "Yeah, I just arrived. Where are you?"

"Every flight from Montevideo to Brasilia was minimum five hours, some twenty-five hours. They have no airline of their own, can you believe that?"

I went cold. "So where are you?"

"Oh, I arrived six this morning."

"Six? How?"

I stepped out to the balcony, gave the guy ten bucks and watched him leave while Njal said, "Only way, I had to get an air taxi. The only airline they have is Aeromas, but it's only air taxis. You choose your time, your own plane. Is very cool. Two and a half hour flight."

I sighed and sat at the table. "Good. You OK? You rested?"

"Sure. I'm at the place. You talk to your friend yet?"

"I'm about to call him. Stay on your toes. I want to get

this done ASAP. If my friend agrees to lunch today I'll message you saying, 'lunch'. Then you move in. Once you are in with the girl, and you have the place secured, send me a message saying, 'I'm home.' Then I'll come over, as we planned."

"OK. I won't move till I hear from you. What about the money?"

"I'll collect it from the bank on the way. I'll call my friend now."

I hung up and ate hungrily. When I'd finished I sat back, drained a cup of coffee and called the number Cyndi had given me for Rocha. He answered on the fourth ring. His voice was cool, with a hint of unfriendly.

"*Aló.*"

"Good morning, Mr. Rocha, this is Jason Devries. we have a mutual friend in Cyndi McFarlane. We spoke a couple of days ago."

"Yes, I remember."

He waited. He wanted me to ask him for a meeting, so we could define our roles from the start, and he could be in the dominant position of strength. Negotiation one-oh-one. If that was his dying wish, I could grant it. I said, "I know it's short notice, Mr. Rocha, but I was wondering if you were free for lunch today."

He sighed, took a moment. "I have a prior engagement, however, as you are a friend of Cyndi's, if it is important..."

I gave a small laugh. "Well, Mr. Rocha, it is important to us, and it is our intention to make it mutually beneficial. Cyndi certainly thought that you would find our project a matter of interest. However, if she has misjudged the situation for any reason, I would not want to encroach on your time…"

He sighed again. "Not at all, any friend of Cyndi's is a friend of mine. By all means, let us meet for lunch. Are you familiar with Brasilia?"

I sat back and let him take the lead. Once he was leading, it would be me doing the granting. I said: "No, this is my first time here. What do you suggest?"

"The Aquavit is suitable. It is quiet and we will have privacy to talk."

"Sounds perfect. How do I get there?"

"It is best if you go under your own steam, so that I am not connected with you at this stage. Take a taxi. Tell him to take you to the Aquavit at the Jardim Botanico. Say one o'clock. You will like it."

"Good, that sounds just fine. I look forward to it."

"Goodbye, Mr. Devries."

He hung up before I could answer. Something told me Mr. Rocha was not going to be as easy to handle as Narciso Terry had been.

I picked up the burner and sent Njal the message, *Lunch @ 1*. Then I lay down and slept like the dead for three hours.

———

A BOTANICAL GARDEN in Brazil is not like a botanical garden anywhere else in the world. It's more like a small country. This one in particular was a vast park fifteen miles across which contained savanna, rainforest rivers and lakes, and every conceivable form of exotic life, both animal and vegetable. It even contained an exclusive restaurant, and by far the most exotic and colorful life forms were to be found in there.

Aquavit was perched on the edge of a three hundred foot lake in a clearing in the middle of one and a half square miles of rainforest contained within the vast botanical garden. It looked like the kind of colonial mansion a nineteenth century tobacco farmer might have had in Indonesia: a single storey A-frame, with highly polished hardwood floors, thick, wooden pillars and bare rafters under a sloping ceiling. The walls were also polished wood, with vast, plate glass windows overlooking the lake and the forest. It was the kind of thing you had to stop and stare at. The Ritz and the Savoy, for all their luxury, could not compete.

I told the head waiter that *el Señor Raul Rocha* was expecting me and he led me across the spacious dining room to where Rocha was sitting by the window, sipping a martini and looking at the lake, like he wasn't aware of me approaching.

I'd seen photographs of him and studied them, but in the flesh he was smaller, slighter, with a small, soft beard and moustache that were turning to gray. When he finally looked around at me, his eyes were large, liquid and brown, like he'd borrowed them from Bambi's mother. He surprised me by smiling and standing, extending his hand to take mine.

"Mr. Devries, it is good of you to meet me here. Please, have a seat, what will you drink?"

I shook his hand. "I'll join you in a martini." I turned to the waiter. "Dry, vodka, shaken, not stirred."

Rocha laughed as we sat. "Like the infamous Mr. Bond. So, I am intrigued, how can the Brazilian Minister for Mines and Energy help a mining engineer from Nevada?"

I looked surprised, smiled and raised an eyebrow. "Any number of ways, I should have thought, Mr. Rocha, but in this particular case, the people I represent have a proposition for you which could be beneficial all 'round."

He raised both his eyebrows at his glass, like it had been an impertinent glass, and said, "That sounds dangerously like bribery, Mr. Devries."

I shook my head. "No, not at all. We simply want to be discreet at this stage."

He looked up and smiled with his doe eyes. "Oh, how disappointing."

We both laughed and I reassured him. "We are old fashioned businessmen, Mr. Rocha, and we have no intention of getting involved in the niceties of local law. We are more interested in conforming to local tradition and making sure everybody gets a fair share of the profits."

"Now you are speaking a language I understand. But tell me, a share of profits in what enterprise?" The waiter brought my drink. Rocha said, "It is the practice of this restaurant to harmonize the food with a wine of the chef's choice. So, for example, the gazpacho with salted codfish fritters will come with a Chilean sauvignon blanc reserve from 2014. I can recommend this very much. The duck confit with fresh corn cream angu comes with a Valpolicella Superiore Tedeschi from 2013. I am not a fan of Italian wine, but this one is very good." He gave a self-deprecating smile. "I am familiar with this restaurant, I live near by and it is like my 'local'. These are my current favourite dishes."

I nodded at the waiter. "They sound perfect."

Rocha gestured with his fingers at the waiter to go away

and smiled at me with his watery eyes. "You were about to explain."

I sat back and sipped my martini. It was excellent. As I set it down I smacked my lips. "Last year a report found its way into our hands. One Samuel Magnusson, a geologist from Iceland, and something of an adventurer, had made his way to Brazil, with a small team of prospectors, and carried out a number of illegal surveys along the Bolivian border, between Rondônia, Mato Grosso and Mato Grosso do Sul: a stretch of some one thousand four hundred miles." I laughed. "Obviously he didn't survey that whole area, but the areas he did survey are within that stretch, as I understand it."

"As you understand it..."

I gave him my most innocent smile. "I may of course have been misinformed. However, the important point at this stage is that the surveys were not authorized by the Brazilian government. The syndicate who bankrolled Magnusson and his team were, apparently, afraid that a by-the-book application for a license might get bogged down in red tape. This was, of course, in the times of the previous administration."

"Indeed. So what did these surveys find?"

I bit my lip and turned my glass around a few times for dramatic effect. "*If* the report is correct, and our experts say there is every reason to believe it is, Magnusson found the biggest deposits of lithium in the world, and then some." I could tell by the expression on his face that he knew what that meant, but I told him anyway. "At current values, lithium is worth between nine and ten thousand dollars a metric tonne. But that is going to change."

"You think so? On what grounds?"

"On two very important grounds. First of all, lithium is going to start replacing oil as the main energy source on this planet, at least as far as motorized vehicles are concerned. But with advances in technology progressing as fast as they are, there is no telling how far it will go, or what lithium will be adapted to." I sat back and studied him a moment. "We are aware, for example, of plans to drive small aircraft with banks of alternating lithium batteries: while one bank runs the motor, the motor charges the second bank. As battery efficiency improves, and charging technology improves, we believe lithium will replace oil across the board. It is conceivable that even houses will be run on lithium batteries."

I leaned forward to give weight to my next statement. "And second, the reserves in Chile and Australia are running down. They were never vast to begin with, but as demand increases for cell phones and motor vehicles, the drain on those mines increases. Put those two facts together, and Brazil becomes the Saudi Arabia of the future."

He tried to hide it, but his big, brown, watery eyes were bright. As with Narciso Terry, I had chosen my lies carefully to appeal not just to the greedy individual, but to the long-term aspirations of Omega—or what was left of Omega. If Omicron wanted to lead the resurgence of his organization, cyborgs and lithium would be at the heart of that enterprise. He gazed at the tamed jungle outside and I watched his jaw muscle bunch rhythmically.

"Are you certain about this?" he said at last.

I gave a small shrug. "I wouldn't be here, and perhaps more to the point, Cyndi would not have given me an introduction to you, if we were not pretty certain."

He nodded. That made sense to him. "What do you want, and what are you offering in exchange?"

I spread my hands. "What my principals want is very simply a partnership. What we want is to pool resources." I laughed. "It may not always look that way, but the American continent is driving toward an ever closer integration. Right now we have the technology to exploit the mines, we know precisely where the deposits are, and we have the money and resources to mine them. But we have more than that. We have contacts that are in a position to control the flow of oil onto the international market and drive up the price per barrel, and so make lithium an increasingly attractive option; and..." I wagged my finger at him. "We can incorporate R&D facilities into the mining process so that we can learn how to synthesize the lithium if and when the deposits run dry. We have everything, Mr. Rocha, except the lithium."

He was quiet for a long time. Eventually he asked me, "Who do you represent?"

I shook my head. "Not yet. If we have the makings of a deal, and you are prepared to work with us, then I can introduce you to my principal. He is here, in Brasilia, at the moment. But we need something pretty concrete from you."

The waiter came with our gazpacho and the wine. He left and we ate in silence for a while. When his bowl was almost empty, Rocha sat back and dabbed his lips.

"Something concrete, like what?"

I echoed his movement and leaned back in my chair, wiping my mouth.

"The people I represent have the same concerns that Magnusson's people had. Even though the administration in Brazil has changed, it is easy for a project like this to get bogged down, and for vested interests to start competing. You have a lot of oil in Brazil, and there are people who are still making a lot of money from that oil. They won't be happy to see lithium mines being exploited. So what we want from you, personally, is the authorization to go ahead with the preliminary stages of the mining, without interference, and with a large degree of discretion and autonomy."

"You want me to authorize it and keep it secret until it is a *fete accompli*."

"Yes. Can you do it?"

He nodded. "Yes. I can do that. How much will you pay me?"

"The precise details are for your conversation with my principal. However, I can tell you that we are prepared to make an initial payment of ten million dollars, and as I understand it, a large share allocation in the company to be formed."

He sipped his wine. He was trying hard to hide it, but there was real excitement in his eyes. I had just told him, in so many words, that not only did Omega have a real chance of reestablishing itself, but that, with a large share allocation in the company, he had a shot at becoming Alpha in the New Order.

But Raul Rocha was nothing if not in control. He set down his glass and gave a smile that said what he was hearing was all words.

"It all sounds very interesting, Mr. Devries, but, with all due respect, you are just the messenger. I need to talk to your boss."

I chuckled. "Not my boss, Mr. Rocha, my principal. Right now, you talk to me and you *are* talking to him. I can arrange a meeting at very short notice. He is keen to meet you. All I need from you at this stage is a firm, oral commitment that you will fast track the project."

He studied my face for a long moment. A waiter came and took away our dishes and the wine. A second brought the duck and the Valpolicella. When he had gone, Rocha shook his head and said, "No."

THIRTEEN

I WENT COLD INSIDE. I SAT WITH MY GLASS halfway to my mouth, staring at him. It was not the reaction I had expected, and if he grew difficult, the repercussions could be disastrous. A delay in the hit would give time for Narciso's body to be found and identified. News of his death would spread through Latin America—and Omega— like wildfire. That, plus my unorthodox approach, could alert Rocha and he would in turn alert the Mexican cabal. If they decided to retaliate, there was no telling where this could end.

I set down my glass, thinking fast about how I could kill him and dump him in the lake on the way home. We would then have to cross six countries plus most of Brazil to get to Mexico, by which time Gonzalez, Zapata and Ochoa would be on red alert. I said: "No?"

"With the greatest respect, Mr. Devries, I cannot make a firm commitment to a man who is, in the end, no more than a messenger. Albeit," he smiled ingratiatingly, "a most eminent messenger, but still a messenger, nonetheless. I will give my firm commitment to your principal, when I have met him and when I have spoken to him. May I know his name?"

I managed to look irritated instead of relieved. I cut at my duck as though trying to repress my anger, stuffed a piece in my mouth and chewed, watching him. After I had sipped my wine, I said, "I come to you with a personal introduction from a U.S. senator—a senator who will, incidentally, be a part of this deal. You are aware of her green credentials."

He closed his eyes and nodded. I went on.

"This is a very delicate affair, very sensitive. We are simply trying to protect our interests, so my principal merely asks that, before he reveals his identity to you, he can be sure of a degree of commitment on your part." I gave a smile that clearly masked displeasure. "It is not a lot to ask."

In his mind, he knew that he held the reins. He controlled the lithium, and we had come to him. He was in control. And I was happy for him to feel that way, because as long as I resisted his meeting with my principal, that was exactly what he was going to push for. He smiled regretfully.

"Clearly, I will not pretend that I am not interested. That would be absurd. And of course, Cyndi's credentials are unimpeachable, as are yours, I am sure. I mean no disrespect. But seriously, to proceed, I must talk to your principal. The most I can say to you, in these circumstances, is that, *prima facie*, I am interested in what you are telling me. But please, let me talk to somebody in charge."

We ate in silence for a while. After a couple of minutes I

nodded and pointed at the duck with my knife. "This is really very good."

He raised an eyebrow at me but said nothing. After another couple of minutes, when I had almost finished my food, I sipped my wine, wiped my moth and said, "Will you excuse me a moment? I'm going to make a call." I hesitated before I stood. "Can I tell him at least that, as you say, *prima facie*, that you are interested?"

He frowned and nodded elaborately. "Indeed, very interested."

I smiled gratefully. "Thank you."

I rose from the table and walked out onto the veranda. I stood where he could see me, but far away enough for it to seem like I was looking for privacy. I called Njal and began to pace, like I was nervous. Njal answered, I said: "Don't talk for a bit, just listen. Here's the situation. Rocha is very interested in meeting you, but he is refusing to give a firm commitment to me, because he feels I am merely a messenger. He says he will only give a commitment after he has spoken to you in person, and knows who you are. I have stressed to him that Cyndi herself gave me the introduction and that I am not merely a messenger. Even so he insists, he wants to meet you in person to discuss the deal, or there is no deal."

I was silent for a bit, walking up and down the veranda like I was listening. Njal said, "So you want me to move in."

I sighed, puffed out my cheeks and said, "I think that's a good idea, but there is still the question of when." I stared up at the sky. "I'll tell him, in a bit, that you are only in Brasilia for a couple of days and that you are willing to cancel another meeting this afternoon in order to see him and discuss preliminary matters. You were hoping that he and I could make some initial progress today, but you fully understand his concerns blah blah, and you can make room for a meeting this afternoon."

"OK, sounds good. I am outside her house. Send me a text if he agrees."

"Yeah, OK. I'll see you in a bit."

He hung up but I stayed on the veranda, pacing up and down, holding the cell to my ear and nodding. Eventually I said, "Yeah, OK, I'll get back to you," made like I'd hung up and walked back into the restaurant with a strained face.

I sat and sighed. "He was hoping that you and I could make some preliminary progress together. He's only here for a couple of days and has other meetings, as you can imagine. However, I told him how you felt and he said that was perfectly understandable. He is going to cancel a meeting this afternoon with an investor and he hopes that you and I can meet him for a drink at the Royal Tulip, on the lakeside by the Alvorada Palace."

"I know it. That's fine. We can have coffee and a liquor, and I must insist you try the brazil nut fragilité with mascarpone parfait and guava. It is sublime and comes with a sauternes Château Gravas, 2008."

I laughed. "I wouldn't miss it for all the lithium on the Enterprise."

He laughed too. "Ah! That is *di*lithium, if I am not mistaken. When we can mine that, we will be truly rich, my friend!"

The mood lightened after that. We finished our duck and the Valpolichella and as they cleared it away, I pulled my cell from my pocket and said, "With your permission, I'll just tell him we're on, and that we'll be there in..." I made a face that was a question and said, "...an hour? Hour and a half?"

"Let us say between an hour and an hour and a half, and that way we will not be late."

I chuckled and nodded, and sent Njal the text. Rocha was having fun, playing hard to get, and who was I to deny him his fun? The text said: *Go in. Take the girl.*

An hour and fifteen minutes later, we stepped out onto the veranda. I placed my hand on his shoulder and smiled as I pulled the keys to my car from my pocket.

"My principal asks that, for the sake of discretion, we go in my car. I hope that's OK..."

He produced his condescending smile again and chuckled. "I have a chauffeur driven Bentley, so I think your principal is probably wise."

We both laughed like he'd said something really funny and we made our way across the gardens to the parking lot. As we climbed into my Jeep, I quipped about how I hoped it wasn't too far below what he was used to, and he made generous noises about how the Jeep was a grand car, and I would soon be rich enough to own a Bentley, like his. He'd had a few drinks and believed he was about to become fabulously rich, not just by Brazilian standards, but on the Gates-Rockefeller standard graph. So, while I drove through the rainforest toward the road, he expounded on the indubitable merits of various American cars, and contrasted them with the palatial luxury of the Bentley. All were found wanting.

While he was doing that, I leaned over and smashed my right fist into his jaw. His eyes rolled and he sagged against his seat belt. It wasn't just that I was tired of listening to him flatulate through his mouth. We were about to join the freeway, and I was going to turn north toward his mistress' house, instead of turning south to go toward the Royal Tulip, where my fictional principal was supposed to be waiting for us. I figured it would be easier all around if he slept through the journey and didn't ask awkward questions.

It was a six mile drive, but it was freeway for most of those miles, and it took a little less than ten minutes to get there. The street, not very evocatively named Shis QI 28 Conjunto 6, was pretty and leafy, and populated by some spectacular, modernist homes. You couldn't help feeling it deserved a better name: something like Palm Drive. I grinned sourly, looking at the unconscious man beside me, and said aloud, "Or Rocha's End."

I pulled into the driveway of a large, white building which had been designed to resemble a cruiser, with portholes and balconies like decks, killed the engine and called Njal.

"Stop calling me, man. We are not supposed to use these damned phones."

"Open the garage for me."

He hung up and two minutes later, the door to the garage started to roll up. I drove through and the blind started to rattle closed behind me. The light came on and a door in the right hand wall opened. Through it I could see a carpeted hallway and, leaning against the jamb, Njal, watching me.

I climbed out and slammed the door. "Give me a hand, will you? Where's the woman?"

He pushed off the doorjamb and walked toward me.

"She's on the sofa. Her arms, legs and mouth are duct taped, but I don't want to leave her too long, you know?"

"OK, just give me a hand to get him inside."

We pulled open the door, I grabbed Rocha under his shoulders, Njal grabbed his knees, and between the two of us, we carried him into the hallway. It was broad and spacious and white. There were a couple of doors and a tiled staircase that rose to the next floor. Njal jerked his head at the stairs. "Living room is on the next floor."

I grunted. Rocha was beginning to moan. I said, "OK, let's get him upstairs."

Upstairs there was a landing with a passage that led off to the left. On the right there were double doors that led to a huge living area with a copper fireplace in the middle of the floor, sliding glass doors and a vast terrace with panoramic views of the lake, and lots of banana trees. There were eclectic, expensive pieces of furniture scattered around the room, and on one of these—a large, white calico sofa—there was a very attractive woman whose ankles were bound with duct tape. She had her arms behind her back and a piece of duct tape across her mouth. Her skin was chocolate brown with a dash of milk, her eyes were large and very dark, and her hair was blue-black, tied in a bun behind her neck. She was staring at Rocha and looked really scared.

We dumped Rocha on a chair and Njal set about duct taping him too. I sat on the sofa with Joelma and looked into her eyes. They were something special.

"Joelma, you speak English?"

She nodded.

"I am going to speak slowly, OK?"

She nodded again.

"I am going to take off your gag..." I made the motion with my hand of removing the tape. Then I shook my head and my finger. "Don't scream. No, *aaaaah!* OK?" She nodded more cautiously. I turned to Njal. "You want to get the money? It's in the back of the Jeep."

He was kneeling by Rocha's ankles, winding tape around them. He nodded and stood.

I hesitated a moment and as he reached the door, I said, "Did you get the weapon?"

He stopped and his eyes went involuntarily to Joelma. She stared back at him. He nodded once. "Yuh."

He left and she looked back at me. I smiled at her and pointed at myself. "I want to give you..." I pointed at her. "Money." I rubbed my fingers together in the universal sign for cash. She frowned and looked at me like I was crazy. I nodded. "Yes, *eu vo dar a vose muito dinero.* I want to give you lots of money."

Her eyes narrowed and became suspicious. She shrugged. *Why?* I smiled and nodded again.

"So you go away. Go to U.S.A."

To say her face was skeptical would be an understatement. I heard Njal's feet on the stairs and after a moment he came in with an attaché case and handed it to me. "We wait till she has gone, yuh?"

I didn't say anything. I opened the case and showed it to her. Her eyes went wide. It contained one hundred thousand dollars, and lying on top of them was a U.S. passport and a ticket in her new name to Los Angeles. I held it up and showed it to her. Then I leaned forward and pulled the tape off her mouth.

She spluttered a few things in Portuguese which I didn't

understand, but I didn't figure they were anything I especially wanted to hear, either. When she'd finished, she glared at me and I could see why Rocha was willing to keep her in a house like this as his mistress. I said:

"All I want you to do, Joelma, is take this money, this passport and this ticket, and go to Los Angeles. Somebody will meet you there and help you."

She was shaking her head like I was crazy. "Why? Why you do this?"

I watched her a moment, and felt a freezing ruthlessness congeal my insides. I said, brutally, "Because we are going to frame you for Raul Rocha's murder."

She frowned, shook her head that she didn't understand.

"We will make it look like you killed Raul Rocha." I mimed as I spoke. "If the cops, the police, catch you, you could incriminate us. The alternative is to kill you too, and we don't want to do that. So the simplest thing is for you to run and get a new identity. So we will make it seem that you killed your lover, and escaped from Brazil."

Her dark skin seemed to turn gray. She glanced over at Rocha. Was there grief in her expression? If there was, it didn't last. It soon turned to fear. She looked back at me, at the money, the ticket and the passport.

"I need house, credit card, bank account, social security number! What about all this?"

I gave a small laugh and shook my head. "Don't worry, we want you to be happy in your new life. The man who is going to meet you will fix you up. Believe me, in Los Angeles you will feel right at home. Have we got a deal?"

She nodded. Njal was pulling on a pair of latex gloves. He took a Glock 17 from his waistband and looked a question at me. I heard Joelma make a small gasp. I ignored her and said, "You got a pair of gloves for me?" He pulled them from his pocket and handed them over. I pulled them on with a snap and said, "Take her downstairs."

He took the tape off her wrists and ankles and helped her to stand. Her bottom lip was curling in and her eyes were flooded with tears. She kept looking from me to Njal with sharp little jerks of her head. He led her from the room. I heard their feet on the stairs. Then I heard a door close.

Raul Rocha had his eyes open. He looked groggy and he was frowning at me. "Why...?"

"Because Omicron must be stopped before Omega reemerges."

His frown deepened. "Who are you?"

"Lacklan Walker. My father was Gamma."

He looked genuinely astonished. "*You?* But we were told you would not come for us."

I stopped dead. "Who told you that?"

His expression was bewildered and for a moment there was a glimmer of hope. "Alpha. Your brother, Ben."

"He's *alive?* Have you seen him?"

He stared at me for a moment, then shook his head. "No. It was a message. A secure message. But there are procedures, checks. Only he has access. He said you had made peace, reached a compromise..."

I put the first round through his heart so it would be quick, then I emptied six more rounds into his chest and belly, to make it look like passion. After that, I carried the gun downstairs.

They were sitting in the kitchen. Joelma was sobbing. I

removed the magazine and handed the gun to her. She held it, staring down at it.

"Pull the trigger a couple of times. Then pull the slide, like this..."

I showed her and she did what I said. Her sobbing became compulsive. After that, I gave her a glass of wine. When she'd drunk most of it, I carried it and the gun back upstairs and set the scene: the bottle of wine and two glasses, each with prints, and the gun tossed on the floor. I removed the tape from his ankles and his wrists, had a look around and went back down to the kitchen. There I made a package of Njal's ID and my Jason Devries documents, wrapped them in a tea towel and weighted the whole thing down with knives, forks and spoons from the cutlery drawer.

While I was doing that, Njal asked me, "What about the bleach?"

I shook my head. "I don't like that anymore. It's not credible. If I were a cop, I wouldn't buy it. It's too professional."

He watched me. His face was expressionless. "Anything else you are planning on changing at the last minute?"

"No."

We bundled Joelma into the front passenger seat of the Jeep, pulled out of the garage and headed for the airport. On the way, as we crossed the bridge, we threw the package into the Paranoá lake. I was now Bill Rogers, an insurance sales-man, and I had no idea who Njal was.

Once over the bridge he said: "Drop me at the next bus stop. I make my own way, yuh? I see you there."

I did as he asked and we watched him disappear down a side street on his long, striding legs. Joelma was still crying. I said, "When we get to the airport, we're going to hug a lot, OK? I'm your boyfriend and you're going back to L.A. We're not going to see each other for a while. You understand?"

She nodded and made a wet noise that sounded like a yes.

"I'm going to see you as far as security. You have a first class ticket and you're a U.S. citizen, they shouldn't give you any trouble. Within the next few hours, the cops will be looking for Joelma Santos. So you keep a low profile and your mouth shut, you don't talk to anybody until you get to Los Angeles, understood? If the cops get any idea of who you are, you could end up going to prison for the rest of your life. Once you're in L.A. you'll be safe, but it is imperative you speak to nobody on the flight. Pretend you have a sore throat. Whatever. Just talk to nobody, OK?"

She scowled at me. "You tell me this already. I say OK."

"Good."

"You can come with me?"

"No."

"Why?"

"Don't ask questions. Just get yourself to L.A."

Next thing, out of the blue, she was screaming hysterically, "*Why you do this to me? Why? You destroy my life! You crazy! Crazy! Crazy! Why you do this to me?*" And then there was a long stream in hysterical Portuguese which I tried to talk over.

"You need to calm down." I struggled to think of calm down in Portuguese or even Spanish, but the screaming noise in the cab was too loud. I said again, "Joelma! Calm down!"

But she just kept going, screaming and pounding the windows with her fists. I had no idea what she was saying, but I was sure she was going to get us both imprisoned or killed if she didn't stop. And then it happened. A police car drew up alongside us, sounded the siren once and indicated we should pull over. I swore profusely, put on my indicator, pulled in to the side of the road and killed the engine.

Joelma had gone very quiet and pale. I said to her, "That was real stupid. I'm going home to the States, Joelma. You are going to prison for the rest of your life, not for murder, but for sheer, damned stupidity."

She stared at me, sniffed and wiped her eyes. One of the cops climbed out of his car and strolled back toward us. He came to my window and indicated I should wind it down. He said something to me in Portuguese.

I smiled apologetically. "*Americano. No fallo Portuguese.*"

He looked at Joelma. "*Esta bem?*"

She nodded, still sniffing.

He looked at me. "Name, driving license."

I reached in my pocket and handed him my new passport and license. I said, "We're Americans."

He jerked his head at Joelma. "*Você?*"

Wiping her eyes and sniffing, she launched into a long exposition while pulling her new, U.S. passport from her bag and showing it to him. I caught snatches. I was her boyfriend. She had to go back to Los Angeles. She wanted me to go with her. I had to stay. She was sure the son of a bitch (me) was seeing another woman. The cop examined her passport. I could see by his face he was growing bored. He handed it back and napped at her in Portuguese that hysterical behavior in moving motor vehicles was the cause of many deaths. She should be more responsible and behave like an adult. To me he said, "You stay in Brazil?"

"For another day or so."

"What is your business?"

I improvised: "I'm an insurance salesman. But my hobby is travel writing and I'm conducting research for an article for a travel magazine." I grinned and laughed. "I love Brazil."

He looked at me as though loving Brazil made me eligible for a good kicking and said, "What is in the case?" He pointed at Joelma's feet. "The attaché case. Open it."

A hundred grand in U.S. dollars was in the case. If we opened it, we would get taken in to the station and questioned, and then everything would unravel. I looked at Joelma. "Honey, have you got the key?"

She sniffed. "I don't have the key. You say you have the key."

The cop snapped. "Open the case."

I started to pat my pockets and I saw his hand go to his piece. I knew I was going to have to kill him, and I didn't want to do that. Outside, I heard the crackle of a radio. I said, "I know I have it somewhere..."

I saw the other cop get out of the car. This was it. This was the moment I either died or killed an innocent cop. My left hand was on the latch of the door, ready to ram him and snatch his piece. The cop by the car called over something in Portuguese. I heard the word '*robo*'—a theft. The cop by the door looked unhappy. He gave me a once over and said, "Be careful when you are driving. Do not argue and drive!"

I nodded. "That's good advice." I turned to Joelma. "See, honey, how your temper always causes problems?"

He turned and walked away, back to his car. I sighed, indicated right and pulled out into the traffic. "Do that again," I said, "and I swear you will spend the rest of your life in a damn jail. Because I will not help you out!"

"*Filho de puta! Cabrão! Asesino!* It is me who save! I save you! You filthy *viado! Bicha corno! Asesino! Asesino!*"

I slowed and raised a warning finger at her. "Don't start again! I swear! Just—don't talk! Just don't!"

She flopped back in her seat and settled to sniffing and sobbing again. After a while, she muttered "*Meu Raul, amorzinho...*" reached down, pulled the attaché case onto her lap and hugged it. "*Meu amorzinho...*"

I parked in the short term car park and accompanied Joelma into the terminal building. There I bought her a sports bag and filled it with clothes that looked roughly the right size. At first I asked her if she liked the things I was buying, but when she just stared at me as though I had finally taken leave of my senses, I bought whatever caught my eye and stuffed it in the bag. When the bag was full, I took her by the arm and led her to passport control.

There I handed her the bag and turned her to face me. "We're in love," I said. "Try to look as though you don't want to tear my eyes out. Give me a hug, make it convincing, and try not to draw attention to yourself."

Her face was twisted and damp with tears. I tried not to imagine what she was feeling. She narrowed her eyes with hatred and gave her head a small shake. Her voice was little more than a whisper. "*Filho de puta...*"

Son of a bitch. She wasn't wrong. She put her arms around me and held me. Then she looked up into my face and kissed me on the lips, she held my head in her hands and whispered close to my ear, so I could feel her moist breath on my skin: "I will find you, and I will kill you."

I watched her step back, away from me, turn and go through passport control.

Sometimes thinking can be the enemy of survival. I didn't think about what had just happened. I turned and walked away to book my flight to Mexico City.

FOURTEEN

It was four in the afternoon in Durango, and we were sitting in the courtyard garden of the Hotel Gobernador, by the pool. It was 90F in the shade, though in the sun it seemed hotter. Njal had a cold beer, and I was on my second martini. The vodka they'd used to dry it up was doing a good job of numbing my conscience, but Njal didn't look happy.

"You keep changing the plan, man. That is a sure path to disaster. You know this."

I drained my glass and signaled the waiter for another.

Njal sighed. "And you are drinking too much."

I pulled a pack of Camels from my pocket. "You mind if I smoke? Or am I doing too much of that too?"

He held out his hand and I shook one free for him. Then I lit up and handed him my lighter. He was waiting for me to answer, so I said, "I'm not changing the plan, Njal. The plan is the same. I'm adapting the strategies to meet the new situations. Were you ever a soldier?"

"My life story is not relevant now, Lacklan. We were supposed to put the body in bleach to delay its discovery. We were not supposed to meet up so soon. We are being seen together, in Durango. We arrived in the same goddamn car, and we are just seventy-five miles from Sinaloa. It's sloppy. It's not like you and that worries me. You said you were OK for the job."

I thought about it and wondered if he was right. I shrugged. "Both hits so far went off without a hitch and ahead of schedule. The only changes I made were to compensate for the early strikes, and to avoid the cops getting too curious. It would have been stupid to stay in Argentina once Terry was dead. Same in Brazil. And as for the bleach, you know as well as I do that Joelma would not have done that. It would have been out of character and the cops would have smelt a rat. It was wrong."

"Yeah, maybe, but what about Mexico? We wound up on the same fuckin' plane, man. If we had stuck to the plan, that would not have happened. And when we got off, instead of ignoring me, you come over, 'Hey, man! I didn't know you was in Mexico! What's happenin'? Don't tell me you goin' to Durango! Me too! Come on, we hire a car together!' That was crazy, man. What got into you?"

"I don't agree. I don't think it was crazy at all. I thought it through for thirteen hours on the plane. I think it was the smartest thing we could do."

"And getting the same hotel and getting drunk, that smart too?"

"Yup."

"So, you better explain why."

"Is that a threat?"

He nodded. "Yuh."

I smiled. Never ask a Norseman a direct question if you don't want a blunt answer. "OK, the one thing we didn't allow for was Joelma being a loose cannon. What you don't know is that after you left she went hysterical, screaming at the top of her lungs that I was an *asesino*, amongst other choice Brazilian epithets. It was so bad we were pulled over by the cops. It was a miracle we got out of there without being arrested or shot." I pointed at him like my finger was a gun. "And *that* was following the plan."

"OK, so?"

"So I got her to the airport, she played her part, but before she left she told me she'd hunt me down and kill me."

"You believe her?"

"No, but I think she is crazy enough to send an anonymous message to the Brasilia PD. And when they find the body, they could well put out a BOLO."

He nodded. "Last time she saw us, we were going our separate ways."

"Exactly. So they will be least likely to be looking for two guys traveling together in Mexico and staying at the most expensive hotel in town."

He grunted. "I still think you're drinking too much."

"Yeah, well, the alternative is worse. We're ahead of schedule, it's been a tough few days and we have twenty-four hours to kill. A miserable, foreign teetotaler sticks out in this town like a hard-on at a nuns' convention. Best thing we can do is go on the town, let off steam and pick up a couple of high-class hookers. Then disappear tomorrow, leaving a false trail."

He grinned. "That's more like the kind of thing I wanna be hearing from you, dude. That's the Lacklan I know."

I agreed with him. It was the kind of stuff I wanted to be hearing from myself. But all I could think about was getting the damn job done and going home. I didn't tell him that. I smiled instead. "OK, so after your next beer, you go out and buy some fancy clothes for tonight. Then we'll book a couple of escorts and go out on the town, have dinner, go dancing. A couple of dudes having a good time. Stay out of trouble. Meanwhile, contact your contact and see if they've collected the goods..."

He nodded and reached for his cell. While he was dialing, I went on. "While you're out, I'm going to ask the concierge if it's cool for women to visit us in our rooms. Then I'm going to ask him the best route to get to Texas..."

He suddenly smiled and spoke into the phone. "Hey, Danny! How you doin', man? Cool, cool, chillin' here in Mexico. Comin' home tomorrow. Listen, I wanned to ask you. Did Mom get back OK...? She did? That's cool. She was lookin' a bit sick, you know? OK, no, that was it, man. I just wanted to touch base. OK, I'll call you when I get home, man. Hang loose, dude." He hung up. "Yeah, she got home OK."

"So where do we collect the stuff?"

"It's about halfway between Mazatlán and Culiacán. There some small farms there on the coast, bays, inlets, streams. They have a small holding, a fishing hut, couple of barns. They good people..." He seemed to hesitate for a second, like he was thinking about telling me something, then went on. "It's about two hundred miles away, so it's gonna be like four hours."

"OK, we collect the stuff mid afternoon. We leave here around twelve noon, get there about four. Then we follow the original plan. We follow the road like we were going to Cosalá. About three miles before Vado Hondo there's a settlement, just a few houses, people minding their own business. Then there's a dirt track that climbs into the hills. We follow the track for about seven miles, till we come to a deep gully on the left. There we lose the car in among the trees. From that point on it's on foot for eleven miles. We need to estimate six hours. We want to get to the forest outside the ranch at about three AM, which, working backwards, puts us dumping the car at the gully at nine PM latest."

Njal nodded. "If we collect the stuff at four in the afternoon, that's plenny of time."

"We don't sleep. We dump our stuff and recon the ranch, lab, whatever it is. Then before first light, we return to our dump and then we sleep. We will have another day for a second reconnaissance before they arrive. By then we need to have the hit figured."

He gave me two thumbs up. "I'm gonna buy clothes. I get you some nice Levis and a cool shirt." He stood. "You fix us up with a couple of nice *señoritas*, man. We can party."

I narrowed my eyes at him. "Did you get stuck in the '70s and just stop aging? What is your story, Njal?"

"I wasn't *born* in the 70s, man. I am Scandinavian. We exist in a time warp. I catch you later, dude."

He left, with his long, loping stride, and I sat and finished my drink, listening to the birds and wondering how much of what I had said to Njal was true, and how much was bullshit. Was I OK for this job? Or was I going to pieces?

I wasn't all that sure. No doubt we'd find out in the next couple of days, but at what cost, and to whom?

The night was uneventful. The concierge had found us an escort company called VIP Escorts, that he said was *muy elegante* and the girls *muy sofisticadas*. The girls in question were called Sandra and Nancy, and took us to a good Mexican restaurant that wasn't superb. According to Sandra, who was cute and dark, it belonged to her uncle.

They both spoke broken English and we spoke broken Spanish back to them; and after the first hour they spoke to each other and laughed a lot, and Njal and I watched and smiled and discussed existentialism.

After dinner Nancy, who was also cute and dark but had dyed her hair blonde, took us to a nightclub that she said belonged to her brother. There the music was too loud to talk, so they danced with each other and laughed a lot. And Njal and I stood and watched and thought about existentialism.

At about two AM they forced us to dance and we made fools of ourselves for half an hour until finally we went back to the hotel.

At nine the next morning, we paid them double what they had asked for and promised to call next time we were in town. They left, looking cute but not really elegant or sophisticated, talking a lot and laughing more. I wondered briefly what Jim would make of our expense accounts when he reviewed them.

I had not seen a single sign that either the cartel or Omega were watching us that night. By the looks of it, they were still completely unaware of our presence. That led me to thinking for the thousandth time about what Raul Rocha had said before I shot him: that Ben had told them I had reached an arrangement with him. That was why their security was so lax. That was why, despite what had happened to Omega 1 and 2, despite the crash of their computer networks, Omega 3 was not on red alert. They were barely on any kind of alert.

So either Ben was alive, despite the fact that I had shot him through the heart and watched him die[1], or somebody was trying to make me, and what was left of Omega, believe that he was alive.

Who?

It was an impossible question to answer on the practically nonexistent information I had. I could speculate: Jim, Gibbons, some as yet unknown member of Omega, even Marni. But speculation got me nowhere, and besides, the real question was not who, but what for?

So far the net effect of this deceit—this game—was the steady and systematic destruction of Omega; and so far that suited me fine. But a war is decided at the outcome of the final battle, not before, and that battle was yet to come.

At eleven thirty that morning, we settled the bill and asked the concierge for the best route to the border with Texas. He gave us elaborate instructions involving the 40D to Monterey, because, he said, Chihuahua was not safe, and then the 85D to Nuevo Laredo.

We listened carefully, made notes on a map, and then loaded up the Wrangler we'd hired in Mexico and took the 40D, like he'd suggested, but in the opposite direction, down into Sinaloa. On the way we stocked up with water, sand-

---

1. See *Kill: One*

wiches and a couple of blankets—provisions we knew we would soon need.

Njal drove. He drove fast and with skill. The road was surprisingly good and cut a deep channel through steep canyons among dense pine forests that seemed to stretch on for eternity. Finally, after a hundred and fifty miles and just under three hours, the landscape began to change. We left the tiny village of La Guasima behind us and the pinewoods began to give way to fields and crops. Then we passed Concordia and Malpica, and we were descending toward the flat, coastal area just south of the Gulf of California. Outside Villa Union, we joined Highway 15, straight and flat, and headed toward Mazatlán, the second drug capital of Sinaloa, and home to Omicron. Of the five heads of Omega 3, he was the one I had come to think of as my real target: General Francisco Ochoa, the supreme commander of Mexico's special forces. He was a dangerous man, and if we failed in this mission, I had no doubt it would be because of him.

Njal put his foot down and we began to accelerate along the freeway. Then, as though he were echoing my thoughts, he said suddenly, "This is it."

I looked at him, then at the open fields that stretched toward the Pacific beyond. I nodded, but I didn't say anything.

We passed Mazatlán on our left and an hour after that we came to a turn off which allowed us to cross the highway and take a dirt track that wound its way past a small lake on the left, surrounded by scraggy trees and shrubs, and then cut through acres of dry, gray dust. We bumped and rattled along that track for about a mile, trying not to kick up too much dust, and all the way I kept my eye on the mirror to see if we were being followed, but there was no one behind us. Just as there had been no one behind us all the way from Durango to Mazatlán.

I shook my head and looked at Njal. "It's been too easy. It has worked better than clockwork. It's been a walk over. They are supposed to be the fucking Illuminati. They're supposed to have eyes and ears everywhere. What the fuck is going on?"

He didn't answer. The track, which had been straight for almost a mile, now began to curl and the ground changed from gray earth to white sand. Then we came to a broad, shallow river, which we crossed, churning up the slow-moving brown water.

I asked, suddenly, "These people who are helping us, do they work for the cartel?"

He shook his head. "She... *They* are smallholders, their land is far away from the plantations and close to the highway. They have nothing to offer the cartel. That's why Jim chose them. They are not at risk, and the risk to us is minimal; and the son and daughter get to go to university in the States, when they are old enough. It's a win-win. I guess. She'll tell you her story if she wants to."

We came out the other side of the river onto something that was barely a track, and followed that around until we came to a small house, set back a way from the road, among palms and eucalyptus trees. It was pretty and well kept, with a nice veranda mostly covered in vines. There were shacks and sheds in back and to the sides, corrals for goats and pens for chickens, and there were a couple of dogs lying in the shade that started to bark as we approached the open gate.

As we drove through, one of them raised his head to the

sky and started to howl, but they didn't get up. They didn't mind sounding the alarm, but they weren't going to fight with anybody. Njal drove the Jeep around the back of the house and parked it where it was hidden from view and shaded by a eucalyptus copse. He killed the engine and we climbed out. As we did that, I saw a woman come out the back door drying her hands on a tea towel. She had dark skin, black hair pulled back in a loose knot, a red, plaid shirt, jeans and cowboy boots. She looked at me with dark eyes and no expression, and said, "Where is Njal?"

I pointed at the Jeep with my thumb. "Right here."

He appeared around the hood and I thought I saw what might have been a smile. "Come inside," she said. "The kids are with my sister. We are alone."

FIFTEEN

THERE WERE PICTURES ON THE FRIDGE. IT WAS A
big, silver fridge with two doors, and it was covered in
pictures drawn in crayon by small kids. There were also
words written in plastic, magnetic letters. The kitchen was
big, floored in big terracotta tiles. A big window overlooked
the back yard, and on the sill there were aloe plants in pots,
flanking a plastic bottle of luminous green washing up liquid
and a jar with brushes in it. A large, pine table with four
chairs drawn around it occupied the middle of the floor. In
the sink I counted three dirty plates, three knives, three forks,
three glasses. A home for a family of three, hiding weapons
for Jim Redbeard, Njal, and me.

She stood by the stove, watching us. "D'you eat? You
want coffee?"

Her accent was more California with a hint of Latino
than Mexican with a hint of Cali.

Njal answered. "We ate. Coffee is good, yuh?"

"Sit. How's Jim?"

Njal pulled out a chair and laughed as he sat. He was at home here.

"You know Jim! Always the same. Always happy, even when he is sad."

I thought the comment was loaded, but she didn't react. She unscrewed the coffee pot with quick, efficient movements. She was slim, but shapely and very feminine, very much a woman and a mother. "Yeah." She said it in a neutral tone tinged with anger. "I know Jim. Does he ever ask after us?"

I pulled out a chair and sat. Njal said: "He thinks about you all the time."

"That's not what I asked, Njal."

He looked at me, raised his eyebrows and grimaced. "He wants you to move back. You know that."

"How would I know that, Njal? He never told me that." She spooned coffee into the percolator, screwed it shut with more energy than was absolutely necessary and put it on the stove. Then she turned and rested her ass against the sink and crossed her arms. "If he wants me to go back, maybe he should tell me all the stuff he tells you."

He raised both hands. "Hey! You asked, I told you. I am not defending the guy, Sole."

"Sure you're not."

"But, I godda say, I do wonder. Why don't you go back to the States? Is better there than here, right?"

She ignored the question and looked at me. "Are you another one of those who believe the sun shines out of Jim Redbeard's ass?"

I smiled and shook my head.

"Well everybody else does, including himself."

"I don't. Clearly, you don't either."

She almost scowled. "Watch your step, friend. Don't jump to conclusions. He's a good man."

I raised an eyebrow at her. "Isn't it time you swept the floor?"

"Excuse me?"

"Eggshells. I seem to be treading on them. He's a great man who thinks the sun shines out of his own ass. It's a fair description. Yours, not mine."

She turned away and gathered three cups from the draining board, put them on the table with milk and sugar, then brought over the percolator and sat to pour.

"I can't afford to go back to the States, you know that, Njal."

"And you know he will pay."

"I don't want his money."

"He already pays for..."

"That's for his kids, not me. I don't use a penny of his goddamn money on myself."

Njal sighed. "Is no good for you to be here, Sole."

"We're not going to have this conversation again, Njal."

"Sell the house..."

She burst out laughing. It was a nice thing to see, even if the laughter was tinged with bitterness. It was more than nice. It was delightful. It made me smile.

"A house and land in Sinaloa? Who's going to buy that? And even if I could find a buyer, how much do you think they'd pay? Ten thousand U.S. dollars? I'd be lucky to get that much!"

I sipped my coffee. It was good and strong. "You get paid for receiving these goods?"

"What do you think?"

"I think you're too ready with a hostile answer. How about you follow your own advice and don't jump to conclusions?"

She was quiet for a bit, looking at her coffee. "Yeah, I get paid."

"Local cartel take any interest in you?"

"Not so far, but I keep a very low profile. Don't worry, you're not at risk."

I drained my cup and stood. "C'mon, Njal. We have a long way to go, promises to keep, and miles to go before we sleep."

He sighed and stood. "It is in the hay shed?"

She nodded. "On the right inside the door. You need to move the top bales, and the tarpaulin."

As I reached for the door, she said, "Robert Frost." I stopped and looked back at her as Njal stepped outside into the afternoon sunshine. She managed something vaguely like a smile. "Stopping by Woods on a Snowy Evening." She gave a small shrug. "Sorry."

I shook my head. "No need. I get it."

We crossed the yard to a wooden barn and Njal heaved the huge door open. Immediately on the right there was a tiered stack of hay bales, about three high at the front and six at the back. Over the front nine bales there was a large, sage green tarp. I pulled it off and between us we heaved off the top three bales, revealing a hollow in the middle with two military green kit bags stashed inside it. I heaved them out and laid them on the dirt floor. Njal pulled the door half closed and leaned on the jamb, keeping watch while I opened up the bags and started taking the stuff out, laying it on the ground and making an inventory in my mind.

There were two Heckler & Koch 416 assault rifles with the AG-HK416 grenade launchers and infrared telescopic sights. There were two Sig Sauer p226s with extended magazines and a Glock 17 with its own high capacity mags, and two suppressed Maxim 9s. There was also an orange osage take down bow with twelve aluminum, broadhead arrows and two strings, and two Fairbairn & Sykes fighting knives. Finally, there were two sets of night vision goggles, two pairs of binoculars, six cakes of C4 with detonators and enough ammunition to fuel a whole revolution. I said: "OK, everything's here."

He turned and looked and I threw him the Glock, a magazine and one of the knives. I took a Sig and slipped it behind my back into my waistband and shoved the knife into my boot. It was good to feel them there again. Then I put everything back in the bags, we carried them to the Jeep and dumped them in the back.

We stood looking at them a moment. Njal sighed. He didn't need to say anything. We both knew. There was no point concealing them. If anybody got close enough to see what was inside the bags, either we would be dead or we would have to kill them. The time for hiding was all but over.

We went back inside. Sole was sitting at the table, staring at her empty coffee cup. She looked up as we came in. Njal shrugged.

"OK, so we are going."

She nodded and pointed to a flask on the table, and a

bottle of Scotch. "I made you some coffee. I laced it, to keep you warm."

I said, "Thanks, for the coffee, and for doing this."

She echoed Njal's shrug. "I need the money, mister."

I glanced around. "How much would you have to sell the house for, to be able to

go back?"

She looked around, like the price might be written on the walls somewhere. "Two fifty? Three hundred? That's the ballpark. Why? You want to buy it?"

"It might have its uses. We'll talk in a few days."

Her face hardened. "I don't want charity!"

"Good!" I snapped. "Because you won't get any from me. Or sympathy, for that matter. Your kids might, but you sure as hell won't! So you can can the attitude." I turned to Njal. "Come on, let's get going."

I walked to the Jeep and heard the door close behind me. As we turned to skirt the house and drive back toward the gate, I saw her at the kitchen window, watching us. I ignored her and accelerated away. One thing I sure as hell didn't need was another woman complicating my life.

It was nearing five o'clock, and sunset was a good three hours away, but the gray dust had turned to copper and the shadows of the trees were stretching long across the flats. As we ground our way back toward the highway I asked Njal, "How far from here to where we leave the car?"

He checked his phone, swiped the screen a few times. "Fifty-five miles. More than half is country roads, and the last ten miles is rural mountain. Hour and a half."

I grunted. "I'd hoped to get there when it was dark."

He gave me a look that said he was struggling to hide the

fact that he wanted to hit me. "Yuh? So, we could have stayed half an hour more with Sole, chill, have a sandwich, you know? OK, so she has a bad attitude. Don't mean you godda fight with her. Do like me. I chill."

I was quiet for a bit, then said, "You're right."

He sighed, pulled a pack of cigarettes from his pocket and fished one out. As he lit up, he said, "Don't do that, man."

"What?"

"Say, 'You right,' like that. Freaks me out. You want a cigarette?"

He handed me one and I poked it in my mouth, turned onto the highway and lit up as I accelerated toward La Cruz, and the turn off for Cosalá. I ignored his quip and started to talk half to myself.

"So here's the bit we haven't planned for, because we couldn't. Two guys in a rented Jeep driving through deep Sinaloa countryside in late evening. Chances of getting stopped by either gang members or the cops—which is pretty much the same thing—are unquantifiable, but possibly high."

Njal inhaled deeply and blew a stream of smoke at the roof of the car. "Down here, not so much, but the closer we get to Cosalá, the higher the chances get. Not cops, but if there are gang members out for any reason and they see us, they could stop us if they think we don't fit."

"OK, here's how we deal with it. Next chance I get, I'll pull over. You grab one of the Hecklers. Keep it up front. If they stop us, we make like tourists and ask for directions to Culiacán. If they don't buy it, we have to take them out. All of them, fast, before they can make a call."

"Yuh, we knew this."

"Good."

We covered the first forty-odd miles without incident and at about six in the evening we started to climb into the hills. It was still two hours till sunset, but because of the mountains, most of the time the sun was behind the ridges, and darkness started closing in early. That at least was a relief.

We passed a sign for a lake called Presa el Salto, and after that the woodland started getting more dense; another three miles and the banks of the road were steep and overgrown, and we were climbing and twisting through the dusk in thick forest, with our headlamps on. A couple of sharp bends after that and we suddenly found ourselves behind a Dodge RAM. I dipped my lights and slowed. My gut was on fire. I was telling myself it was probably just some farmers going home from the fields, but I couldn't recall having seen any fields for several miles. I glanced at Njal. He cocked the HK and popped a grenade in the launcher. I cocked the Sig and put it between my legs on the seat.

The hazards on the Dodge came on and it began to slow and move into the center of the road. Njal said, "We gotta kill them."

I slowed too and wound the windows down. The Dodge stopped and I stopped ten feet behind it. I covered the Sig with my right hand and leaned out the window, smiling. The driver's door opened and a big guy in an Italian suit climbed out. He had curly hair and a moustache. He looked Spanish, or Middle Eastern. The passenger door opened and a taller, slimmer guy with long hair and dark olive skin climbed out too. His suit looked expensive, like his pal's, and

I caught the glint of a weapon as he walked around the back of the car. Through their rear window I could see two heads: two who didn't feel they had to get out. If there was going to be trouble, all four would have gotten out. Maybe we'd be OK.

Moustache shrugged and said something in Spanish, like *what's happening? Where you going?*

I broadened my smile and said, *"Americano, perdido, Culiacán?"*

He stared at me for a long moment with hard, unfriendly eyes, then spoke in English.

"What the fuck?" He looked across at his pal with the long hair. "Culiacán. They want Culiacán." Then to me, "You goin' north into the fuckin' mountains. Culiacán is west on the plain. This is Sinaloa, amigo. You ever heard of Sinaloa? Is not smart for two *gringos* to be drivin' around at night in Sinaloa in the countryside."

I grimaced. "Can you advise us how to get back on the right road for Culiacán?"

He looked at his pal and grinned. To me he said, "You got money? How much money you got?"

I made a face of confusion. "I don't know, a hundred bucks?"

But his eyes were already traveling to the back of the truck and he was frowning. "What you got in the sacks there?"

"Those?" I said. "Oh, Njal, take out the truck."

Moustache was still frowning at me, trying to work out what I meant, when I plugged him between the eyes. Ponytail was not slow to react. While his friend folded to the ground, he ran and rolled behind the back of our truck. Njal sprayed a short burst of automatic fire and shattered the windshield of the Jeep, then plugged a grenade through the back window of the Dodge. The detonation lifted it a foot off the ground and blew the doors off.

By that time I was out and walking to the back of the Wrangler with my Sig in my right hand and the Fairbairn & Sykes fighting knife in my left. Ponytail came around the trunk to meet me, holding his Eagle out in front of him with both hands. I weaved to my left as he fired and slashed the blade up the back of his right wrist, severing the tendons. His hand went into spasm and curled in on itself. The gun dropped and he was left gaping at the blood streaming from the gash. I kicked him hard in his nuts and as he doubled up, I shot him in the back of his neck. It all happened in less than three seconds.

Njal came around with his Glock drawn and shook his head at me. "This is a fucking mess, man."

"How far are we from where we dump the Jeep?"

"About fifteen miles."

"Shit!"

"We got to assume they are part of the gang and they were going to Cosalá. We got to assume they are expecting them and they will come looking for them."

"We have two options, and only two."

"Turn back or continue."

I nodded. "You can go back if you want. Take the Jeep. I can continue on foot."

"Don't be a fucking asshole, man. Come on. We are wasting time."

We clambered in, skirted the wreck of the Dodge and took off at speed along the road. Dusk was closing in. Njal was looking at his phone. "The problem is when we get to the settlement. There we can be seen. We need a goat track. These hills are full of goat tracks. Look..." He said it to the phone. I glanced. He was looking at satellite images. "Up ahead there will be a track on the right, go slow. It climbs that hill and goes to Camoa on the other side. We can leave the Jeep up in the forest. Then we go on foot. It will add another mile to our walk, but we start walking an hour or two before we expected."

"OK, we do that."

The turning came out of nowhere, concealed by dense pines. I slowed and turned in, and we began to grind and bump up the track. It was rutted, narrow and winding, and in the failing light, progress was slow and difficult. The headlamps were out of the question, but at times, on our right hand side, we were mere inches from a steep precipice that plunged down into a gorge that was practically a canyon.

After almost two hours, we finally broke out of the trees onto a plateau, and far below, on the right, we could make out the few, winking lights of Camoa, way down in the valley. I stopped, then reversed back into the cover of the forest and found a space among the trees and ferns where the Wrangler would be hidden from view. Then we pulled out the kit bags, packed them with the food, the water and the blankets, slung them over our shoulders and set out on the long trek toward the ranch, or the farm, or the lab—or whatever it was that Zapata had up there.

It was a long, difficult night. We didn't talk and we rested as little as we could. It was a twelve mile trek, through dense woodland, scrambling down steep hills and clambering up canyons that were at times almost vertical. At times we would come across narrow tracks that we were able to follow, and then we would walk ten paces and run ten paces, alternating, and we would make fast progress, but at others we were battling our way through trees and ferns, and moving at barely a mile an hour.

At shortly before midnight, with aching legs and sore backs, and scratched and bruised arms, we broke out of the forest onto a high ledge and looked down at the lights of Cosalá. Above us, the sky was almost black, with no moon, peppered by billions of minute, icy stars. Below it, the tiny village winked, and looked oddly warm and comforting.

I was perspiring with the effort of the climb, but it was cold, close to freezing. We sat to rest for a moment, and had a drink from the flask of coffee and whiskey Sole had prepared for us. We both gazed down at the village in silence, in our own thoughts.

After a while, Njal asked, "What are their lives? How many people are there? Five, six thousand? They are ruled by the drug lords and the drugs trade. How do they live? In constant fear of the cartel lords. Who is going to set them free? How many of them are a part of it? How many can imagine something different?"

I took a swig. Felt the sweat chilling on my back and shuddered. "I don't know. Sometimes I wonder, Njal, if Omega is the cause of all this evil, or just a symptom. Are we fighting against Man's innate nature? Is there any point to what we are doing?"

He nodded slowly for a bit. "You know the answer to that, Lacklan. Just like I do. The point is the fight. As long as we are fighting, people will keep thinking that maybe there *is* another way." He looked at me and grinned. "We are hippies, my friend. Hippies with guns."

"Now we're hippies? I thought we were Vikings."

He stood and heaved the sack onto his shoulder again. "Vikings were just hippies with axes."

And we set off down the track and into the valley.

Another half hour of descent, and two hours of steep climb, found us in a clearing, surrounded on three sides by dense pine forest, and on the fourth, bordered by huge, gray rocks. Beyond the rocks was a steep drop of maybe two hundred feet or more. It was hard to tell in the dark, but down there, in the blackness, a handful of lights winked and glimmered around a floodlit courtyard.

We dropped our bags in among the trees, made a simple, makeshift camp, and then returned to the rocks. There we fitted our night vision goggles and looked down into the eerie, green blackness below. There was no doubt, it was Zapata's *Castillo del Diablo*.

It was set in a wide clearing, surrounded by forest on all sides, with only a narrow, winding track connecting it to the outside world. As well as the protection of the trees, it had a high perimeter fence that seemed to consist of a steel frame with wire mesh. I spoke quietly, "Two gets you twenty the fence is electrified."

"No doubt."

Inside the fence there was a space of about seven feet which was laid with rolls of barbed wire, and after that there was a perimeter wall eight feet high, made of solid concrete.

Njal grunted. "It's not a ranch or a lab, it's a fortress."

Within the wall there were a number of buildings. At the center was a large, Spanish style villa, with corrugated tile roofs, a veranda and a central patio. Directly opposite the front porch, at about fifty or sixty paces, was the double gate that gave access to the compound: one gate in the wall, and the other in the perimeter fence. Beside the inner gate there was a guards' hut and beside that I could see three military Jeeps parked up against the wall.

Behind the villa, at about seventy paces distance, was a large, rectangular prefab that must have been at least four thousand square feet, fifty by eighty, and over by the far wall there were two more, smaller prefabs; one looked like a garage with two roller blinds; the other had the look of a barracks. They and the villa were all floodlit by spots, and in their light we could see armed men with dogs patrolling the grounds. They weren't in jeans and sweats, either. They were in military combat uniform, and they were well armed.

I said to Njal: "How many do you see?"

"Two at the gate, two at the door of the house, two at the big prefab, two at the door of the smaller prefab. So eight stationary. Then there are..." He paused a moment. "Four patrolling with dogs, so twelve total. It's taking them..."

He went quiet and we both checked our watches. Eventually, I said, "Four minutes."

He nodded. "Yuh, four minutes. One goes and one comes, so there is always somebody. It is floodlit, so they can all see each other." He removed his goggles and turned to face me. "Come, we go back to the camp. I don't like to talk here."

We returned to the cover of the trees, pulled the blankets from the kit bag and each took a slug of hot coffee with whiskey.

"OK, what's your assessment?"

"There is a barracks, I figure maybe sixty feet by thirty. You don't need a barracks this big for ten men, or even twenty men. There are for sure more men in there. So we have minimum twenty men, probably more. They look like professional soldiers and well armed, with four, maybe eight dogs, electric fence, barbed wire, high wall, and no way in. And to make it more complicated, all the guards are visible to the other guards all the time. My friend, Lacklan, my assessment is that this attack is impossible. It cannot be done."

I sighed. "Yeah, that was my assessment too."

SIXTEEN

WE SLEPT FOUR HOURS AND WOKE BEFORE THE SUN
had climbed over the wooded mountaintops. It was cold
and the ground was wet with dew. We had a breakfast of the
remains of the coffee laced with whiskey and made our way
to the rocky outcrop to peer down at the facility that
Samuel Zapata, Xi, called *el Castillo del Diablo*: the Devil's
Castle.

As we took up our positions and I adjusted my binoculars, men in military fatigues started emerging from the
barracks. They were supervised by a sergeant barking orders.
The guards who stood sentry at the gate and on the doors
were all replaced, but the patrols with dogs were withdrawn.
Clearly they were only deployed at night.

At eight twenty, a small group of four men and two
women emerged from the house. They were having some
kind of discussion, stopping and starting as they walked and
talked, making their way toward the big prefab at the back,
drifting apart, while one or two spoke in animation to each

other, then coalescing again as others returned to join in the discussion.

By the time they'd reached the corner of the villa, another man had emerged. He was short, overweight, with balding, dark hair and a moustache. He stood on the porch and ignored the group who continued their slow drift toward the large building.

I watched him, but Njal said, "Deep in discussion. Ages, twenty-seven to thirty-five, jeans, T-shirts, sweatshirts, trainers, the guys are unshaven, the women not wearing makeup. Two of them are definitely Latino, but some of them could be European, especially the women."

I glanced at him. "What's your point?"

He didn't look up from his binoculars. He said, "Geeks, nerds, scientists."

I frowned. "You sound pretty sure."

"Who else has intense conversations at eight in the morning?"

I focused on them again. He was right. They had that indefinable look about them that said this person talks about up quarks and negatively charged electrons and quotes from the Lord of the Rings.

"You could be right. It would fit with the prefab being a lab. What the hell are they doing in there? The place is huge."

The whine of a diesel in low gear made me look over toward the gate. A red Toyota pickup was bumping and rattling up the path, out of the trees and toward the gate. An electronic buzz and a clang preceded the slow opening of the outer gate. The truck rolled in and the gate closed laboriously behind it. A second, louder buzz and the inner gate rolled back to let the truck drive in. It came to a halt in front of the villa, and the short guy with the moustache stepped down from the porch to meet it, as two guys swung down from the cab.

I said, "The guy with the moustache is Zapata."

"Uh-huh. And the two guys from the Toyota are giving him bad news."

He was right. They were spreading their hands and shrugging their shoulders, like they were making excuses. Meanwhile, the guy who was probably Zapata was waving his hands and shouting.

I said, "They found the truck last night and they've been looking for who did it. So far they've found nothing."

Njal nodded, but didn't say anything.

We watched as Zapata slapped and kicked the two men and they cowered away from him. He shouted something, pointing at the gate, and they clambered in their truck and drove away.

After that, he did more hollering at the sergeant. The sergeant did some hollering of his own at the troops and marched off toward the barracks building. Five minutes later, he was mustering all his men, with dogs, in front of the villa. I felt a hot, sinking feeling in my gut.

Njal said, "Thirty-two men, plus eight sentries on the doors and the gate, total forty. Four dogs."

"His guests are coming tomorrow. He wants us caught before they arrive."

Njal sighed. "But we want them to arrive before we attack."

"We need Omicron. This whole damn operation is

about General Francisco Ochoa. We need to take him down."

"Those dogs worry me." He turned to look at me. "We call it off. While they are searching for us, we go hit Ochoa."

I thought about it and shook my head. "Let's stay cool. In twenty-four hours we'll have all three of them in the same place with twenty pounds of C4 and enough artillery to invade a small country. Plus, I want to know what the hell they have going on in that lab."

He gave something like a smile, shook his head and looked back down at the complex again. "They are leaving. Two Jeeps and all the men except the sentries."

We watched them stream through the gates at a jogging run, then start to fan out into the forest, to right and left. There were seven patrols of four men, and two Jeeps.

I did a rapid calculation in my head. "They'll start close to the perimeter fence, then they'll start spiraling out, the four teams with dogs taking the lead. It's going to be slow work and heavy going. They won't get up here till late afternoon, at the earliest."

He put down the binoculars and rested his chin on the back of his hands. "But they will find us."

"We have the advantage here, Njal. Jungle warfare is all about staying hidden and using the element of surprise. Right now we know where they are, but they don't even know for sure if we're here at all. We use the bow and the Maxim 9s."

He nodded, but then shook his head. "If we start picking off the troops, Gonzalez and Ochoa ain't gonna show."

I was quiet for a bit. "I'm not sure that's true. We hold off till late afternoon. Let them find our flask, an empty kit bag, some cigarette butts, leaving a trail moving away, back toward where we left the Wrangler. Let them think we're trying to escape. Ochoa will come for sure. He'll want to be there at the capture, and at the kill. My bet is Gonzalez will too. They'll come today."

"Yuh?" He nodded. "That's good."

We went back to the camp, shared out the weapons, and put the C4 and the spare ammunition in one of the kit bags. While we worked, I told Njal my plan.

"I'd have liked to do a reconnaissance before the attack, but we can't afford to do that now. So we draw the troops away from the facility, and this afternoon we start picking them off silently, group by group. So even they won't know exactly how many men they have lost or are losing."

"They will be in radio contact with each other."

"Yeah, but they'll also be trying to observe radio silence. Every crackle and every conversation gives us a location."

"OK."

"We take out a couple of teams, then we start moving back toward the facility. If we come across more teams, we take them down too, but that's not our priority anymore. With most of the men in the field, we go to the rear of the facility, where the lab is."

He frowned. "But we can't get in that way. We have the fence, the barbed wire and the wall. We need come in through the gate. Is the only way."

I shook my head. "If we go in through the gates, we will never make it to the lab. We'd get trapped between the fortified troops at the facility and the returning patrols behind us. No, we set small charges on key supports on the fence."

"It's electrified, remember?"

"We put the explosives in empty plastic water bottles. When we detonate them, the fence falls across the barbed wire and rests against the top of the wall. It also shorts the electricity so we can use it as a ladder. We have to be fast. We scramble up and drop over the wall behind the lab."

He grinned, then laughed. "Good plan. Cool. So, next, we don't want nobody escaping and we don't want nobody coming in through the gate, so we take out the guards' hut where the controls for the gates are."

"Exactly, you do that while I take out the guards at the lab and the barracks. Then we move forward to the back of the house and take out the guards on the door at the house and, if they are still alive, the guards on the gate. We do it fast and efficient."

"It's good. I like it."

"We hope by then Gonzalez and Ochoa will have arrived. If they haven't, we take Zapata and we decide what to do next. Either way, we photograph and film the lab, then destroy it."

"What about the nerds?"

I sighed. "Logically, we should take them out."

"Logically..."

"Let's find out what they're doing... If they are prisoners, or if they don't know what they're involved in..."

"Yuh, OK, I hear you."

We left no trace of our presence at the site by the rocks, but we left a subtle trail, something only a pro would be able to follow, leading away from the woods near the compound back toward the valley to the south of Cosalá, and the track that led to our Jeep. All the while, in the distance, we could hear the occasional howl and bark of the dogs, slowly, steadily getting louder.

By late afternoon, as the sun began to sink toward the mountain tops, and the shadows of the peaks started to stretch across the valleys and the canyons, the howls and barks grew louder and more excited. The dogs had picked up our scent, and the soldiers had started to find clues that we had been there: an ill-concealed cigarette butt, half a boot print, a crushed fern or even the discarded kit bag. All of them, to a trained special ops soldier, would be evidence of a prey who was close to panic. That, as darkness started to close in and we heard the dogs getting excited, that was when we started to work our way back along the trail we'd left, searching for a spot to wait for them.

We found it deep in a gully where a narrow, beaten track forded a mountain stream. The slopes were densely wooded with pines, and down by the watercourse, the shade and the moisture had made the ferns grow thick and tall, some reaching up to five feet in height. It was quiet, dark, and the smell of damp, rotting leaves and pine needles was strong on the air. There was no sound but the lapping of the water, and the whining and howling of the approaching dogs.

Njal took the left slope, scrambled up and hid among the ferns behind a large pine tree. I took the right slope, on the far side of the stream, set up the bow, strung it and nocked an arrow. Then we settled to wait.

We didn't have to wait long. Within five minutes, a squad of four soldiers in camouflage came down the path at a half-run. The guy in the lead had a large Alsatian on a chain and was being dragged along by it. The three guys behind him were all carrying assault rifles. The dog crossed the ford and started to go crazy, running around in circles, sniffing the spot where Njal and I had split up. The soldiers immediately started scanning the trees. I had already selected my mark and had him tabbed. I drew back to my ear and loosed in a single fluid movement. There was a slight rattle as the arrow slid over the wood, and a whisper as it slipped through the air. I saw my mark frown and half a second later, the broadhead had buried itself in his chest, slicing through his heart, and punched out of his back. His body gave a tremor and I heard him say, softly, "*Ay....!*"

Then there were two quiet, *phut! phut!* sounds. The dog keeled over and his handler frowned down at him an instant before his forehead erupted in blood, brains and gore.

By that time, I had nocked my second arrow. The two remaining troopers were paralyzed with confusion and growing fear. Death had come out of nowhere and three of them had gone down in a split second. I drew and loosed. Again there was the rattle and whisper followed by a second suppressed double tap from Njal and the two soldiers went down.

We ran silently to the scene of the carnage. Silently, we picked up each body between us and carried them in among the ferns, behind the trees, and, using a couple of their canvas camouflage hats, we carried water from the stream and washed away the blood.

After that we carried on up, following the track, but keeping in among the trees. Soon, after maybe ten minutes, we heard the crackle of a radio. The sun had dipped behind the mountains and it was getting dark in the forest. It was hard to make out any detail among the foliage, but the sounds of muttering voices carried with clarity, seeming almost to be enhanced by the closeness of the woods. Njal signaled to me that he had eyes on something over on the right. Without having to speak, we each backed away, separating, in among the tree trunks to where the ferns were thickest. There I picked up a small branch and broke it. The snap was like a gunshot echoing under the canopy. The voices stopped instantly. I knocked an arrow and we waited, motionless and silent.

They took about a minute to come. They were not sure if what they had heard was a man, or some forest creature. A crack was not enough to call for back up, and they had heard nothing before and nothing since, so they proceeded cautiously, one step at a time, being quiet, listening. They appeared through the green shadows, spread out in a line, their weapons cocked and trained forward. These had no dog, only their assault rifles.

The way they held their rifles made a shot at the heart impossible. A barb through the belly would be a slow, painful death, and a noisy one. This would have to be a headshot, and that would take skill. I drew back to my ear, measured the distance, breathed out, saw the arrow hit its mark and loosed. It happened in a second, but time seemed to slow. The soft rattle of the arrow on the wood, the four men frozen, listening for that second sound, the whisper of the feathers though the cool, dark forest air, and then the cruel thud as the long, razor-sharp barb rammed home through his eye and shattered the back of his skull.

Njal was quick. Two double taps: *phut-phut! Phut-phut!* followed instantly by four eruptions of black-red blood from two of the soldiers. By then, I had drawn again and loosed a second arrow, which skewered its mark through his back as he turned to run.

Eight down and one dog. That left twenty-four men and three dogs, plus the guys back at the facility. We left these bodies. It didn't matter anymore if they were found. The longer the teams delayed, searching for us in the woods, the better. We set off at a quick march, keeping away from the tracks, heading as directly as possible toward the Devil's Castle. Now it was time to open the gates to Hell.

SEVENTEEN

We climbed for fifteen minutes through the woods without coming across another patrol. We could still hear the dogs. But they had grown more distant and were falling behind us. They thought they were chasing us in our escape, but we were driving for their heart. Soon they would pick up our scent again and start to follow, realizing what we had done, but by that time I hoped we would be storming the compound, and it would be too late.

It seemed we had a clear run, but when we were about ten minutes from the back of the enclosure, we heard the distinctive rustle and crackle of bodies moving through the undergrowth. I laid aside my bow and pulled the Maxim from my belt, and we both hunkered down.

We saw them after another two or three minutes. There weren't four, there were eight, about fifty paces away. It looked like they had met up and decided to stop and have a smoke. I couldn't make out what they were saying, but they started exchanging cigarettes and several of them sat on the ground to light up. There was a lot of shoulder shrugging and hand waving and I figured the sergeant was the subject of discussion.

I looked at Njal and he gave his head a jerk toward the slopes to my right: climb up and circle around them. There were too many to take silently, and there was no telling how long they might sit there. I nodded.

Very slowly, by degrees, one step at a time, we moved away from them and then started to climb and circle around. After another five minutes, we came out of the woods and onto a clearing dotted with shrubs and clumps of tall grass. It was about thirty feet across and at the far end fell away suddenly into the valley, where the *Castillo del Diablo* was located.

The sun had gone behind the mountain peaks some time back, and though the sky was still clear and blue, the valley was in deep shadow and evening was closing in. We dropped on our bellies and crawled to the edge of the clearing, where we could get a view of the complex. It was quiet and very still. Our view was from the rear, so we could see the two guards by the gate and the two at the barracks door, but the other four were hidden from view.

I had a look around and was satisfied that we had plenty of cover to make our way down. I glanced at Njal and pointed, but he wasn't looking at me. He shook his head and jerked his chin toward the far side of the valley. I followed his gaze and saw, about half a mile away, the two jeeps moving along the track beyond the trees, headed toward the compound gate; but they were not alone. They formed the vanguard and the rearguard of a small convoy of vehicles.

There were two Range Rovers and a Land Rover, with a

military Jeep at the front and another at the rear. I peered through my binoculars. Each Jeep was occupied by two soldiers, one driving and the other riding shotgun. They ground their way slowly up the track and now we began to hear the whine of the diesel in low gear. It was not possible to make out who was in the cars. What I could see was that the Range Rovers had just a driver and a passenger, while the Land Rover seemed to be full.

Njal said, "You were right. They have come early for the hunt."

"And they've brought reinforcements."

"The Land Rover."

"This changes things."

"How?"

I spoke fast. "We have about five minutes. You position yourself on the slope above the gate. They are going to have to stop while the first gate is opened. Four grenades, hit the Range Rovers first, then you spray them with automatic fire.

"Meanwhile, I carry out the plan we already discussed, but as well as taking out Nu and Omicron, you will be providing a distraction while I get over the wall. Then we close in and wipe them out."

He sighed, then nodded. "You keep changing the plan, man. It's freaking me out."

"We'll talk about it later. Now let's do it. We're on the clock. Go!"

He crouch-ran back to the cover of the trees and I scrambled down the slope toward the fence. I ran, stumbled, fell, scrambled and ran some more. I wasn't as worried about being heard as I was about being late. There was a hill and a forest between me and the two patrols and they were not likely to hear me. But if I was late with the charges, Njal would be in trouble. Serious trouble.

I reached the bottom of the hill and fell flat on my belly. I was fifty yards from the perimeter fence and through it I could see the barbed wire and the wall. I lay still and listened. There was only the distant barking of the dogs, still searching for us in the failing light. I grabbed the five charges I had prepared earlier, a pound and a quarter of C4 stuffed into each of five plastic water bottles, with remote detonators patched into my cell phone.

I ran. I had no time to be fancy or skillful. I wedged a bottle into the mesh beside each of the mainstays. It took me a whole minute to complete the whole thing and then run like crazy back to the cover of the trees. I wasn't seen. I pulled out my cell and laid it on the ground, ready to detonate. Then I pulled the HK grenade launcher from my shoulder, loaded a grenade, took a deep breath and pressed OK. The detonation was like a smack in the face. It's not like the movies. There is no rich, slow, rumbling fireball. It's a loud smack, and then a plume of smoke and dust. But before that happened, I had fired the grenade.

I had not been able to shape or position the charges, so I had no idea which way the fence was going to fall. The grenade took care of that. It crashed into the central mainstay near the top and exploded, hurling the fence back. A shower of electric sparks and crackles ripped the air at either end, and then the whole structure started to sag and fold in on itself. I watched it fall back across the barbed wire and settle gently against the wall, and again, I ran.

As I ran I could hear the staccato rattle of automatic fire punctuated by exploding grenades. I leapt onto the fence and started to scramble up toward the top of the wall, pulling the 416 from my shoulder as I went. The fence began to give and slip as I approached the top. I jumped, made the wall, hauled myself over and let myself drop down on the other side. I hit the ground, rolled and ran to the corner of the prefab. I was aware that the explosions had stopped. The gunfire had reached a crescendo a few seconds earlier, but now it had also stopped. There was only silence.

I peered around the corner at the dusty yard. All I could see was the back of the villa. I crawled on my belly to the next corner. Now I could see the unguarded door of the barracks, and sharp to my left, the door of what I assumed was the lab. Nothing else, nobody else.

Then I heard the rumble of diesel engines. My gut was pierced by a hot stab of fear, not for myself, but because if the trucks were moving, it meant Njal had not destroyed them, and that would only have happened if he had been captured, or if he was dead.

They came around each side of the villa: the two military Jeeps, the two Range Rovers and the land Rover, fanning out so there was nowhere to go. And behind them, what looked at a glance like twenty to thirty soldiers were following at a run. I was completely surrounded, penned in on three sides with an eight foot wall behind me. A strange certainty settled on me, that Njal was dead, and here, today, was where I was going to die too. The realization came with a kind of peace. My only regret was that I had not finished Omega before I died.

Then I remembered something Jim Redbeard had said to me, laughing, quoting some Norse god: *Fearlessness is better than a faint heart for any man who puts his nose out of doors. The length of my life and the day of my death were fated by the Norn long ago!*

So, time to die.

I bellowed like some demented creature, scrambled to my feet and charged, spraying the trucks and the soldiers with automatic fire as I went. In my ears I could hear a mad voice howling, "*Odin!*" and dimly realized it was me. As the trucks rocked, windows shattered and soldiers ducked and scattered, running for cover, a flash of clarity told me what I had to do. I turned, blasted the lock on the prefab and hurled myself at the door. It burst inward and I rolled as the outside of the building was struck by a hail of fire. Above me, the windows imploded and glass sprayed under the torrent of burning lead.

Then there were shouts and the shooting stopped. I scrambled to the nearest of the shattered windows and peered out.

The trucks had come to a halt forming a makeshift barrier. The men were either sheltering behind them or lying flat on the ground, their weapons trained on the building where I was hiding. For a moment nothing happened. Then there was movement. The far door of one of the Range Rovers opened and a man got out. I couldn't make out any detail. Doors slammed and he was joined by another man from the other Range Rover. I saw Zapata and figured the other two were Gonzalez and Ochoa. There was some talking, more movement of people and two men came through the gap between two of the trucks. One of them was the tall, lanky figure of Njal. I smiled. So much for my intuition. So much for time to die. His hands were bound behind his back and his face was bruised, but it was also defiant, and, above all, he was alive.

The man behind him was tall, strongly built and dressed in military fatigues. He had the bearing of brass and I recognized him as General Francisco Ochoa. This was Omicron. For an insane fraction of a second I thought about shooting him in the head, but then the image of Sergeant Bradley, the gigantic Kiwi who had mentored me and guided me in the Regiment, came into my mind, scowling at me: "Choose your battles, and never pick a fight you can't fuckin' win. We leave the fuckin' suicide missions to the ragheads, right? We prefer to come home alive... sir."

Come home alive. That was looking like a tall order.

Then Ochoa had a pistol in his hand and was pointing it at Njal's head. I felt sick and lined Ochoa up. If we died today, he was coming with us. I shouted: "Shoot him and you're next, Ochoa! And I have nineteen pounds of C4 here, that I will detonate in this lab. So think hard about what you do next."

He looked over his shoulder at where Zapata was standing with Gonzalez. He said something and they all laughed. Then he turned back and shouted to me.

"No need for nobody to die today! We know who you are, Mr. Walker. All you godda do is come out with your hands up and we send you home."

I laughed. "*What?*"

"You didn't get the memo, huh?" There was more laughter. "The war is over, Walker. We all friends now. You didn't know, so I'm gonna forget what has happened here today. You come out, you and your pal here go home, and I never wanna see your face again in Mexico. That's the deal. Let's not make it any more complicated than it needs to be."

My head was reeling. Questions crowded in from every side. I spoke without thinking, shouting to him, "How the hell do you know who I am?"

"Come on, Lacklan! Who do you think you are up against? We ain't playin' games here! Come on out. You are my guests. We have some dinner, a glass of wine, you sleep in a comfortable bed tonight, and we send you home in the morning."

I could see Zapata and Gonzalez still grinning behind him.

"You're out of your mind, Ochoa! How stupid do you think I am?"

He laughed out loud. "Pretty stupid! Stupid enough to take on Omega! That's real stupid, Lacklan. But ask yourself: I have about forty guns here, most of them assault rifles, I got grenades, I got two Range Rovers and a Land Rover, two Jeeps, and you are one man. So you ask yourself, do I really need to negotiate with you? If I storm you right now, you gonna die in five minutes. So why am I tryin' to persuade you to come out peacefully? Ask yourself."

"Because you want to preserve what is in this damned lab, that's why, Ochoa, and you know that if you attack, I am going to blow this place to hell."

"Not so. You got a powerful friend, Lacklan. He wants you alive."

I told myself he was trying to fuck with my mind and shouted, "Screw you, Ochoa! The war is over when Omega is finished! I came here for you and Xi and Nu, and I will take you down, you son of a bitch, or I'll die trying!"

He sighed. "You will do neither, Lacklan. You are powerless."

He turned and said something to one of the grunts, who ran over to the Land Rover, climbed in and fired up the engine. He turned the truck and reversed it to where Ochoa was standing, so it had its back angled toward me. Ochoa then dragged Njal over to the truck, and uncuffed him.

"OK, have it your own way. You got your pal into this situation, Lacklan. You caused him a lot of trouble because of your obsession. Now you're gonna cost him his life. He is gonna die of thirst, or worse, of suffocation. You ever watch anyone die like that, Lacklan? Is a horrible way to die." He yanked Njal's arm up and cuffed it to the corner of the roof rack. Then he took a second set of cuffs from his belt and manacled Njal's other wrist to the other corner of the rack, so he was effectively crucified.

Ochoa turned toward me and pointed at Njal. "In that position, he is gonna be in crippling agony in his arms, in about ten minutes. In fifteen minutes he's gonna be crying like a baby girl. It's gonna take him two or three days to die of thirst. He might die of suffocation before that. Either way, you gonna have to sit there and watch him die in agony. But all you gotta do to stop it, is come and have some dinner with us. We answer your questions. You ask what you like. And your friend too. The war is over, Lacklan. Don't kill your friend for no reason."

Njal spoke for the first time since he'd been dragged in. He raised his voice and shouted, "Lacklan! What the fuck are you waiting for? Shoot the motherfucker! And the other two over there! Do the job!"

He was right. It was what I should do. It was what I had

come here to do. Three clean shots. Then spray the troops and if I was still alive, detonate the C4 and do as much damage as I could to the prefab. The job was the imperative. We were soldiers. We were expendable. We expected to die.

But I wasn't going to do it. Today was not our day.

Ochoa shrugged. He turned away and said something in Spanish. Four soldiers ran and took up positions around the square. The other troops began to fall back and Zapata and Gonzalez started making their way toward the villa. Ochoa followed, and called to me over his shoulder.

"Try to release your friend and my men have orders to shoot him, not you, him. *This is the result of your obsession!*"

This last he shouted as he disappeared around the side of the house.

I looked at Njal. With his arms in that position, as exhaustion set in, his back and chest would quickly go into spasm. Suffocation could follow anytime within a couple of hours or a couple of days. It depended on the person. It was one of the most painful deaths known to man. With dehydration added into the deal, he would be in hell long before he died. But if I tried to release him, they'd shoot him, and there was no way I could take them out first.

My only option was to surrender to Ochoa. I didn't buy his bullshit about the war being over. I didn't know what his game was, but I knew for sure what it wasn't, and it wasn't peace and brotherly love. Neither did I buy the suggestion that Ben was alive and looking out for me. I could tell by the way Njal was standing and moving his back and arms that the cramps were already starting. I had to do something, and I had to do it fast. But what?

Then I looked behind me.

EIGHTEEN

THE LIGHT FROM THE SPOTS OUTSIDE FILTERED IN through the broken windows, casting twisted shadows and partially illuminating the interior of the prefab. It was like something from a science fiction movie. It was a vast, hangar-like building, maybe eighty feet across and at least fifty feet deep. Mostly it was open space, but at the back and to the sides there were cubicles, some only fifteen or twenty feet square, others considerably bigger.

There were benches. Some were clear, others contained computer terminals and still others were littered with what looked like electronic equipment. Whatever this was, it was not a cocaine processing plant.

I glanced out the window. Nothing was happening. I moved into the hangar and started to explore. Most of what I saw meant nothing to me. There were dozens of workstations, many of which had clipboards beside them with annotations which I could not read. Most of the annotations referred to PT 1 through PT 5, but there was no indication of what the PTs were.

All the workstations had computer terminals, and these seemed to be connected by a network of cables duct taped to the floor, leading to a single bank of hard drives which I eventually found housed in a small room in back of the building. It took up the whole of one wall fifteen feet across, to a height of nine or ten feet. The capacity must have been immeasurable.

Clearly this computer had not been networked with the main Omega computer I had destroyed in Brussels. That of itself was interesting, and suggestive of what Jim had said about Omicron. This operation was independent: independent of Omega, but within Omega.

I took my cell from my pocket and photographed and filmed what I could see, plus all the annotations I could find. I tried switching on some of the terminals, but could not get past the password request.

Then, in the dim light filtering through the windows, I became aware of a series of doors along the right hand wall, furthest from the entrance. I moved over to them and found them locked. I blew out the first lock with the Maxim and stepped inside. It was pitch dark, but there was a noise. It was a rhythmic noise, like slow, heavy breathing, but it wasn't like organic breathing, it was somehow artificial. I felt by the door and found a switch. I flipped it and the room was flooded with light.

It was about fifty feet long and fifteen or twenty feet across, taking up the whole side of the building. The walls were white and the lights were stark and harsh. The entirety of the back wall was taken up by five glass boxes positioned at waist height on white, steel stands. Each stand had a word and a number stenciled on it. The nearest said: Prototype 1, the next was Prototype 2, and so on until Prototype 5 at the end. These, then, were PTs 1 through 5.

Beside each stand with its corresponding glass box was a stack of electronic equipment, including what appeared to be monitors connected to a pump, or a number of pumps. Cables and tubes inserted into the glass boxes, and from there were connected to brains.

My head swam and I felt suddenly sick. I stepped out of the room, found a dark corner and vomited. I gave myself a minute, then returned to the room and forced myself to examine each one.

Each one was different.

The first was too small to be human. It was slightly bigger than a large grapefruit and was not divided into two hemispheres. I became aware that it seemed to be contained within some kind of plastic cling-film. It was moist and seemed to pulse gently.

The next two were slightly bigger and looked like pictures I had seen of human brains, only like the first, they were not split into two parts. I wondered if they were simian.

The fourth was huge, bigger than a human brain, but the fifth was unmistakably human. As I looked at these prototypes, my skin went cold and I realized what I was looking at. I had seen another part of this same research at the John Richard Erickson Institute, the night I'd killed Senator McFarlane's husband. But there, they had not removed the brains from their subjects. They had opened up their skulls and carried out their experiments, but they had left the brains inside their tortured, harrowed subjects, and closed them up again afterwards. I had wondered then, what exactly the research was for. Now I knew. They were trying to make cyborgs.

The voice startled me. I had not heard anyone approach. It was a sweet, feminine voice. It said, "They are not in pain."

I turned. There was a young woman, maybe in her late twenties, standing in the doorway. She was one of the group of what Njal had called nerds. She said, "They don't suffer. You need a body to suffer. Anxiety, fear, loneliness... They are all organic. You need a body..."

I spoke without thinking. "And a soul."

"What?"

"To be human," I said. "You need a soul in order to be human."

She shrugged. "I'm a scientist. I don't know about souls. I do know that these brains were going to die, and we saved them. Now they are part of something greater."

"Really?"

She pointed to PT 1. "This was *Chucho*. He was Xi's Labrador. He had leishmaniasis. Out here, that is fatal for a dog."

"You're a member of Omega?"

She shook her head. "I am nowhere near rich enough. But I believe in their vision, in the project. I want to be a part of the New Eden when the time comes." She gave a small, pretty laugh. "That might be sooner than we expected. Did you read the latest IPCC report?" I had a bizarre sense of being at some kind of cocktail party discussing current affairs and the latest exhibits from the Brains Trust. She saw my expression and pointed at PT 2. "That was Chita, a chimp who was injured in Africa. We flew her out here when they notified us. Next to her is Odo, he was a gorilla, shot illegally by hunters. The big one there..." She smiled. "That is Mogli, an Indian elephant. People don't realize how smart they are. They're smarter than dolphins. Of all the animal kingdom, they are the closest to humans in intelligence and self-awareness. Did you know that?"

I pointed at the last one. "And this one? What's his name? Or was it a woman?"

"He was very hard to get hold of. We had to pull strings. He was a prime subject. He had no family left, no fixed address, no friends..."

"You mean a homeless guy, easy prey for parasites."

She gave a small shrug. "I guess you could say that. He was unlucky enough to be at somebody's house when there was a home invasion. He got shot. If we hadn't got him, he would have died."

"That...",I pointed at it and realized my hand was shaking. "That is being *alive?*"

She frowned. "Organically, he is alive. Who are you to judge the quality of his life? You..." She gestured at me and gave a small, contemptuous laugh. "You who are consumed and twisted by hatred, you who try to solve every problem by killing and torturing people, you who exist in continuous suffering and turmoil. *You* are going to judge the quality of his life?"

I shook my head, not sure how to answer her, knowing only that she was wrong but not knowing why. "How can you call that life?"

She gave a small, patient sigh. "Every morning he has a cup of coffee and a couple of croissants. While he is having his breakfast, he does the cryptic crossword. Today he had roast lamb for lunch. He never suffers anxiety, fear, loneliness; and his mind is ever active, exploring, studying. He never kills anybody, and he never hurts anybody. How about you, Mr. Walker? What have you done today?"

I frowned and narrowed my eyes. "Are you seriously advocating *that* as a way of life? He may *think* he had coffee and croissants, but they were illusions. They were not *real!* His life, what you call his life, is not *real!* OK, so you need a body to suffer, to feel anxiety, distress, fear. But you also need a body, and those emotions, in order to feel honor, compassion, empathy, love!"

She snorted. "Was it that honor, compassion, empathy and love that led you to kill twelve men in the last twenty-four hours?"

"No."

She smiled. "Lacklan, your friend is out there suffering. He is in considerable pain. Soon he will be in agony, and it is only going to get worse. Release him. Release us all, Lacklan. The war is *over*. Come in, we'll bring him down, have something to eat, a drink. Talk to us, we will answer all your questions."

I stared at her a long time. "I killed Ben," I said finally.

She nodded. "Yes."

"He was my brother."

"Your half-brother."

"They keep telling me he's alive."

"Come inside, we'll explain everything."

"Is Ben alive?"

"Come inside..."

"Go, tell Omicron I will come inside if he answers that question. I need to know. What I do next depends on the answer to that question. I am prepared to let my friend die. I am prepared to take my own life and destroy this lab..." I saw her go pale. "But I need to know, is Ben alive? If he is, that changes things..."

She took a deep breath. "All right, Lacklan. I'll go and ask him, and I'll bring you the answer. Then you come inside, but please, *please*, don't do anything that will hurt these minds. They are a treasure and you have no right to destroy them. Let's please step back from the abyss, and stop destroying lives."

I gave a small nod, like I agreed. "This is your project, right?"

"Yes."

"You must be brilliant. What are you, twenty-six, seven?"

"I'm twenty-eight. I have an IQ of one seventy."

"You knew Ben?"

"Lacklan, I knew Ben. We were close. All he wanted, all I want, is to save lives, save the best of humanity."

"What's your name?"

"Calypso."

"Go, talk to Omicron. I'll wait for you." As she turned to go, I looked at the floor and sighed. "Calypso?"

"Yes...?"

"Please, let my friend down, answer my question about Ben, and I will come in."

She looked at me for a long moment, searching my face. I let her see my exhaustion, my confusion, the sickness I felt at the endless death and suffering I had caused—was causing still. Finally, she nodded and left.

I followed her shadow through the huge hangar and

from the window, I watched her step out into the yard. She called a couple of guards and spoke to them, and as she made her way to the villa, they took Njal down and dragged him away, after her, toward the house. Then I turned and looked around me at the cold, clinical horror they had created. You didn't need to be a cyborg to exist without human emotions. Humans were more than capable of that.

I looked deep into the shadows and wondered how many more of these independent, un-networked computers they had set up around the world. There was still Omega IV and Omega V in Africa, and China.

But Omicron, Jim had said, Omicron was the key to their resurgence. Without Omicron, they would be finished.

It took her just fifteen minutes and she came back across the yard, with her long shadow stretching out before her across the dust. She looked just like somebody's daughter, like the girl next door, in her jeans and her sweatshirt and her boots: pretty, young, nice, sweet-tempered, smart.

She stepped through the door and smiled at me.

"You saw that your friend was taken down."

"Have you killed him?"

She laughed and rolled her eyes. "Not everybody is as obsessed with killing as you are, Lacklan! The whole purpose of our organization is to stop the killing and the suffering. Omicron said come inside, and he will tell you about Ben."

"So you are Omega?"

"I told you, I am associated with Omega. I am not a member of the cabal. I have no letter."

"Is he OK?"

"He is fine. He's very strong. He's sitting at the table, eating roast chicken and drinking beer."

"Why won't you use his name?"

She frowned, shifted slightly and her face went into shadow with the light from the spot outside leaning across her chest and belly. "What?"

"You keep calling him my friend. Why won't you call him by his name?"

She gave a little snort of a laugh through her nose, shrugged, gave her head a little shake. "I don't know his name."

I nodded. "Oh."

I raised the Maxim and shot her in the head.

If she knew my name and not Njal's, that let Jim off the hook as their informer. That was all I'd wanted to know.

I walked across the spot-lit yard, with my shadow stretching out behind me. The four guards watched me with incurious eyes, just doing their job, questioning nothing. I came around the villa and climbed onto the porch. Two guards stood there, flanking the door. They pointed their weapons at me. One of them frowned.

"*Donde esta Calypso?*"

"In the lab." I jerked my head toward the prefab. "Checking everything is OK."

"*Manos arriba!*"

He gestured I should put my hands up. I did and they frisked me and found nothing. Then they grabbed my arms and shoved me through the door. Inside, they dragged me across a large, terracotta entrance hall, through tall, double doors and into a dining room.

There I saw a long table. At the head was General Ochoa, Omicron. Behind him was a window, in front of him was a large balloon glass of cognac. On his left was

Zapata, Xi, the head of the Sinaloa cartel, and next to him was Gonzalez, Nu, governor of the free and sovereign state of Sinaloa. They too had glasses of cognac in front of them. Opposite them, on Ochoa's right, was Njal, eating hungrily and watching me with curious eyes. In front of him he had a stein of beer, half empty.

The general said, "Where is Calypso?"

"She's in the lab. She wants to make sure I haven't damaged anything. She said she wanted her team over there."

He raised an eyebrow. "You said you had I don't know how many pounds of C4 and you were going to destroy the lab. I know you had an automatic weapon..."

I looked at him like he was stupid. "Yeah, I didn't think it was smart to walk into a house full of armed men carrying C4 and a Heckler and Koch. They're in the lab, with Calypso. I handed everything over to her."

He turned to one of the guards and rattled something in Spanish. I gathered he was telling them to get the team and go over to the lab, to make sure everything was OK. Then he turned to me as the soldiers left the room. "Sit. Are you hungry? You see we have not hurt you or your friend. We just want this to end, Lacklan."

"Yeah. I'm hungry. I want what he has." I jerked my head at Njal. "Calypso tried to sell me the same line. So did Ben, before you. But frankly, the only thing I am interested in right now is whether Ben is alive or not. My father was Gamma. Ben was his son, my brother. I eventually discovered he was also Alpha. I killed him. I shot him in the heart and I watched him die. Why do I keep getting messages claiming to be from him? Why do you keep trying to sell me the line that he is still alive?"

General Ochoa leaned his forearms on the table and rumbled a deep sigh. He stared into his glass and finally said, "Alpha is dead, Omega is finished. You..." He gestured at me with his open palm. "You are the destroyer. But death must be followed by rebirth and regeneration. Ah-Puch, the Mayan god of death and regeneration, takes our lives and then gives them back to us. It is the eternal cycle of creation and destruction."

I sighed. "Is there a god in your universal pantheon for plain speaking? It is not a complicated question. Try to give me a plain answer. Is Ben dead or alive?"

He leaned back in his chair and smiled. "Ben, your brother, Alpha, is alive."

NINETEEN

RAISED VOICES CAME TO ME, ALONG WITH THE tramping of feet, people in the hallway. The front door opened, people filed out, then the door closed again. Moments later, through the window behind Omicron's head, I saw the nerds, accompanied by a handful of soldiers, hurry past, headed for the lab. A moment after that, a pretty, young maid came in with a tray. On it there was a plate of roast chicken with French fries and fried vegetables. There was also a stein of beer. She placed it in front of me and withdrew.

In my head, I was counting footsteps. I turned to Njal and raised my stein.

"The length of my life and the day of my death were fated by the Norn long ago."

He smiled and raised his glass too. "I ask only to live like a hero, and die well."

It was about thirty paces from the back of the villa to the

entrance to the lab. I put the stein to my lips and took a long pull, counting twelve, thirteen, fourteen. I put down the stein and stared down at the chicken. Eighteen, nineteen, twenty...

I looked at General Ochoa, then picked up my knife and fork. "You must think I am real stupid, really gullible, to believe that you can take a man who's been shot twice in the heart and fix him so that today he is still alive. I am not that stupid, Ochoa."

I cut into the chicken. Twenty-eight, twenty-nine, thirty. I stuffed the chicken in my mouth. Give them a few seconds to get inside. Chew. Wipe my mouth. Drop my arm and press.

Nineteen pounds of C4 makes one hell of a detonation. Four pounds will destroy a bus. Ten pounds can destroy a house. Nineteen pounds, placed with skill, tore through the lab, ripped open the computer bank, incinerated the team of scientists and the soldiers, and brought down the prefab in a pile of smoldering, splintered rubble. It shook the house and shattered the glass in the window, making people shout and scream and scramble to their feet. I didn't see it, not then, but I heard it. I was expecting it and even so, it stunned me. But Ochoa, Zapata and Gonzalez were not expecting it. Ochoa slumped forward, covering his head, then jumped to his feet. Zapata covered his head with his arms and Gonzalez staggered from his chair and fell to the floor.

I got to my feet and moved around the table to where Gonzalez was lying in a heap in the fetal position. I had the knife I'd been using for the chicken in my hand, but I didn't bother with it. I'd planned to cut his throat, but instead I stamped with my heel on the back of his neck and snapped his vertebrae. His legs jerked a few times and he lay still. By that time I was standing behind Zapata.

Across the other side of the table, Ochoa had charged Njal and they were wrestling while the general screamed for his men. Out in the hall, there was chaos and confusion, with shouts and running feet. I knew we had bare seconds. I grabbed Zapata's hair and yanked his head back as I rammed the knife in through his carotid artery and out through his windpipe. His body jerked and spasmed as he tried to stand and his arms flailed. I wrenched the knife out and a geyser of blood erupted from the big, gaping wound, spraying the walls and the ceiling.

I threw him to the floor and jumped on the table, going after Ochoa. He and Njal were locked in a clinch. Ochoa was going for a take down in the hope his men were about to arrive. His hopes were not unfounded. The door burst open and four men rushed in, pointing their rifles and shouting. I made a split second decision. I knew they wouldn't shoot Njal for fear of hitting their general. I flipped the knife, grabbed the blade and hurled it. It slammed home into the nearest soldier's eye. He screamed and fell back and I jumped at the guy behind him.

There was a burst of fire that went wide and hit the ceiling. I grabbed the barrel of his rifle in my left hand and levered it away from me as I kicked him hard in the nuts. As he doubled up, I arced the barrel high over my head, brought it down facing the door and snatched at the trigger, spraying the doorway with lead. One soldier went down. The other fled, screaming for support. My guy was still holding onto his rifle, clutching at his balls with his left hand. Ten points for tenacity, but it wasn't going to save his life. I kicked him in the head, wrenched the weapon free and blew his brains out.

Njal and Ochoa were on the floor, struggling to get an arm lock on each other. I took two long strides and kicked Ochoa in the ribs, grabbed the scruff of his neck and dragged him to his feet. I snapped at Njal, "Weapons!" and he scrambled, collecting up handguns and rifles from the dead soldiers. I smashed my fist into Ochoa's kidneys. His knees buckled. I shouldered the assault rifle and Njal read my mind and threw me a Glock. I snapped, "Cover the window. We're going out the door," and shoved the general ahead of me toward the hallway. I rammed the handgun into the small of his back and snarled, "Tell them to stand down. I want their weapons on the ground. One twitch I don't like and I blow a hole in your gut. You won't die quick, you son of a bitch, but it will hurt. I promise you that!"

He raised his voice. He was short of breath. He was in pain.

"*Tiren las armas. Hagan lo que dice. Tiren las armas!*"

I knew enough Spanish to get the gist. He was telling them to drop their weapons and do as I said. We stepped into the hallway. There was half a dozen soldiers there. Their weapons were on the floor and they looked mad. I bellowed at them, "*Fuera! Fuera de aquí!*"

They moved toward the door and backed out into the night. Njal collected up a few more guns and we stepped out after them. He was behind me, walking backward, keeping his weapon trained on the soldiers. I pressed the Glock hard into Ochoa's back. "You let me live, I'll do you the same favor. But you do exactly what I say. We're going for the Land Rover. We leave here in the truck and I'll let you out when we're clear. But right now you do exactly as I say or you and your men die. Do you understand me?"

"I understand."

"Tell your men to get in the barracks."

He gave the order. They tried to argue, but he yelled at them and they filed away, around the other side of the villa, toward their quarters. We moved around the near side and I saw the lab for the first time. The roof had caved in and the walls had crumbled. Thick smoke was rising from the mess, like there was a fire burning inside. There were dead soldiers scattered outside in the dirt, some dismembered and smoldering.

There was a crowd working to clear the mess and get inside, to look for survivors. Obviously they hadn't heard the shooting from the house. Now there was an exchange of shouts with their colleagues on their way to the barracks, and the guys working on the ruin turned to stare at us, still struggling to comprehend what had happened.

I shoved the barrel into Ochoa's back again. "Tell them! Tell them to join their pals in the barracks, and give you the key."

He was getting worried about where this was going. He had good reason. Flames started to lick up from the prefab, small at first but growing fast. I snarled, "Do it."

"*Vayan,*" he said. "*Enciérrense. Denme a mi la llave.*" There was a moment's hesitation and uncertainty. Then he shouted, "*Vayan! Me va a matar si desobedecen!*"

Go, he'll kill me if you disobey. That worked. They backed away toward the barracks. There were about fifteen of them. They filed inside, and the last one gave the general the key and closed the door. It wouldn't hold them long. They would break the windows and get out. But it would slow them down at least.

"Lock it!"

I shoved him up to the door. He fitted the key and turned it twice, speaking as he did it. "You are crazy. They will alert the authorities. You will never leave the country."

"Keep talking like that, General, and you won't see the dawn. If they follow, you die. Tell them!"

He shouted to them and I dragged him stumbling toward the Land Rover. As we went, Njal muttered, "He is right. We let them live, we don't leave the country."

Ochoa erupted, "You are a fool, Lacklan! We were willing to send you home. What is wrong with you?"

"I don't like people who remove other people's brains. Now shut up!" We had reached the Land Rover. I pulled open the back door and growled, "Get in! Lie on the floor on your face. Njal, get in with him. If he moves, kill him."

Ochoa moved to climb in, then turned suddenly, smashed his shoulder into Njal's chest and ran screaming for the barracks, shouting, *"Ahora! Ahora! Ahora!"*

Somewhere glass shattered. Njal shouted, *"Shoot him!"*

There was a crack, then two more. Dust spat up from the ground around us. Njal grunted and knelt down. I heard him say, "Not today…"

I knelt beside him. He scowled at me. *"Get him! I will not die for nothing!"*

"You're not going to fucking die! Get up!" I dragged him to his feet, hurled him in the back of the Land Rover and slammed the door. Ochoa was at the barracks, fumbling with the lock. I took aim. He wrenched the door open and I missed the shot. A soldier went down instead, but all the guys behind him came storming out. I let off a burst and five guys fell. Then I clambered behind the wheel. The engine roared, I floored the pedal. Slugs like hailstones pelted the chassis and shattered the side windows as we hurtled toward the gate. I heard Njal's voice from the back, weak and breathing hard.

"The gates are locked, Lacklan. How you gonna get out..."

"I don't plan to."

I spun the wheel and screamed around the villa in a cloud of dust. I reached back and grabbed one of the assault rifles Njal had collected. There was no windshield because I had shattered that earlier. I rested the magazine on the window frame above the dash and came around the back of the villa, on the barracks side, to the sight of some fifteen soldiers, all with their backs to me, charging after their general to where they thought I was, when I was actually behind them. I could hear Njal laughing and realized I was laughing too. And to our crazed laughter was added the laughter of the AK-47 I was holding as it opened up, spitting death. The hail of lead tore into the running soldiers, spewing up great fountains of blood and gore, crippling, maiming and killing as the men went down.

And then it wasn't the bullets killing them, but the wheels of the truck as I crashed into them and rode over them. I spun the wheel again and again as the few remaining men scattered and fled, and I went after them, picking them off, mowing them down in hot hails of death.

Finally, there was no one left. No one but the general,

lying in the dust, staring at me. I climbed out of the truck and walked toward him.

"Get up."

"Why...?"

"You granted me my life when you could have killed me. I'll give you the chance to die with honor."

He got to his feet and squared up to me. For a moment we stood in the floodlit yard, staring into each other's faces under the black sky. Then he did what I knew he would do. He bent, pulled his Bowie knife from his boot and charged me, screaming. I stepped to my left, gripped his wrist in my left hand and smashed the heel of my right into his nose. The pain made him gasp and stagger back. I kept pace with him, still holding his wrist, and smashed my knuckles into his wind pipe. His eyes bulged as he struggled to draw breath. He dropped the knife and tore at his throat with both hands. I bent and picked up the big blade with the serrated back. I took a large step toward him and rammed the blade home, up to the hilt, into his chest. He shuddered, then fell on his back.

I looked down at him, where his bulging eyes were staring unseeing at the emptiness of space. Flames were dancing in his eyes from where the lab had started to burn.

"I stabbed you in the heart, Omicron. You're dead," I said. "And so is Ben."

I walked back to the Land Rover and opened the back door. Njal was lying very still.

"You still with me, pal?"

After a moment he said, "Yuh..." but his voice was weak, like he was very tired.

I closed the door and got behind the wheel. As I drove toward the gate again I asked him, "Where are you hit?"

He answered like he was half asleep. "In the chest. Left. Is not my heart, cause I ain't dead, right?"

"Right. You stay with me, Njal. Don't you go to sleep. You understand?" I pulled off my shirt and handed it back to him. "Press this against the wound to stem the flow of blood."

He took it.

"I'm OK... Just getting kinda sleepy..."

I stopped at the gate and swung down from the cab. I ran to the guards' hut, found the green buttons to open the gates and hammered on them. The gates groaned and creaked, rattled and buzzed as they rolled open. I climbed back in the cab and drove through, into the blackness, with the cones from the headlamps picking out the road ahead, and the twisted, diabolical shapes of the trees as they leapt out at me. I spoke as I drove.

"I'm going to take you to Cosalá, pal. We'll get you a doctor. You're going to be OK."

He didn't answer.

I went on, "It's probably a through and though. No vital organs. Your heart's OK, and your lungs..."

I should have stopped, should have turned and looked. I should have checked how he was. I should have examined the wound. But I couldn't. I couldn't turn around. I kept driving, careening down the dirt track, willing the damned truck to go faster, not wanting to see what I knew was behind me. It was not today. He had said so: not today.

"They have to have a doctor, Njal," I said. "We'll wake him up. We'll drag him out of bed, pal. Don't you worry. I'm not going to let you die. There is no way you get to Valhalla before me. Not today..."

My voice sounded strange and twisted in my ears, and ahead the lights of the village, growing closer, were blurred because there were tears in my eyes and my face was wet, because behind me there was only silence. Not even the sound of breathing.

EPILOGUE

THE MOON HAD NOT RISEN YET. THE SKY WAS almost black. The number of stars was astonishing, like gold and silver dust cast over infinity, incredibly far away. The ocean, a sheet of black glass, lapped gently against the hull of our small sloop. The sails were furled. The breeze was chill on my skin. The world seemed an empty, cold, wet place.

Sole came up from below, wrapped in a blanket. She handed me another and sat next to me.

"He'll have to come soon. The moon is gonna rise, then it's not safe."

I studied her a moment, then put the blanket around my shoulders. "It is never safe for you. Why do you live here?"

"I'm from Sinaloa. I was born here. I was more at risk when I was sixteen, eighteen, till I moved to California. Now I am old. In the cartel's eyes I am old. Nobody is interested in me."

"Your kids?"

"They'll go with their father before they are at risk."

"Jim?"

She nodded. "He is my husband."

I smiled. "Tough break."

She smiled too, then laughed. "Good man, terrible husband. Like you, I guess."

"I guess. I don't know if I'm a good man. I am tired of killing. I am tired of all the death."

She reached under her blanket and pulled out a pack of Camels from her shirt pocket. She shook one free and offered it to me. I took it. She flipped an old steel Zippo and we lit up.

"What were you doing there?"

I shook my head.

She said, "I know about Omega. Jim is my husband, remember?"

"I can't talk about it."

She sighed. "Cosalá, that's Zapata, *el Vampiro*. He has a ranch up there, and it's no secret he is close pals with the governor and General Ochoa. So I figure that was your job. What went wrong?"

I took a deep drag and released a stream of smoke over the black sea. "Compassion went wrong. We hit a senior member of Omega. Professional logic dictated we take out his mistress too, make it look like they killed each other. But we didn't want to kill an innocent woman. So we framed her for her lover's death, but gave her a new identity and a new life in the States. It was a costly mistake, not just financially." I gestured at her. "Just like Jim talks to you about Omega, I figure this guy spoke to his mistress, gave her information, people to contact if she was ever in need..." I shook my head. "I don't know. Maybe he even introduced her to other members. But I figure the minute she got off the plane in L.A. she called somebody, and when we struck, they were waiting for us. It was stupid and naïve of us. And Njal paid the price in full."

She nodded and sighed. "Being noble is a weakness, Lacklan. But it is also a strength. You just gotta learn to be noble and smart." She gave me a gentle punch on the shoulder. "You gonna die anyway, right? People who are bad, and people who are noble but stupid, die thinking their lives were wasted. People who were noble and smart, die knowing their lives were worth something."

I nodded. "That's wise. But a bit late for me."

"It's never late, dumbass."

I looked at her and laughed. "No?"

She smiled with hooded eyes. "Nope. It is never early and it is never late. It is always now. No more, no less."

"Zen."

"Nope. Truth. Give yourself a break."

We were quiet for a while, smoking and watching the northern sky, waiting for her husband. My mind drifted. I thought of Njal sinking to his knees. His quiet voice, "Not today..."

"What?"

I turned to Sole, realizing I had spoken out loud. I shook my head, then said, "It never ends, Sole. You eliminate one cell, one group, and then there's another, and then another. And you keep killing them, but they keep coming back. And you begin to realize that it is not Omega that's evil, it's people. And you are not killing Omega, you are killing people. And..." I gave a desperate, humorless laugh. "The reason you are killing them is because *they* plan to kill..."

"...people..."

I looked at her and nodded. "I have become my enemy."

"If only it were that simple, Lacklan, but I think there is a lot more to what Omega do than killing people. Killing is the least of their evils."

"I know, you're right, Sole. But I don't want to become like them. I am tired of the killing, tired of being the destroyer."

I looked away, to the north, and saw one star that was brighter than the others. I was surprised to feel a pang, and a twist of resentment at its appearance that I could not quite place. I would have been happy to spend the night on that yacht, talking.

I turned to her and said, suddenly, with a strange sense of urgency, "Sell me your house."

Her eyebrows shot up. "What?"

"Your house, sell it to me."

She shook her head. "I told you I don't want charity."

"And I told you, you won't get any from me. The house would have its uses for operations against the cartel. For real, Sole. And you and your kids could get away, somewhere safe."

"Are you serious?"

"Listen, my old regiment, the DEA, the Feds, the CIA, not to mention me and Jim, we could all use that house."

She was frowning, hesitant.

"Please," I said, and surprised myself. "Let me do something useful that does not involve killing people. Let me do this."

She nodded. Then she smiled and she nodded again.

"OK, thank you." Then there was mischief in her hooded eyes. "But it won't be cheap."

"Good. I hate cheap things."

Soon we could hear the drone of the twin engines, and the great hulk of the Grumman Albatross came into view. We watched it settle on the water, among great spouts of luminous foam, and it came gently to a halt fifty or sixty feet away. Sole started the outboard and coasted over to the door in the rear of the plane. As we drew level, it opened and Jim stood looking out at us. He nodded at me and smiled at Sole.

"How is he?"

She shrugged. Her tone was hostile. "Lucky. Lacklan has offered to buy my house. I told him yes."

He regarded me with curious, bright eyes. "Good," he said. "I've been trying to convince her to sell that place for a long time. Where's Njal?"

I said, "I'll go get him."

When I got below, he was sitting on his bunk. He was dressed, but you could see the bandages under his shirt.

"We going home?" he said.

"Yeah, pal. We're going home."

"Good."

He stood and I helped him up the stairs and onto the deck. He was still weak and groggy from painkillers. Jim helped him into the plane and they hugged. Then Njal disappeared into the bowels of the aircraft, muttering something about how he was going to lie down. Jim regarded me.

"Let's go."

I said, "Joelma blew the whistle on us. They were expecting us."

He nodded. "I figured that. We're debriefing her now."

I went to move, but hesitated. "Ochoa said Ben is still alive." The hull of the yacht tapped the side of the plane. The waves lapped. In the east, the orange rim of the moon peered over the world and warped. "I keep hearing he's alive. I get messages from him. They said the war was over, and I just hadn't got the memo."

He glanced past me at the moon. "They're playing with your head, Lacklan. Don't let them get to you. We need to go. The moon's rising. We also need to talk. We almost lost Njal."

"I know." I glanced at Sole. "I'm going to stay and deal with the buying of the house. I'll see you back in L.A. Give me a couple of weeks."

He nodded a few times. Then snorted a small laugh and nodded a bit more. "OK, call me." He looked at Sole. "You too. Keep me in the loop."

We watched the plane speed across the water, then rise up into the black sky, growing dim as the drone faded. Then we hoisted the mainsail and the jib, and headed slowly back to shore. I found a bottle of Jameson's down below and poured us each a shot, then sat beside her and watched the moon slowly rise over the horizon.

"Where are you going to stay?"

She asked it looking at the moon, but then turned to face me. She had no expression, but there was humor in her eyes.

I took a deep breath and puffed up my cheeks. "It's funny you should ask. I was wondering the same thing about you, once the contract is signed, while you sort out a new school for the kids and everything... I guess I could rent you a room..."

"Oh, you gonna rent me a room in my own house?"

"But it won't be your house. It will be *my* house."

"Not if I don't sell it to you it won't!"

"Great! Now you tell me. Now the plane's gone."

"We can call him back!"

"No, don't do that..."

And so it went, as we sailed slowly along the golden path to the moon.

Don't miss 9MM JUSTICE. The riveting sequel in the Omega Thriller series.

Scan the QR code below to purchase 9MM JUSTICE

Or go to: righthouse.com/9mm-justice

NOTE: flip to the very end to read an exclusive sneak peek...

DON'T MISS ANYTHING!

If you want to stay up to date on all new releases in this series, with this author, or with any of our new deals, you can do so by joining our newsletters below.

In addition, you will immediately gain access to our entire *Right House VIP Library*, which includes many riveting Mystery and Thriller novels for your enjoyment!

righthouse.com/email

(Easy to unsubscribe. No spam. Ever.)

ALSO BY BLAKE BANNER

Up to date books can be found at:
www.righthouse.com/blake-banner

ROGUE THRILLERS
Gates of Hell (Book 1)
Hell's Fury (Book 2)
Ice Burn (Book 3)
Judgement by Fire (Book 4)

ALEX MASON THRILLERS
Odin (Book 1)
Ice Cold Spy (Book 2)
Mason's Law (Book 3)
Assets and Liabilities (Book 4)
Russian Roulette (Book 5)
Executive Order (Book 6)
Dead Man Talking (Book 7)
All The King's Men (Book 8)
Flashpoint (Book 9)
Brotherhood of the Goat (Book 10)
Dead Hot (Book 11)
Blood on Megiddo (Book 12)
Son of Hell (Book 13)
Merchant of Death (Book 14)
Extinction C-14 (Book 15)

HARRY BAUER THRILLER SERIES

Dead of Night (Book 1)
Dying Breath (Book 2)
The Einstaat Brief (Book 3)
Quantum Kill (Book 4)
Immortal Hate (Book 5)
The Silent Blade (Book 6)
LA: Wild Justice (Book 7)
Breath of Hell (Book 8)
Invisible Evil (Book 9)
The Shadow of Ukupacha (Book 10)
Sweet Razor Cut (Book 11)
Blood of the Innocent (Book 12)
Blood on Balthazar (Book 13)
Simple Kill (Book 14)
Riding The Devil (Book 15)
The Unavenged (Book 16)
The Devil's Vengeance (Book 17)
Bloody Retribution (Book 18)
Rogue Kill (Book 19)
Blood for Blood (Book 20)
The Cell (Book 21)
Time to Die (Book 22)
The Reaper of Zion (Book 23)

DEAD COLD MYSTERY SERIES
An Ace and a Pair (Book 1)
Two Bare Arms (Book 2)
Garden of the Damned (Book 3)
Let Us Prey (Book 4)
The Sins of the Father (Book 5)
Strange and Sinister Path (Book 6)

The Heart to Kill (Book 7)
Unnatural Murder (Book 8)
Fire from Heaven (Book 9)
To Kill Upon A Kiss (Book 10)
Murder Most Scottish (Book 11)
The Butcher of Whitechapel (Book 12)
Little Dead Riding Hood (Book 13)
Trick or Treat (Book 14)
Blood Into Wine (Book 15)
Jack In The Box (Book 16)
The Fall Moon (Book 17)
Blood In Babylon (Book 18)
Death In Dexter (Book 19)
Mustang Sally (Book 20)
A Christmas Killing (Book 21)
Mommy's Little Killer (Book 22)
Bleed Out (Book 23)
Dead and Buried (Book 24)
In Hot Blood (Book 25)
Fallen Angels (Book 26)
Knife Edge (Book 27)
Along Came A Spider (Book 28)
Cold Blood (Book 29)
Curtain Call (Book 30)

THE OMEGA SERIES
Dawn of the Hunter (Book 1)
Double Edged Blade (Book 2)
The Storm (Book 3)
The Hand of War (Book 4)
A Harvest of Blood (Book 5)

ABOUT US

Right House is an independent publisher created by authors for readers. We specialize in Action, Thriller, Mystery, and Crime novels.

If you enjoyed this novel, then there is a good chance you will like what else we have to offer! Please stay up to date by using any of the links below.

Join our mailing lists to stay up to date -->
righthouse.com/email
Visit our website --> righthouse.com
Contact us --> contact@righthouse.com

 facebook.com/righthousebooks

x.com/righthousebooks

instagram.com/righthousebooks

EXCLUSIVE SNEAK PEEK OF...

9MM JUSTICE

CHAPTER 1

I WAS IN TUCSON, ARIZONA, FOR NO PARTICULAR reason, standing on a corner admiring a girl in a flat bed Ford who had slowed down to take a look at me. She gave me a wink and I smiled. The lights changed and she drove away, out of my life forever. That's the way it happens sometimes.

It was one of those Arizona days, when the sun scorches the sky to a blue that is almost white, and the palms stand motionless in tall, thin silhouettes, over broad streets of low houses. I was strolling, with my hands in my pockets and no particular direction. No particular direction had led me, without realizing it, from America's Best Value Inn, on the East Benson Highway, south to the Fairgrounds district, along South Park Avenue. I was on the corner of East Fair Street, smiling to myself as I watched her drive away, when I caught sight of a small group gathered outside Cora's Golden Café, across the road, about fifty or sixty yards away.

Like a lot of places in Tucson, Cora's Golden Cafe was set back a ways from the road, among a broad patch of dirt with a parking lot out front. Something about the group made me pause to look at them. There were four guys. Their hair was cut real short. They had the dark, olive complexion of Latinos and all four of them looked lean and athletic. I thought their attitude and manner seemed aggressive, even threatening. None of them looked much older than twenty-five.

They were talking to two girls. One of the girls was wearing jeans and a T-shirt. Her hair was long, loose, a bit wild. She seemed to be mad and was waving her hands a lot, cocking her hips and her head as she spoke. The gestures made me smile. She looked like a handful.

The other girl was holding her arm. She seemed maybe a couple of years older, though that may have been because of her clothes, and her manner. She was wearing a pale blue dress, her hair was cut to her shoulders and she seemed to be trying to reason with the boys. A small crowd had gathered outside the door to the café, watching, waiting, like people at a circus.

Before I knew what I was doing, I had started to cross the road. The far sidewalk was a strip of dirt with patchy grass growing on it. There were traffic lights and a big tele-graph pole blocking my way. I loped across the blacktop and saw one of the boys move forward and push the girl in jeans. The girl in the dress stepped in front of her, blocking the boy's way. The others closed in. I noticed a couple of them were wearing hoodies. The other two had short sleeves and I now noticed they had tattoos. I had started to run. They were thirty paces away now, and I began to hear a different sound, the throbbing of ugly music played too loud in a car.

It was approaching from South Park Avenue toward me,

and without knowing why, I knew it was important, and I knew it was bad. I went from a jog to a sprint. The girls were backing away, toward a white truck. One of the boys had his hand behind his back, reaching under his hoodie. I shouted. They didn't hear me. I could feel my Sig Sauer heavy under my left arm. They were fifteen, twenty yards away, still backing toward the white pickup. I shouted again. On South Park Avenue, a customized Lincoln Continental came into view, traveling fast. I pulled my Sig and shouted again. The Continental veered suddenly, accelerating fast across East Michigan toward the far entrance of the parking lot. They all froze, staring at the car that was speeding toward them. I heard myself screaming, *"Get down! Get down!"*

The girl in the jeans turned to stare at me. She was frowning, like she didn't understand what I was doing there. Everything seemed to slow right down. I saw every detail of her face. I saw her long, unbrushed hair waft as she turned her head. I saw the small crease between her eyebrows as she frowned.

I shifted my eyes and saw the Continental screeching past behind them with the windows open. I knew what was going to happen. I screamed again, *"Get down! Get down!"* running, gesturing with my hands. But it was too late. It was like firecrackers going off inside the car. Brilliant flashes of light illuminated the cab and the diabolical faces of the men holding the assault rifles. The crackle filled the air. The small crowd scattered. One of the hoodies went down where he stood. The two guys in T-shirts ran a couple of paces before they fell. The second hoodie made it a little further and died at the sidewalk.

The girl in the jeans fell staring at me, with wide,

shocked eyes. The Continental lurched out of the parking lot and sped away, fishtailing slightly along South Park, leaving littered, scattered bodies behind it.

I stopped running, staggered to a halt and knelt by the girl, reaching for my cell. I felt for a pulse in her neck. It was a faint flutter. She blinked, panting softly. I saw she had a bullet wound in her belly, but the blood was pooling underneath her. It had gone right through.

"Take it easy," I said, "I'm calling for help. You're going to make it."

"911, what is your emergency?"

"Drive by shooting in Cora's Golden Café parking lot, corner of South Park Avenue and Michigan, six badly hurt, probable fatalities..." I glanced around me. The girl with the blue dress had gone. "Five," I said. "Five casualties."

The girl was looking at me. She was frowning again. I could see her hand moving slightly, like she was trying to lift it. I took it in mine and smiled at her.

"My name is Lacklan. I'm going to help you. The ambulance is on its way. You're going to be fine."

Her lips had gone very pale and she was trying to move them. I said, "Don't try to talk, you can tell me later. I'll be there at the hospital when you wake up."

She blinked again, with the ghost of a smile, and whispered, "Celeste, nice..." She took a couple of breaths and whispered again, "...nice to meet you..."

Then there was a slight rasp as her lungs emptied, her eyes lost focus and her hand went heavy and cold in mine. I sat and crossed my legs, holding her hand in my lap, waiting with her as the distant sirens wailed across the Arizona afternoon. Close up, she was more like eighteen than twenty. She had on a blue and violet plaid shirt and a thin string of beads around her neck. She had boot cut jeans and brown cowboy boots. Her eyes, now lifeless, had been bright and curious, and a dark chestnut brown.

Vehicles were pulling into the parking lot: four patrol cars, lights flashing and sirens crying out, three ambulances, a Ford Focus. I looked down at Celeste and realized my face was wet. I gave her a rueful smile she would never see and said, "See you in Valhalla, Celeste."

There were cops walking toward me with their weapons drawn, shouting at me to raise my hands and lie face down. I put her hand carefully back on the ground, raised my own hands and turned to lie on my face.

They didn't ask me any questions. They just cuffed me, took my weapon and bundled me in the back of a car. From there I watched how they put her in a bag, zipped it closed over her head, lifted her onto a gurney and wheeled her to one of the ambulances. I watched also, a little later, as a woman in her fifties came running up East Michigan Street and into the lot, screaming and shouting as she went. A couple of cops crowded her. She appealed to them, looking up into their faces, saying something, and they led her to a man in a blazer and chinos. He listened to her for a moment, then called over a female police officer and the woman was led toward the ambulance where Celeste's body lay. Her mother, sent to identify the body.

The guy in chinos and the blazer was walking toward me. I figured he was fifty, not in great shape, and he'd been around the block a few times—too many times maybe. He opened the car door and helped me out, then showed me his badge.

"Detective Mike Shannon, Tucson PD. You make the call?"

"Yes."

"What's your name?"

"Lacklan Walker, my driver's license is in my breast pocket."

He reached in and pulled it out, examining it. "Captain, huh?"

"British SAS."

He glanced at me, curious. "You an American?"

"On my father's side, yeah. Is that relevant?"

"I don't know yet. Tell me what happened."

I tried to keep the edge from my voice. "I witnessed a multiple homicide, called it in and tried to help one of the victims. Unless any of those things is a crime in Arizona, how about you take the cuffs off?"

"You were armed."

"Like everybody else in Arizona, New Mexico and Texas. I have a license and the weapon has not been fired. Besides, you'll find that these people were killed with an assault rifle, my weapon is a 9mm, a Sig Sauer p226 Tacops. I don't believe you have any reason to arrest me, Detective, and given that I have every intention of cooperating with you, as of right now this is a false arrest and you're breaking the law."

"Keep your panties on, Captain." He turned me around and took off the cuffs. "We have gang wars around here. You can't be too careful. They told me you were sitting beside the girl, holding her hand?" He gave it the intonation of a question and narrowed his eyes at me, like he thought my behavior was weird. I gave him a rundown of what I'd seen, then shrugged.

"She looked like she was in trouble with the guys, her friend—"

"The one in the blue dress."

"Yeah, the girl in the blue dress, she seemed to be trying to help her. I got the impression they were not the intended victims of the drive by. The boys were. I tried to help the girls, tell them to get down, but I was too late. When I got to her, while I was calling 911, she was still alive. She couldn't be more than eighteen or nineteen. She said her name was Celeste."

He nodded like he understood. "Which way'd the woman in blue go?"

"I don't know."

He frowned, sucking his teeth and staring at his notes. "You're a very observant man, Captain, the detail here is remarkable. Comes with that kind of training, I guess."

I shrugged. "Maybe."

"But you didn't notice where the woman in blue went."

"No. I was surprised. When I called it in, I said there were six victims, then realized she wasn't there."

He showed me the notebook. "I'm going to need you to sign the statement." He pointed at the crossroads. "The station house is just on the intersection."

I stared where he was pointing, then at him. "That is a damned confident drive by, on the doorstep of the police station."

He jerked his head, indicating I should follow and we walked to his car as the last of the bodies was being lifted into an ambulance and the Crime Scene team started their minute search of the parking lot.

"These kids believe they are invincible. They have more coke than they know what to do with. Take enough of that stuff, you start to think you're God. Add to that the fact that they are backed by the power of the Mexican cartels, sometimes I think we're fighting a losing war."

We climbed into the car, slammed the doors and he pulled away. After a moment, I said, "In the southwestern states, you are."

He raised an eyebrow at me. "I'd like to take every politician in Washington, D.C., and have each of them watch a son, a daughter—some loved one—die from addiction to heroin. It's not just the death." He pulled onto the road and accelerated toward the intersection. "It is the slow destruction of the person, of the mind and the character, that comes before the death. I'd like those son of bitches to have to go through that and then explain to me why we can spend three trillion dollars invading Iraq and Afghanistan, while we sit on our asses and allow this flood of death to seep through our border."

I didn't answer him. I had no answer. My answer used to be Omega[1], but with Omega all but finished, the only explanation was that this was human nature. This was the human condition. We lived in Hell, a hell of our own making, because we were too damn cruel and too damned greedy to create anything better.

He parked in the station parking lot and led me through the crowded building to the detectives' room and then to his

---

1. See *The Omicron Kill*

desk. There I sat while he typed fast into his computer and printed my statement. He handed it to me and said, "Read it, Captain, and if you agree, please sign it."

I read through it, signed it, and handed it back to him.

"I need my gun back. It hasn't been fired, so it's not part of your investigation."

He picked up the internal phone and after a moment said, "Yeah, this is Shannon, Sig Sauer Tacops p226, just brought in from the shooting outside Cora's Café..." He waited, turning a pencil over in his fingers. "Send it up, will you? No, it's not going to the lab. We're returning it to the owner. Thanks."

I'd been watching his face. Now I said, "You know who did this."

It wasn't a question and he nodded. "The four boys are part of the *Iluminados* gang. They're at war with Jesus, Pedro and Pablo Santos, the *Santos del Diablo*."

"A turf war."

"What else? They both buy heroin, coke and other shit from Mexico. They're probably buying from the same supplier. They sell it locally to the local users, and they also sell it on to suppliers in L.A., San Francisco, Chicago, New York, Washington..." He shrugged and spread his hands. "Right across the nation. It's the commodity everybody wants. Heroin for the losers and coke for the winners."

"They're making a lot of money."

"Thousands, tens of thousands every week. That's why they are at war."

"They're that hard to bust?"

"Hey, don't give me a hard time, Captain. Tucson PD thanks you for your cooperation, but I don't need lessons in law enforcement from a British soldier. Guns ain't the only thing they buy with the dough they're making. You catch my drift?" He glanced over my shoulder. "Here's your piece. Be careful what you do with it."

A uniform approached and put the weapon on the desk. I holstered it and went to stand, but stopped with my hands on my knees. "What about the girls? Do you know who they are? Were..."

"Why?"

"I'd like to pay my respects to Celeste's mother. I think she'd like to hear her daughter's last words. I'm figuring she's the woman who turned up while I was waiting in the car. Her last memory of her daughter is not a nice one right now. Maybe I can improve it."

He sighed and sat forward, leafing through his notebook. He spoke as he did it. "The girl was Celeste Martinez. Her dad was killed about sixteen years ago, shot by a cop. He was involved in narcotrafficking across the border. She and her mother have stayed clean ever since... Here, the mother is Estrella Martinez, she lives on East Michigan, eleven-oh-two."

"Thanks."

He watched me stand and narrowed his eyes at me, like he wasn't sure if he thought I was OK or a pain in the ass. "She'll appreciate it. But don't get involved, Captain. Don't turn superhero on me."

"I'm just passing through, Detective: see the sights, try the food and I'll be on my way."

I left the detectives' room feeling his eyes on the back of my head. I rode the elevator down to the lobby and stepped out into the bright, Arizona sunshine, thinking about Celeste Martinez, knowing Detective Mike Shannon was not going to punish her death, knowing her death could not go unpunished.

CHAPTER 2

IT WAS A SHORT WALK TO ESTRELLA MARTINEZ'S house, along East Fair Street and down Freemont Avenue. Hers was the third house along. It was set behind a chain link fence and a front yard that was mainly dust and scrubby grass, shaded by velvet mesquite and yellow palo verde trees.

She was not alone. There was a small crowd of women, children and young teenage girls in her front yard, all talking at once outside her door. Her door was open and I could see and hear more people inside. I went through the gate and they all went quiet and watched me as I stepped inside the house.

There was no entrance hall here. It was one room, with a kitchen in pale, faded green on the left and a living area on the right, with a threadbare sofa, a couple of armchairs and a TV. A crucifix and a Virgin Mary were both nailed to the wall.

Sitting on the sofa was the woman I had seen in the

parking lot. She was crying and had a couple of women on either side, holding her and patting her hand. They were also crying and by the looks of it, their good intentions were leading Estrella Martinez straight to hell. There were other women and young girls sitting around, looking at me.

"Estrella Martinez?"

Several of them pointed to the woman I had recognized. She looked at me, blinking and stifling her sobs. I said:

"I was with your daughter when she died. I tried to help her." They all started talking to her at once and I heard the words *es verdad* a couple of times from the young girls. They were telling her it was true.

Her expression changed. There was a hint of longing, like she thought because I had been with her daughter when she died, in some crazy way I might be able to bring her back. I took a step closer. "Can we talk for a moment, alone?"

There was an explosion of chatter then, with everybody talking at the same time, and through it all, I got the idea she was asking them to leave us alone and they didn't think that was such a good idea. Eventually they all filed out, eyeing me curiously and a little suspiciously, leaving the living room empty and the front yard full. I closed the door behind them, crossed the room and sat next to her on the sofa, half turned to face her. She spoke first.

"You were with my Celeste when she...?"

Her eyes flooded and I nodded. "Yes. Do you want to know what happened?"

She hesitated, then closed her eyes and nodded.

I told her how it had started, how I ran toward them and tried to make them get down, how Celeste had stared at me and time had seemed to slow down, how in that moment we had seemed to know each other, to live a whole life of friendship in an instant, as death had closed in on her. I found myself speaking to her, perhaps as I imagined I might have spoken to Celeste, in a way I had never spoken to anybody. Through it all, she kept her eyes closed and cried as I spoke, but it wasn't the convulsive sobbing of intolerable grief, though that was there, for sure. But rather it was the helpless weeping that comes with the emptiness of letting go.

I told her how I had sat beside her at the end and held her hand, how I had told her my name and she had told me hers, just before she went. I realized then that I too was crying, and that she was holding my hand.

I dried my eyes and my cheeks with the sleeve of my free hand and asked her, "How old was she, Estrella?"

"Just nineteen, last May, a little Taurus bull. So obstinate, so much temperament, but always laughing and happy. One minute a storm! The next minute sunshine. Such a good daughter."

"You raised her alone..."

"Yes, my husband..." She shrugged. "Better alone than in bad company. My friends tell me, 'Oh, you raise Celeste all on your own!' I tell them, 'No, I have help. Celeste help me. Celeste and Jesus help me. Now! Now, she is gone with the Angels, I am alone."

I nodded. "Did she work? Did you depend on her financially?"

She pulled a handkerchief from her apron and dried her face, then blew her nose. "I depend on her for money, to make ends meet. But she didn't know how much. Now she decide to go to college, and I didn't know how I was gonna cope, but I didn't tell her. I didn't tell her nothing. I believe Jesus would help me."

"What was she going to study?"

"Child psychology. She loved the children. Even when she was a baby, she love the babies." She stopped talking a moment, staring out the window but seeing some scene in the past. "She want to work with kids who had lived through a trauma, like her. You know, is very bad here. Here in Arizona every year there is more violence, coming from Mexico, with the drugs. Mexicans are good people, but the people who come with the drugs are bad. She don't want to know nothing about that. She want to help the victims and the children. I don't know what I am gonna do now she is gone."

She let go my hand, pulled a handkerchief from her pocket and blew her nose. I sat a moment remembering the big, brown eyes staring at me, frowning slightly, as the shape of the black Lincoln Continental closed in, as death claimed her and she became collateral damage. She wasn't even the target. She was killed because she happened to be there, in the way of their greed.

A hot coal of rage had started to burn in my belly.

"Estrella, she was with another woman, dark hair to her shoulders, a blue dress... Any idea who she was?"

She shook her head. "I don't know. Could be anybody."

I nodded, then asked, "Do you know who did this?"

Her face became drawn. What little color there was turned to gray, but she didn't answer.

I went on, "It was the *Santos del Diablo*. Do you know who they are?"

Her eyes narrowed. "Who are you? Are you *policia*? FBI?"

I smiled and shook my head. "No, I'm a friend of Celeste, and I'm mad that they took her on the day I met her. I'm not a cop."

"Don't go after them, Mr. Lacklan. Don't do nothing stupid."

I allowed my face to become reassuring. "I don't plan to do anything stupid, don't worry. I just..." I sighed and shrugged. "I just want to know."

She turned away from me and gazed out the window, where the sun was starting to stretch the shadows of the mesquite trees long across the dust. "Celeste was not involved in any of that. But everybody around here knows who are the *Santos del Diablo* and the *Iluminados*." She turned back to me. "The *Santos* are Jesus' gang. He was a nice boy, I know his mother, but when he turn thirteen he become a monster, killing dogs, killing cats, fighting with knives. When he was sixteen, he form his own gang with his cousins Pedro and Pablo, and he make this blasphemous name, the Saints of the Devil."

"Is it a big gang? Are there many of them?"

She raised an eyebrow at me and sighed. "*Ay!* I don't know. If you want to know you gotta ask the *Iluminados!* Talk to Carlitos. Maybe you can become one of them and join all the killing."

I smiled and squeezed her hand. "I have done all my killing, Estrella. I was in the army, and I am done with that."

She smiled back, but she shook her head, looking me in the eye. "You are a good man, Mr. Lacklan, but you are lying. You are still a killer, and God has chosen you to do his killing for him. You want to know where are the *Iluminados*?"

"Yes."

She stared at the carpet for a while and I thought she might start crying again. She didn't. Instead she said suddenly, in a loud, hard voice, "You go to the bottom of Freemont Avenue, where it makes a corner, there, in the bend, they have their club." She raised her face to look at me and added, bitterly, "If you go to talk to them, a *gringo* like you, they will probably kill you. Then you can ask Celeste all your questions in person."

"I doubt I'll see Celeste where I'm going, Estrella. Thank you for talking to me. I only knew Celeste for a few seconds, but I know she was a very special person, like you."

She patted my hand, I stood and left the house.

Outside, the crowd had scattered, but you could still see the odd knot of two or three women and girls gathered at their gates, talking and glancing at the house. I turned into Freemont and walked the three hundred and fifty yards to the end of the street, where it turned east. To the right there was a broad expanse of wasteland that separated Freemont from South Park, a hundred and twenty yards away. To the left there was a row of nine houses, each set in its own plot of desert. Ahead of me was a house of the same sort, but the front fence had been torn out and where the yard should have been there were half a dozen bikes and a couple of trucks, all painted with desert scenes, saguaro cacti, death's heads and cannabis leaves. They were anything but original.

The front door was open and there was a guy in black jeans, a black T-shirt and a long black ponytail leaning on the doorjamb watching me. To complete the picture, he was holding a bottle of Coronita.

To the left of the door there was a green, molded plastic table with two chairs of the same design. They were occupied by a bare-chested kid of about eighteen whose arms and face were tattooed with variations on the theme of skulls, eagles and snakes, and a third guy who'd cut the arms off his denim jacket and embroidered it with more unoriginal designs from Hollywood Mexico. They all watched me step onto their forecourt and walk to within two paces of the guy in the door.

"I need to talk to Carlitos."

They muttered obscenities at me in Spanish, then the guy with the ponytail spoke in a deep baritone.

"Fock you. Get outta here or we gonna cut you bad."

"I need to talk to him about the *Santos del Diablo*."

"What the fock you know about the Angels, *pendejo*?"

I spoke very quietly, holding his eye. "Maybe I didn't make myself clear. I didn't say I needed to talk to a long streak of bat shit with the IQ of a laxative. I said I needed to talk to Carlitos. So how about you stop playing tough guy, and you run along and tell your boss he has a visitor."

He spat elaborately on the ground and stepped out the door. He didn't put his beer bottle down and that was a mistake, because I knew he was going to smash it in my face. He was two paces away and I let him take one and a half. Halfway through his second step, when he had only one foot on the ground, I smashed the heel of my boot into his kneecap. He staggered and stumbled, making a keening noise, gripping at his dislocated knee. I grabbed his ponytail with my left hand as he went down and twisted him savagely around, pulling my Sig from under my arm and shoving the muzzle into the back of his neck.

The two guys who'd been sitting at the plastic table were now on their feet. Again I spoke quietly.

"Now, I came here for a talk. I didn't come here looking for trouble. But trouble found me. So, how I deal with that trouble depends on you boys. I don't want to hurt anybody, and I don't want to blow anybody's brain out of their face, but if that's what you make me do, then I'll do it. Only it seems a shame, as all I want to do is talk to Carlitos."

They just stared at me, waiting to see what I was going to do. Ponytail meanwhile was whimpering like a girl and doing small hops on his good leg. I jerked my head at the denim jacket and said, "Go tell your boss he has a visitor. Tell him what happened."

"I can see for myself what happened, *gringo*. What do you want?"

He was maybe thirty, slim, hard, with short hair and the kind of unremarkable face you might see at a checkout, or behind a million desks across the U.S.A. Only this one masked the mind of a psychopath.

"I want to talk to you about the *Santos del Diablo*."

"What do you know about the Saints?"

"I didn't come here looking for trouble, Carlitos. I came here to talk. Tell your boys to stand down and I'll let this asshole go. Any trouble and I'll shoot you first."

He told them in Spanish and I dropped Ponytail to the ground, where he curled up, gripping his knee and screwing up his face. A small group had gathered inside the house, behind Carlitos, and now they came out and helped Ponytail hop and hobble into the house. Carlitos jerked his head at me. "Talk."

"I saw what the Saints did to your men in the parking lot. They also killed a girl, an innocent bystander. She was only nineteen."

"So what?"

"I think they should pay."

He smiled. It wasn't a nice thing to see. He looked at his two guys sitting at the plastic table. "Can you believe this guy? He comes here, to my house, he breaks Toni's knee and threatens me with a gun, because he don't like to see a girl die." They started to laugh. "What am I, your fockin' psychotherapist?"

I let the laughter die down.

"I can hurt them. I'm a pro. It's what I do. But I need some help from you."

Now his face flushed. "Hey! *Pendejo*! Look around you! What you see? We all pros here. We kill people. Is what we do. Now do yourself a favor and get the fock out of my house before I cut you open!"

I sighed. "Come on, Carlitos! I'm offering you something here. It's going to cost you nothing but some information, and maybe the loan of a couple of your boys."

"You out of your *fockin' mind? The loan of a couple of my boys?*"

I could see I was getting nowhere. I shrugged. "Suit yourself. At least tell me where he and his saints hang out. I plan to make him pay, with or without your help."

"What the fock do I look like to you? A fockin' public information service? What the fock, man?"

Suddenly I'd had enough. Two strides took me over to

the table. I took a handful of the bare-chested kid's hair and dragged him yelping to his feet, but before he could get his balance, I had slammed my fist deep into his solar plexus and spun him around with his back to me, retching and gasping for air. They had still not reacted by the time I'd kicked him in the back of the knee, pulled my Fairbairn & Sykes fighting knife from my boot and prodded the tip of the blade into the side of his neck, over his carotid artery. He was on his knees, gasping and whimpering and holding his hands out like he was trying not to fall over. I looked at Carlitos.

"Have I got your attention? One push and the blade goes through his artery and severs his windpipe. Believe me. I don't see any pros here. Give me an excuse and I'll decapitate this pussy and shove his head so far up your ass you'll look like a fairground attraction. Now, I'm done trying to reason with you. Where do I find Jesus and his saints?"

Carlitos wasn't staring at me, he was staring at the kid kneeling in front of me. His expression was one of fascination, like he was wondering if I would really do it. Fortunately for the kid, his pal with the denim jacket spoke up.

"Don't hurt him, man. He ain't done nothing to you. They hang at Jesus' place on South Fair Avenue, by the railroad, corner of East Fairground Drive. You can't miss it. They always got their bikes and trucks parked at the side of the house." He hesitated a moment and frowned at me. "What you gonna do to them?"

"Too late. Now you'll have to read about it in the papers."

I pushed the bare-chested wonder onto the dirt and he curled up in the fetal position in a strange echo of Toni before him. Carlitos snarled at me, "You jus' made yourself a bad enemy, *gringo*."

I slipped the knife back into my boot. "Tell it to your therapist. My beef is with Jesus and his angels, Carlitos. Stay out of my way."

I turned and walked back up Freemont, toward South Park, America's Best Value Inn and my Zombie.

I was going to need my Zombie.

CHAPTER 3

To look at, the Zombie is a matte black 1968 Mustang Fastback. But under the hood it has twin lithium ion batteries driving two electric engines that deliver eight hundred bhp—one thousand eight-hundred foot-pounds of torque—straight to the back wheels. It will accelerate from standing to sixty miles per hour in just over one and a half seconds, and has a maximum speed of two hundred miles per hour. She is a brutal beast, but best of all, she is totally soundless. Which is what you want if you are looking for a silent kill.

There was nobody in the parking lot when I got to the inn. I had my car sitting in the shade of some mesquite trees, backed in with the trunk to the fence. The trunk of my car is where I keep my kit bag, a habit from the old days with the Regiment, which I never quite shook off. I opened the trunk, then pulled open the bag. In it I had my spare Sig Sauer p226, a Maxim 9 and the big Smith & Wesson 500, with plenty of ammunition. I also had my Heckler and Koch

416 assault rifle, my hickory take down bow and eight out of the twelve arrows I'd had to begin with. The other four were in Sinaloa somewhere.[1]

I had a bunch of detonators, some remote and some mechanical, but no C4—that was back in Sinaloa too—and I also had a pair of binoculars and some night vision goggles. You never knew when night vision goggles might come in handy. Other than that, my kit was pretty depleted. I could have restocked it weeks earlier, but I hadn't wanted to.

I took the binoculars and the goggles and closed the trunk, pulled my Camels from my pocket, poked one in my mouth and lit up with my old brass Zippo. Then I leaned on the roof of the car, thinking. I hadn't restocked because after the hits in Argentina, Brazil and Mexico, I had decided that I'd had enough. Just like I had left the Regiment two years earlier because I'd had enough. I was tired of killing. I was tired of waging war against Omega, only to find that even as they withered and died, human evil flourished and prospered. Omega did not create human evil. Human evil had created Omega.

Yet, here I was again, checking my kit bag, making an inventory, assessing what equipment I was going to need, what equipment I was going to need to return to doing once again what I was best at—killing.

For a moment I thought of settling my bill, climbing in my car and driving north, to Wyoming, where I still had the small house and workshop I'd bought when I got back from England. Then I thought of going back to Boston, to Weston, to the house I'd inherited from my father, with my

---

1. See *The Omicron Kill*

cook and my butler and the gardener, to take charge of the family estate. I smiled. Rosalia and Kenny would be pleased. It would be peaceful. New England in the summer was a good place to be. Maybe it was time, after all...

And then I thought of Celeste, that face, strangely familiar, her eyes searching mine, that sense of a lifetime of knowing each other, passing in an instant. All she had wanted was to stem the evil and the violence that was spreading like a dark tide across the land; all she had wanted was to do something good, something valuable, and she had died because we live in Hell, and in Hell evil must always prosper.

It was not time. Not yet. I still had work to do. I climbed in behind the wheel, fired up the powerful, silent engines and pulled soundlessly out of the lot. I cruised down South Park and turned west on East Fair Street, past the cop shop and over the railway lines.

There I found myself at a broad intersection with a lot of open wasteland running beside the tracks, and stretching between one fenced off house and another. I was in the heart of the city, but I might have been in some remote town in the desert. On the right of the road there was a house behind a chain link fence, mostly concealed by trees and bushes. Diagonally across, on the corner, there was a long, low orange shack that had once been a club and still bore the name *El Sinaloa*. Now it was boarded up and covered in graffiti.

I pulled over opposite, on the stretch of dirt beside the railway track, and killed the engine. I had a pretty clear view of the house Carlitos' boy had told me was Jesus' place. It was about two hundred yards down the road, on the corner.

There were a couple of the mesquite trees that grow just about everywhere in Tucson, which would partially hide me from their view at this distance. I put the binoculars to my eyes and studied the place for a while. There wasn't much to see. As the kid had said, there were some bikes and trucks parked at the side of the building—a low, sprawling mess of a place, with a lot of junk in the yard, a couple of sheds and a long, low porch. I could see people, mainly guys, sitting around, talking, drinking, not much else. Except that after half an hour they had a visitor. Some guy pulled up in a Toyota, left the engine running, went in and came out five minutes later, then drove off.

I kept watching and after a couple of hours I'd noticed that there was a steady flow of people who would turn up like that. Some came on foot, others in cars or trucks. Once it was a couple. Most of them looked like hell and had an air of urgency about them. You didn't need to be Sherlock Holmes to deduce that they were coming for their hits.

After three hours, the sun was low on the horizon and dark shadows were stretching long through bronze light, across the blacktop and the dust. I had counted twelve visitors in that time. If they were selling Mexican brown, they were taking twenty-five bucks a paper. That was just three hundred dollars in three hours. By drug dealer standards, that was not a fortune. For the kind of turnover Shannon had been talking about, they had to have some other kind of outlet.

They did.

When the sun had gone and the dark had closed in, I crept a bit closer. One by one, six of his boys left the place, some on foot and some in their vehicles. I figured they were being dispatched to street corners and dives around the city. That would up his income by at least six hundred percent. Now we were looking at in excess of a grand an hour. That was more like it.

Among the people I saw at his house, there were three guys I noted in particular who stood out from the rest. Their clothes were a bit sharper and by their manner and the way they spoke to the rest of the gang, they had authority—were telling, not being told. They gave orders and were obeyed, and nobody sent them out to street corners. They stayed back at the house and received the cash. One had a ponytail and a goatee and was a little older, none had visible tattoos and all dressed sharp. I figured these were Jesus and Pedro and Pablo.

I spent the next three days observing them and the house, sometimes from my car and sometimes from the wooded wasteland that bordered the track at the back of the Fairgrounds shopping mall. The routine seemed to be the same every day, and the guys I had decided were Jesus, Pedro and Pablo rarely seemed to leave the place. In fact the youngest never did, and the other two rarely, except in the evenings. But on the fourth day, the Friday, the routine changed.

At ten o'clock that night, the three of them came out onto the porch and stood talking. Meanwhile, two of their boys went to one of the sheds at the side of the house and after a couple of minutes, the black Lincoln rolled out. Then one of the three, it could have been Jesus, Pedro or Pablo, I didn't know yet, skipped down the steps from the porch and climbed in the back of the Lincoln.

They turned out of the yard and headed south. I

watched the other two go inside and I followed the Lincoln. Pretty soon it pulled onto the Nogales Highway. They didn't drive fast, and from what I could make out they weren't blasting rap music either. I figured they were not looking to attract attention, but even so, it surprised me they were using the Lincoln only a few days after the hit at Cora's Café. I kept back and left my headlamps off. To them I would be almost invisible.

After six or seven miles, the city lights began to give way to the impenetrable darkness of the desert. We passed the Desert Diamond Casino and the Monsoon Nightclub, set back from the highway on the right, and then, about a mile farther on, they pulled off the road into a large, concrete parking lot that was flanked on three sides by floodlit palm trees, tall, thin and strangely eerie against the night sky.

On the fourth side there was a two-story building that would have looked more at home in Vegas than in Tucson. It was a strange cross between a Greek temple, a Roman villa and a Rococo French palace, but over the Palladian entrance there was a vast, neon image of a cowgirl in a red shirt and blue shorts riding a brown bull. She was holding a cocktail glass in one hand and a lasso in the other. The club was called the Cowgirl Rodeo and by the looks of the parking lot, it was popular.

I slowed and pulled off the highway and onto the shoulder. From there I watched them climb out of the Lincoln and go inside. When they were out of view, I drove in and parked near the exit. There I sat for a moment and thought about what to do next. Finally I climbed out of the Zombie and went into the club.

Like all clubs of that type, it was an antechamber to the

ninth level of Hell. There was a perpetual throbbing noise that made it impossible to hear anything else, and red and blue pulsing lights made it impossible to see anything clearly, except a great mass of black silhouettes with their arms in the air, jumping up and down to the infernal pulse. Dotted around the room there were retro cages, reminiscent of the discos of the '70s, where naked girls were dancing, and, in a kind of pulpit above the bouncing throng, there was a guy illuminated by electric blue light, who seemed to be a DJ.

I pushed through the crowd and found the bar, where I ordered a whiskey. As he poured it, I scanned the room and saw there was a balcony. Up on the balcony there were sofas and armchairs, and dark alcoves.

I looked around for the stairs that led to the upper level. I found them over on my right. They had a red and gold rope hung across them at the foot, and a big black guy in a dinner jacket and a bow tie who didn't let you past that rope unless you had an invite.

I took my drink and strolled over to him, leaned close and shouted, "What's upstairs?"

He let his head drop to one side, like I'd asked to get down from the table before I'd eaten my spinach. "Non o' yoe business is what's upstairs, mother focker. Now beat it."

I thanked him and returned to the bar. I didn't have time to finish my drink though. Two minutes later, the guy who was either Jesus, Pedro or Pablo came down again with his two boys. It was the first time I'd seen him closer than a hundred and fifty or two hundred yards. The two boys went ahead. One was older, maybe in his late thirties, craggy, with a moustache and a hard, wiry body. I told myself he was the dangerous one. His pal was a good ten years younger. He had a red bandana and expensive cowboy boots on the outside of his jeans. He might be dangerous in ten years, if he lived that long.

Behind them came Jesus, Pedro or Pablo. You could tell he had ambitions and aspirations by the way he dressed. He had short, well groomed hair, an expensive jacket that might have been Hugo Boss, with a collarless shirt, designer jeans and what looked like hand made boots. I wondered if he was Jesus, but decided as I watched him that he was dancing in somebody else's limelight. He was either Pedro or Pablo.

The boys opened a path for him through the crowd and they left the club. I looked around again, studying the clientele. This wasn't the kind of place you came to play with silver spoons. This was the kind of place you came for a snort. I figured right then there was probably a case upstairs with a couple of kilos of coke in it, and Jesus' right hand man was probably leaving the place forty grand richer.

He visited another couple of clubs that night, one out in the desert just past Summit, and another near Valencia West. By the time we got back to the city, the eastern horizon was turning a pale gray. I let them pull ahead and made my way back to the inn. There I fell into bed and slept like the dead for four hours.

In my dreams I could see shadowy, semi-human creatures by moonlight, inky black, highlighted in luminous blue, filtering across the border. They gathered, like a coven, around the amorphous, stygian shapes of their trucks, muttering and murmuring. They brought death with them, they cloaked themselves and everything about them in death. They were the emissaries of a vast tide, a slow tsunami of evil that was engulfing the continent.

I awoke understanding that they must have a supply line from Mexico. The most effective way of winning a battle or a war is to destroy the supply lines. I needed to find the Saints' supply line and choke it off, and then kill Jesus, Pedro and Pablo—and anyone else who stood with them. I had been watching them for four days; pretty soon they would have to take delivery and I would get a glimpse of their source of supply. Then I would plan my attack, and execute it.

It and them.

I rose, went to the shower and stood for ten minutes lathering myself and waking myself up with alternating blasts of hot and cold water. Then I dressed, had some coffee and returned to my vigil on South Fair Avenue, by the old Sinaloa Club. Nothing much happened till noon. Then I saw a white Ford truck nose around the corner and park outside Jesus' house. I put the binoculars to my eyes. Through them I saw the door open and a girl get out. She was in her early to mid twenties and, unusually, she was wearing a pale cream dress rather than jeans. Her hair was dark and cut to shoulder length. She was the girl who had been with Celeste when she was shot. Only then her dress had been blue.

She crossed the sidewalk and as she arrived at the gate, one of the holy trinity stepped out to meet her. It wasn't the guy I'd followed the night before. This one was younger, maybe in his early twenties. His clothes looked expensive, but like his pal's they were understated: jeans and a grandfather shirt. He and the girl hugged and he kissed her cheek. They spoke a moment, laughing, then went inside.

There was no mistaking the intimacy and the closeness. It was in the body language, in the way they stood together and spoke to each other. It was in the laughter. They were close.

I lowered the binoculars and sat pinching my lip. Two questions sprang into my mind: A, who was she? And, B, if she was close to Jesus, why the hell didn't Detective Mike Shannon know who she was?

I didn't have much time to think about it. A couple of minutes later, she came out of the house again, climbed in her truck and drove up the road toward me. I slid down in my seat and stared at my phone, like I was writing a message, trying to keep my face hidden, but as she passed she slowed, and in my peripheral vision I saw her staring at me. Then she drove off.

Scan the QR code below to purchase 9MM JUSTICE
Or go to: righthouse.com/9mm-justice

Made in United States
Orlando, FL
02 January 2026

76166286R00159